MW00936928

1

To Chupe, our third amigo, who couldn't be there.

Contact: Dragan Radulovic, Radulod@aol.com

Cover designed by: Tatiana Radulovic
Edited by :Petrana Radulovic

On the Road Again

In what follows, the names, the places and the events, they are all true. It all happened, the way I wrote it. And it was easy to write. All I had to do is to remember, but memories, they are sometimes jumbled.

The Afghan

He was probably Hazare his head shaved and his face oriental looking, almost Chinese, but his clothes and his demeanor were definitely Afghan. He was one of the few that spoke a word of English among this bunch, and now that the bus had stopped, and while we all looked for a shade, he waved at us. The driver was fixing the tire. This was the second one that blew off in the last few hours. And by now we knew the drill: get out and find the shade. Except, there were no trees or bushes or buildings, only the sun, high above our heads, and the bus, in the middle of the desert, casting its tiny shadow. And our Afghan friend, saving the spots for us. Our feet were dusty, our faces scorched by the sun and dry air. One could not see any sand dunes, just a rocky plateau, stretching forever, with some mountains in the distance. But the sand was everywhere, in our hair, in our pants, in our ears. There was no road in sight, and one only wandered how the driver knew where to go. No tire marks, no signs of humanity. A deserted landscape, an Afghan bus, with a flat tire, bunch of locals and two of us.

The wind was howling, which was a welcome relief, save for the dust in our eyes. Squatted down, fighting for the few inches of the shade with the Afghans, we waited. There was not much talk, just a grunt or two, with our heads between our knees, we weathered the wind. We were low on water and had no idea where this bus was heading. But we were not scared. None of our companions carried any water and none of them seemed worried. And our friend, it appeared, had some standing among this bunch. After all he saved the two spots for us, and the locals, wicked and unapproachable as they were, did not object. He obviously liked us and for this I have to thank Yuri. For my companion was as tough as a nail, and toughens, it was revered in these parts.

Yuri was the one that spotted him that morning, hours earlier, when we stopped at the first of the outposts. A shanty barrack in the middle of nowhere, but with some freshly baked naan and surprisingly, some cold Coca Colas. For indeed, there, halfway between Zahedan and Quetta, in the middle of Baluchistan, a desolated outpost, just a few pieces of plywood, a shack actually, had a cooler, with soda bottles at the bottom of an icy barrel of water. The heat was already unbearable, and this was manna from heaven. The sodas were just ten rupees and we were getting thirty rupees for a dollar. That morning in Taftan. The locals, the rowdy bunch, thirsty as hell, swarmed the patron, grabbing the bottles from the bottom of the icy pool. But not him. He waited, and when crowd thinned, he came, picked a bottle and held it in his hand, measuring. And then he returned it back. He picked another one, which too he held, for a while, only to discard it as well. Then he left. Without drinking. Apparently the sodas were not cold enough. We saw what he did and we nodded, and he offered a thin, veiled smile and nodded back, appreciating our admiration.

Later, on the next stop, the same thing repeated itself, the shack, the naan, the sodas and the thirsty bunch. This time the sodas were cold enough, so he drank. And so did we, except we ran out of rupees very quickly. The patron and the suspicious companions would not talk to us, let alone take our dollars for their rupees. But he did. He offered twenty rupees for a dollar, two sodas for a dollar, which here under the desert sun, at high noon, was nothing short of miracle. I took the deal but Yuri stopped me.

The rate is thirty rupees a dollar, the guy is robbing us blind, he said.

Are you fucking kidding me? Twenty rupees, thirty rupees, who gives a shit. We will get the cold sodas for pennies either way, I replied in disbelief.

Nobody is gonna make a fool of me. He stood firm. *If you want to take a deal, take it. I don't care.*

Which meant that I could not take the deal. Those were the rules. So, looking rough and tough as we did, myself bearded and with a pony tail, Yuri, with his shaved head, bald with mean mustache, standing a foot taller than the rest of the crowd, we declined the deal. The Afghan, he walked away. Unimpressed. We played down the whole incident and nonchalantly left the shack, set on the dusty desert floor, somewhere nearby, in the shade. We stayed there for a quite some time, never looking back at the crowd, never acknowledging their existence. We stood our ground, but it was not easy, we were thirsty as hell and we knew, all too well that right there, a few feet away, there were ice cold Coca Colas. Then he came. With two sodas in his hands, one for each of us. Free of charge. A gift from him. We nodded, and he nodded back.

Monica

We didn't see any leopard. Now, to be fair, Ned never promised we would see one. He only said that the leopard might come to drink at this creek. The locals told him so. So we snuck out, early in the morning, to ambush the beast. What a stupid thing to do. But he never came. Maybe we frightened him, or more likely the locals exaggerated, as they often did.

The sun was slowly rising behind the palm trees, their black silhouettes against the orange sunrise. We walked back, along the beach. The Indian Ocean was calm that day and the jungle of Goa was slowly waking up, with bird calls breaking up the silence, and with the leopard nowhere in sight. It was a low tide, ocean floor exposed, and the hard sand easy to walk on, with thousands of tiny little creeks forming on the beach as if the jungle floor was draining into the ocean. On the way back, we had to cross a river, rivulet actually, just a foot or two deep, a stream that cut our path along the beach. Ned the giant, he carried Monica. Like a doll she was, sitting comfortably, hanging on his left arm, the way a kid would do on a swing. The rest of us just pushed through. It is there where we met the fishermen, their long, wooden canoe-like crafts marooned on the sand, them working on their catch, still entangled within the nets. We all saw them but it was Ali who spoke first:

Fish, we get fish. I make fish-stew for you guys.

This meant that we should get some fish. Ali never had any money. The Turk was a funny fellow, likable and strange at the same time, a mix between a menacing looking Ottoman and silly court jester. He was short, stocky and bold, his head shaved and his beard too, save for a large goatee. And his eyes. He had those strange,

9

evil looking, light brown, almost orange eyes. And a big gold earring. That was the menacing part. He also wore those baggy Indian pants. We all did, but his had stripes, and he walked kind of funny, like a clown, and his colorful shirt did not help. We made fun of him but he did not seem to mind. Penniless as he was, he courted the westerners, and we tolerated him. We all knew that this was Ali's ploy to get himself a meal or maybe even a place to crash, for one can endure the beach bed for only so long. Ned was in a good mood:

Yeah, man, I'll buy some. We eat at my place. Tonight?

Ned's place was a cottage, a bamboo shack at Baga Beach. A nice place actually. We all stayed at Baga, but we rented the rooms at Inns. These rooms, they were fairly clean, with the usual cockroaches on the bed sheets and geckos on ceiling, sleeping nets to guard us against mosquitoes, and the inevitable fan above our heads. Ali slept on the beach, of course. But Ned had a semi-permanent place, which made sense, him being almost a local. The place was colored orange, inside and out, the floor was just the hard pressed earth, with no tiles or flooring. There was running water but not for drinking. Monica made most of the place, she arranged for a little kitchen and cabinets, some hippie decorations, wind chimes and similar stuff. There was a small terrace and a sitting place in the back, with a garden of sorts, palm trees and sand. We did not mind crashing there, but she did not look too happy. And it was funny to see the exchange, between the giant and his porcelain doll, him sensing that he might have crossed the line. For a few seconds, they walked along, next to the rest of us, silently, and one could have felt the chills that went through his spine. None of us dared to say anything, for who would risk offending our fair lady. So Ned finally spoke. He had to:

Monica, you OK?

I am not cooking. Let him make that Ottoman stuff, the one he did the other day.

Ali, hear that? The Ottoman stuff.

Ali heard it all right. His whole face was jovial, his cheeks happy, his head swaying from one side to the other. Yes, Ali was happy. He would feast that night. He sped up his pace, now gesticulating something to the fishermen.

One more thing, I'll set up the place, but you keep the count down. O.K.?

She was referring to the last party they had and all the bums of Goa that crashed in. Ned, the gentle giant he was, with his seven-foot-frame and those large arms and huge hands, as big as shovels, he had welcomed everybody. Sipping a cold beer and passing a joint, he had sat in a corner, telling stories, about Kashmir and Afghanistan. But it was Monica who had done all the work, with the drinks and the snacks, like a busy bee, charming and attentive, making sure that all was well and that those few possessions they had were not stolen or broken. The crowd was huge and dumb hippies showed up with a guru, who, painted all blue and red, danced and chanted and the hippies, god bless them, they kept drumming their drums. This was all amusing, a noise in background at first, but after a while it became a nuisance. Later we realized that their guru was actually a village idiot. We made fun of the hippies, who like us, were fooled by a fool, for nobody could tell the difference between a holy man and an imbecile. Ned knew, of course, he recognized the man, but cool as he was, he did not say a word.

We bought some fish. Ali picked the smaller ones, the Baitfish and some Smelts, and I chose a nice size Kingfish which I saved for the grill. The fishermen gutted the smaller fish for us and filed the King. Later we stopped at the market for some vegetables, spices, and potatoes. Ned bought us some pakoras: lamps of onion, eggs and spices, deep fried, and served in a nicely rolled newspaper. The Times of India, I think. It was a perfect breakfast and with these snacks we went to our beach, at Ben's hut, where we sat, rolled the joint and just killed time. Ned ordered his usual, King Fisher and Arack, a beer and a brandy, early in the morning, under the palm tree shack, on the beach, in the shade, Ned, Yuri and I. And some dope. Monica left with the fish back to their cottage. We stayed there, talked about our travels and our adventures. It was hard to compete with Ned's tales, the times he spent as a guest to an Afghan drug lord in Kush Mountains. It was difficult to imagine Monica, a tiny porcelain doll, among the scoundrels of Afghanistan. But then again, with a seven-foot giant at your side, strange things can be accomplished.

We watched the locals preying on Australian tourists. Many of whom came to experience the wild side, the vacation outside the tour guides and resorts, to be the outlanders like us, drifters from one country to another, *"with no direction home, like a complete unknown, like a rolling stone"*. Tony, the German, as we called him, was with us. Once, he was like them, on his two week vacation, a break from his engineering job, but he had an epiphany: *Fuck career*, he said, *I ain't going back to my office*, he said. So, he stayed. This was six months ago. These westerners, the outlander wannabes, were Ned's main source of income. Ever so suspicious of the locals (and who is to blame them) they resorted to him as a supplier of dope and as a shopping guide. Ned had a deal with local shop owners and was getting a cut for any tourist he brought in.

Hey, man, looking good, looking good.

We teased Ali, who worked on the dinner. The crafty Turk dug out a large hole in sand, right there a few steps away from us, filled it up with dead palm trees brunches and lit the fire. Normally the locals would have objected to a bonfire in the middle of the day, in front of Ben's hut, but Ali was with us, so they let it slide. He had this large clay pot, which he filled with a layer of fish, a layer of onions and potato, and a layer of herbs and spices, and then he repeated this, again and again. He worked methodically and patiently. By the time he was done with the pot, the fire had died out and he asked for some wine which he pored over the fish. The clay pot, now covered with a heavy lid, went into the ground. He carefully arranged the hot wood charcoal around the pot and then covered the whole thing with sand. And waited. His whole face lit up, his cheekbones smiling he replied

Looking good, looking good.

We asked him to come and join us, but he refused. He laid down on sand, leaning on his elbows next to the pit, guarding the dinner, which was to cook for hours to come. The mysterious Turk just stared at the ocean, sun now slowly going over it, toward the horizon. We did the same, just a few feet behind. The conversation died down. We sat there peacefully, sipping beer and smoking pot.

Later that night, we feasted on the Ottoman stew, which put my grilled Kingfish to a shame. We kept the word and the crew was smaller, a dozen of us with no fake hippies in sight. She served the drinks, the food, entertained the guests, bubbly and charming, green eyed fairy as she was. Cockney Boy showed up: *this ain't my cup of tea* he said, but came he did. The "boy" was in his seventies, recruited from East London, during the WWII, he was stationed in India, some half a century ego, never to return back. Now he drifted from place to place, a walking legend he was. Stoned to his bones, he played a game of chess with the German. Dylan was playing in the background, the incense, lit to ward off the mosquitoes, mixed with the hashish saturated the air. The chess match become intense, the two of them, face to face, deep in their thoughts, chess pieces on the board, and all of us gathered around, watching.

Whose turn is it? Ned asked, but nobody answered. So we watched, silently, not to disturb the players. After a while, I asked Cockney Boy:
You gonna play or not?
Not my turn, he replied.
Mine neither, the German retorted.
Does anybody know who's turn is it? Ned asked. But nobody knew. We were all stoned, and we had all forgotten whose turn was it, the players too, each waiting for the other, to make the move.

Hay, Monica.
Yeaaas dear, she replied mockingly, walking by between the guests, her head turned toward me.
Hey Monica, how's going?
It is going fiiiiine, she teased me.

Then she came closer and sat on my lap and started gently messing up with my hair. Like a child, playing, with both her hands in my hair, pulling it out of my ponytail and letting it all lose.

Nice hair, look at these goldilocks, like Tarzan, he is.

She teased me like that, her green eyes locked on mine, all innocent and playful, yet flirting and suggestive. I had a joint in one hand and a beer in the other, and green-eyed tiny princess on my lap, messing up my hair, now completely over my face up to my shoulders and in my eyes and mouth.

Hey, stop that, it's in my mouth.

But she did not stop, she continued like that for a while, she gazed at my eyes, her face just inches away from mine, she wiggled her body on my lap, gently caressing my hair, teaching me a lesson, of sorts.

It is going, fiiiine, I told you so.

She stood up, kissed me on my forehead, like my mom would do, and then she left. Her figure gently swayed under her sari, and once she reached outside, she threw me another glance, over her shoulder, one green eye, fixed at me for a second. I felt a bit confused and embarrassed, and I glanced at Ned, who was next to me. But he did not care. Two of them have been through this type of play a million times. I guessed.

The night went on like this for a quite some time, more people come and some left. The locals arrived trying to sell us some things, but once they saw Ned, they veered off, knowing for sure that these were the wrong westerners. Two Swiss girls, cute blonds, stopped by trying to flirt off some heroin, but with no luck. Monica made sure of that. We made plans for the future and exchanged our favorite tales. Cockney Boy, with his impenetrable slang, told about Kashmir, the Himalayas and the times he almost got married. We countered with Tanager and the thieves of Morocco. Monica, she spoke about Afghanistan and the mountains, and how beautiful and peaceful life was over there. And as she did so, the conversation would stop. All of us, awestruck, mesmerized by her, we would listen, intensively. But she did not seem to notice the effect she had on people. Or she did not care. I couldn't tell. It was almost a dawn and the day was long. *How about that leopard?* someone said, *should we try again?* We laughed, knowing that it was time to leave. A glance over my shoulder, two of them waving. I could still picture her, standing there in her colorful sari, our fair lady and her giant.

A few years later, she paid us a visit at my home town. My parents prepared the dinner and Yuri was there too. We reminisced about Goa, good old times and the times before that. My mother was mesmerized by her: *So charming, so well-spoken and so pretty. She even helped with the dishes, what a girl,* was what my mother said. Little did she know that they were in trouble. Ned was in a prison, on serious drug charges, and she had come to visit him, now lost without her giant, like a little bird without a nest. She died a few years later, a drug overdose. I think.

The Princesses

I married Isis on the fifth day of May, But I could not hold on to her very long, So I cut off my hair and I rode straight away, For the wild unknown country where I could not go wrong,.... Dylan was playing on our tape recorder. A feeble, naked light bulb and its yellow glow, over our heads, heavy curtains on the windows, two plain steel-framed beds, a shabby night cabinet in between, a water sink in a corner, and the ceiling fan and the *flap, flap, flap* sound it made. And Dylan, whining in his nasally voice from a cheap tape recorder. We sat on our beds, half-naked, sweating in this heat, contemplating our predicament. Neither of us panicked but we both knew that we might have bitten more than we could chew. For the time being we were okay, somewhat safe in this room.

Earlier, we ventured outside, on the streets of this megalopolis, for a short walk, a few blocks around the hotel, reasoning that under this scorching heat there would not be many people and that our presence would not be so obvious. We were wrong, the people noticed us. They seemed very intrusive, either staring straight at us, or passing by, only to turn around as if asking, did I just see that? We stuck out, and how could we not, blond hair, ponytail, earring and all. I was advised to remove it, and maybe I should have listened. That old Armenian, at the border, he gave me a look, a sad, worrying look, as if saying: *Son, are you sure you are going in like that?* So we snuck back into the hotel, as soon as we could, holding on to the provisional safety of the room.

It did not start this badly. Two days ago, when we entered, all our fears disappeared. The policeman at the border was rather pleasant, spoke very good English and just asked if we had any pornography or playing cards. He even said that it was not a problem if we did, as long as we threw it away. Both of us carried large knifes, but that was not an issue, apparently. He wished us well, never commenting on our looks. This surprisingly welcome entry, it continued. Later, we took a room in the border town of Maku, as well as a bus for the capital, the morning after. And there were no problems. People stared at us, but we were used to it. The locals often did that, stared at us. Overall, they were rather pleasant folk. Military checkpoints were frequent, every few hours, but that too, was understandable, the country being at war. The soldiers would enter the bus and check our passports. The clean-cut pictures in there did not resemble our ragged look but they never said anything. It was only when we arrived at the capital that things had gone wrong.

We could not get a room. The usual approach did not work. Even getting a local taxi proved difficult since none of the drivers would speak to us. Finally, since the mighty dollar talks, we got one, but we could not find a hotel that would take us. We struck a deal with the driver; we would pay double as long as he found a hotel for us. And boy did he try. But nobody would take us. He would drive to a fancy western-type hotel, walk into the reception, and we would see him gesticulate something to the receptionist, pointing toward us and then, through the glass doors we would see the receptionist, shaking his head, as if, *no, I cannot take them*. And then we would try another place, and another. As time passed, the driver become more and more nervous, realizing that he too had probably bitten more than he could chew. His meter was running high, and we were not paying a dime until we got the room. And by the look of us, he knew better than to try to trick us.

The hotels and inns become seedier and the neighborhoods grew shabbier but with no luck. Nobody would take us. Sleeping on the streets was nothing new for us. The weather was dry and nights warm, but sleeping on these streets, it was out of question. Khomeini's pictures and menacing looking Mullahs stared at us from the posters plastered all around the city. The driver became agitated, he spoke loud and fast, in Farsi. We could not understand a word but we knew, all too well, what he was saying. He wanted the money and he was backing out of the deal. Which of course was not an option. So we had a discord. He mentioned police and he threatened. We doubled down, figuring out that he was in more trouble than we were, if it came to police. He backed off, and finally managed to find this dump. So we got a place, but barely, and we knew that it was a close call. The alternative, sleeping on the streets of Teheran did not look good. Not good at all. And we were worried.

The two of us had been through some rough times and dire straits, so we knew what to do. In fact, there was only one way about this, which was to do nothing. To keep calm and wait it out. For more often than not things tend to work out on their own, as long as one is patient enough. So we waited. Uneasily. There was not much we could do to kill the time. Unlike that time in Marrakesh, smoking a joint was not an option, so we made some tea instead. We had a small gas burner and some tea leaves, for one tries not to drink water in these parts. Squatted down on the wooden floor of this shabby hotel room, we lit the burner and boiled some water. We used the sink to wash ourselves, mainly by splashing the water over our backs. There were no towels, of course, but that was not much of a problem. Standing there wet, with a ceiling fan on, in the desert heat, it was rather pleasant. Eventually, it was hunger that helped. We did not eat anything since we left Maku, which was the day before. So, after a few hours, when sun had lost most of its vigor, we ventured out. We had to.

Looking for a meal became the imperative and inquisitive glances from the locals did not have the same effect any more. There were no outlets, stores or restaurants of any kind nearby, but a few blocks away we discovered a busy city block, with a park and people, some sitting on benches and some sipping tea in the shops. It was there were we met our first, friendly, Teheran locals. Our dollars were exchanged and the rate was astronomical; much higher than the official one. We suspected that buying local currency on black market was illegal, and we knew that in this country one could get hanged for a trivial offense, but we had to eat and the locals did not seem to worry. So we got our Rials and we went hunting.

The restaurant owner, his mustache smiling, kept bringing more and more dishes, dill flavored rice pilafs, lamb kebabs, roasted eggplant. And we ate like hungry bears. All too happy, he praised his food, which was good. We knew he was overcharging us and he knew that we knew, but we did not mind, the whole feast costing us a buck or two. As we ordered more, the locals gathered around, curious about our looks as well as our appetites. None spoke any English but they gesticulated, laughed and mimicked our behavior. We laughed back, buying a round of sweets, baklavas and pistachio puddings. With some tea we concluded the meal. Later, our bellies full, our first contact with friendly locals established, we ventured out to the park.

One learns not to stare at girls in a traditional Muslim country, so we kept our gaze down. We did our part, but the princesses did not oblige. I am not sure which one of us noticed it first, but very quickly it became obvious that it was not the Iranians and their inquisitive stare that made us so uncomfortable earlier on, it was the Iranian women. We would diligently turn away our gaze, as we have learned to do so through our travels, but here, there were so many of them. Women and girls were everywhere, walking freely and gaping at us. So, after a while we decided, to hell with it, we will return the stare.

Every now and then, a Persian princess would appear, walking in our direction, in her high heels, her perfect nose and pale face showing under hijab, with her flawless make up and manicured hands. Her dark eyes fixed on us, she would stare and approach, with no hesitation. And we would stare back. Little shaken, as if wandering how dare these bums confronting a princess like that, she would lower her gaze. But only for a second. Now even more determined, fixing us up with her dark eyes, she would come ever so closer. It was magical, and a bit intimidating, at the same time. A bit hesitant, we would offer a smile, her eyes still locked on us, she would smile back, adjust her headscarf with her immaculate hands, and offer a gentle nod, tilting her head as she passed by. Sometimes, after passing, she would glance back, as if saying, did I just see that?

We knew that in this empire of Mullahs we could not hope for more, but, in some sense, it was even better this way. Sitting on the bench we savored the forbidden fruit: agreeable princesses passing by, the late afternoon prayer echoing in a distance, and the enormous orange sun, sinking slowly at the horizon. Little by little, the late afternoon turned into dusk, and more and more locals came out to get some cool air. As the sun disappeared behind the distant mountains, orange glow just hanging there, this megalopolis came to life. There were a few ice-cream parlors, candy shops as well as tea shops and restaurants, visible across the street, on the other side of this small park. Their lights sparkled, attracting the kids and the families, who swarmed around. The kids, mainly the pre-teen boys, ran nearby chasing the football, while the younger ones, stayed closer to their mothers and ice-cream shops. The elderly, they sat outside the tea shops, smoking, sipping their beverages, chatting, passing the time. In the distance one could see the desert, preparing for a starry night, another one from the remaining thousand, Sinbad, Aladdin and Sheharzaad included. Sheharzaad in particular.

Rickshaw

That is too much, you overpaid, she said.

No, it's OK, I just gave him four rupees.

Three is enough, he would have done it for two.
You overpaid, the fat Nigerian girl said.

I felt bad for the skinny youth, pedaling his rickshaw tricycle up and down the hills of New Delhi, for a mere dime, which was how much the three rupees fetched. But that was the rate and she was right, there was no point of changing it, for one cannot change India, one can accept it or get the hell out of it. Ever since we landed, these two were onto us, determined to help. Their pretty faces and pleasant demeanor on display with their curious Nigerian accents, they took the charge, called for a taxi, knew where to get cheap hotels and it what neighborhoods; authentic, not westernized, and yet not exactly shanty towns. Yuri and I, we played the role of confused tourists and let them do all the work; this arrangement they did not object to. Two of them were apparently students, coming back for a semester. They talked about their country and their lives, the usual small talk, the kind two of us abhor. So we zoned out, with their yakking in the background, answering the inquisitive questions with our shorts "yups" or "nopes". This was part of a role play, them so happy to score two white boys and us, content to have someone do the usual ground work. Any new city comes with the usual challenges, getting the logging and figuring out the transportation. And of course, to decipher the locals. Intriguing, suspicious and always puzzling locals. Never failing to surprise. Delhi was not an exception, not by any means. And we were happy to follow the lead, them clearly knowing what to do.

As we took a taxi from the airport, the tentacles of this gargantuan city began to appear, a splendid cacophony, an orgy of scents and sounds engulfed us. The slick buildings of the airport gave a way to shanty towns. From a speeding car one could see the water buffaloes lazily bathing in canals and children playing near them; a cart, pulled by an ox, moved along the canals, slowly, with a pace made for a man, not for a machine. A dark skinned man, walked along the ox and children running around. So many children. The flat landscape, the palm trees and their silhouettes above the shanty towns, endless fields of shanty towns; people sitting in front of their homes, shacks of tin and plywood scraped together, gazing at the highway; an occasional empty stare from a women laboring in a canal, and a wave from a child.

Watching camels pulling the huge hay carts on the highway, sharing lanes with automobiles, the haze from burning wood and the scent that came with it, the mist of vapor from morning dew, awakened by the sun, the first shops and neighborhoods appearing on the side of the road, the crowded city streets that followed, the crossroads where red and green lights do not matter, the cows and the holy men walking by, passing the taxi, now stuck in traffic, watching all of that I knew that we have made it. I knew that finally we had arrived, and that India would be all we hoped it to be. He saw my gaze, he saw my smile and I could tell that he agreed. But, being the cooler of the two, or maybe just more cautious, he kept the hype down.

You gonna crash again, he said.

He did not have to say anything, his look told it all, the two of us never needed to talk much. He was referring to my last crises in Lahore and the one before, and one before that, Madrid, Casablanca all over again. Lahore, just a few days ago, hit me really hard. It hit him too, but he was always tougher, ever since we were little kids, he handled himself better. In Lisbon, a few years earlier, after we were robbed, left unconsciousness in a train, for hours, drugged possibly by that sneaky Arab, offering us drinks and sandwiches, or the Venezuelan, who quietly sat in the corner, we never found out. Either way, his money was gone but thankfully not his passport. Mysteriously, none of my stuff was taken. It was some bizarre drug they used, since we could see that the police stamped our passports at Spain-Portugal crossing, but we could not remember the event. Apparently, we were able to take the passports from our bags, and communicate to the police, both in Portugal as well as the Spanish border, and yet, neither of us remembered a thing. Shaken by this we flinched, but only for a day. We decided to press on, toward Africa, with half the money, no credit cards, and one-way ticket. We split the cash and he paid me back by smuggling a brick of hashish from Morocco. He did not even blink crossing the Moroccan border, although we both saw *Midnight Express*. Cool as cucumber, he carried that brick across Europe, over countless border crossings and into our communist country.

In Lahore, we hit a wall, and hard. It was a Gypsy curse at its worse. *Let all your dreams come true*, says gypsy, for it is a journey that matters and not the goal, and when one reaches the goal, achieves the dream, more often than not, one realizes that it ain't much of a dream. And then it hits you. *What a fuck am I doing? All this effort and for what?*, is what you think and it messes you up. Lahore was like that. We could see that we had made it, that Lahore, for all practical purposes, was India, and although the sounds and the colors were there, something was missing. It all felt like: *So what? Here we are, we made it, we traveled from Europe to India, by bus, across Turkey's lawless Kurdistan, over Iran, while it was at war with*

Iraq, through Afghanistan, smuggled among the Mujahedeens, and what now? Where is the fun? What to do? We tried visiting some local monuments, parks, mingled with the locals, befriended the scorpion guy, a street performer who let us hold the palm-sized poisonous creature in our hands, but to no avail. It all felt empty. Even the local food did not taste as good.

We suspected, at that moment, that the true goal of our journey, India, her majesty, would likely yield a Lahore type disappointment, for why would Delhi be any different from Lahore. But two of us, stubborn and resolute, we pressed on. If for no other reason than to extend the journey, for a bit, and prolong the inevitable, Gypsy curse that lurked at the end. However, even that was impossible to do, in that shithole. There was no way out. One cannot traverse the India-Pakistan border. There are no buses they said, there are no trains they said. There is a road and yes, there is a railway, but buses do not go and nor do the trains. They haven't for years, decades even. And as much as we tried, the answer was always the same. No passage. The best we could do was to book a convoy that travels once a month but that required permits and paperwork and who in his clear mind wants to spend a month in Lahore? Our adventure, to get to India via buses and trains, and to avoid the planes, had to be scrapped. We had to book a plane, we had to become the stupid tourists, the very one we detested, and it felt bad. And we both crashed, except that he managed to keep his cool much better than I, but then again, he always did.

The poor rickshaw boys, panting and huffing, one with two giant westerners on his puny, clumsy tricycles, and another with two fat Nigerian girls and ton of their luggage, finally unloaded us at a small square at the mouth of a street. Our street. And what a street this was. The patchouli scent, mixed with sandalwood and rotting vegetables and cow dung, scents from the shops, two fat Nigerian girls navigating along the crowded street, cows and people and scents and the fruit stands and tea shops, and people sitting, sleeping on the floor, leaning over the balconies, small scooters zigzagging along, between the cows and the people and the shops. The splendid, chaotic mess of sounds and aromas.

Two of them brought us to their room in a not-too shabby hotel, thirty rupee, or something like that, a dollar a night, I think it was. *But you don't have to pay, you can stay with us, as long as you want.* Two steel frame beds and a fat Nigerian girl sitting on each, their cute faces and pleasant smiles asking for company. And we would have obliged, after all we owed them a favor, but this was the age of AIDS and two of them, fresh from Africa, made us certain to pass. They could not understand why we would decline: *Why a different room?,* they asked. We felt sorry, we mumbled some half-cooked excuse and left the room. Outside was India, the majestic flower, waiting to be plucked.

Grandpa

It was cold. Very cold. I had not brought any winter attire, and my long-sleeved, denim shirt was the warmest thing I had. Traveling to India, via the deserts of Iran, in the month of August, who on earth would have imagined that we would need warm clothes? But here, in this bus, it was cold. This late at night. High in the Afghan mountains. Or at least that was our guess, for we had no idea if we were in Pakistan or Afghanistan. The bus had stopped some twenty minutes ago and this was clearly not one of the regular rest-stops. There was nothing outside. Just an empty gorge, high in the mountains, and from what I could see through the bus window, there were no trees or bushes, just the usual Afghan stone desert, within the walls of some mountain range. A good portion of folks went outside already and were now scattered in a dark, probably searching for some cozy place to sleep, cuddled in their shabby blankets. The rest of us stayed inside.

By now we had realized that, inadvertently, we had booked a bus that illegally smuggled Afghans into Pakistan. Their plan was to spend a night hiding in some godforsaken corner in order to avoid the authorities and then sneak into Quetta, during the morning rush. That was our guess. We had no idea. We were not even sure the bus was going to Quetta, we did not even know what Quetta was. Al Masher told us yesterday that this was a bus to Pakistan and that it went to Quetta. One way or another, we had to spend a night here and we made it as comfortable as we could. With many seats now empty, Yuri left and found a spot some few rows behind so I had our two seats for myself. I stretched across, with my head resting near the window, laying on my back, with my legs, out in the aisle, resting on the luggage that the Afghans kept in there. The ride, so far, was the strangest and bumpiest one we had ever witnessed, the bus driving over the unpaved, pothole infested road, for the better portion of the last twenty-four hours. This overnight rest, and in such cozy and quiet conditions, was god sent. Except that it was cold.

The rest of the passengers, the ones still in the bus, made very similar arrangements. There were legs crisscrossing the aisle through the whole bus. Just as I dozed off, I heard him for the first time. There was this Afghan, far at the rear, walking down the aisle, trying to get out. *Fuck, now I have to move and wake myself up.* I was contemplating, if I should go back to sleep, or if I should wait for him to pass. I waited. But he moved so slowly, the aisle being crammed with crisscrossed legs resting on the luggage blocking any easy passage. I could hear him mumbling and pushing his way through, closing on my position. It took forever and I was so tired and sleepy. He spoke softly as he navigated through the corridor, each time waking some of the Mujahedeen, who would mutter something harsh and then the fellow would proceed further down the aisle, toward the bus exit, and closer to me. Half awoken, between dreams and reality, I could hear him, slowly advancing, until he was at my legs. He just tapped them, pushing me with his knees, assuming that I would lift up my legs and let him pass. But my legs, and my whole body, were nicely positioned, and I refused to move. I figured, if he really wanted to go out, to the bathroom I presumed, he should just step over me.

But, he did not do that. He pushed me again. Very gently, for in these parts any physical contact carries a weight and one must be very careful how one conducts oneself. I ignored him again, but he kept pushing and mumbling. He pushed very gently, and very persistently. I had had enough. I opened my eyes and lifted my head a bit. Then I saw him. He was an old, frail man. A skinny, tiny little Afghan grandpa, he was. Apparently, it was hard for him to step over me and probably that was the reason it took him forever to navigate these few rows in order to get out. I felt bad for the old man, so I decided to help, which was not that easy. In that tiny little bus, I was on my back, my legs blocking his way across the aisle. I had to lift my legs off the parcel in the middle of the aisle, pull them up, and pretty much twist my whole body, since the seats were small. And there I was, in a very compromising position, with my legs pulled up, my knees on my chest, squatted, as if on a toilet seat, but lying on my back. It took him forever, to step over that parcel. Now irritated, in that strange, folded position on my back, I waited for him, to finally clear the parcel and leave the bus. But he did not do that.

Instead, after a few adjustments, he decided to just sit down on the very same spot I had lifted my legs off. I thought he needed room to get out of the bus, but he was actually looking for the place to sit. The Mujahedeen, apparently, had chased him out and now he took my leg-rest as his seat. *What the fuck! That is what I got for being nice.* I was on my back, squatted in this strange uncomfortable position with my knees on my chest, with no place for my legs, and this moron had just took my place. *Fuck you*, I thought, *if you wanna be rude, so will I.* So, I stretched out and rested my legs right on his lap. After all, he was sitting at the exact same spot where my legs where just moments ago. *There you have it, my legs on your lap. Deal with it.* I was ready to confront him and yell back at him after he objected. But he did not object. Not at all. Instead, he adjusted his position, and with my legs on his lap, he leaned forward, hugged them, and used them as a pillow. And there I was, lying on my back, across the two bus seats, with my legs resting on an old man's lap, him leaning over, hugging my legs and his head, gently resting on my upper thigh. An Afghan grandpa and I. It was quite cozy, and it was not cold any more.

Turkish Curse

The bus had stopped, in the middle of nowhere, late at night, with no roads, no lights, no houses of any kind, a small lamppost, in the distance with a naked twinkling light bulb. The passengers were disembarking and so did we, our eyes, still accustomed to the bus lights, now gazing into emptiness. There was nothing there, just a dark endless plateau, a bit chilly, this high in the mountains.

What the fuck? Where is the outpost? I asked.

Yuri just looked around, as confused as I was. Was this the last stop? Did our thirty-six hour journey, non-stop through Turkey, just end? We had no idea where we were. We shouted at the driver:

Hey you, is this a rest stop? Are we to change buses here?

But he did not understand. Of course he did not. And in his authentic Turkish manner, he responded by chasing us off the bus. We guessed that this must have been the last stop, since everybody got out, took their luggage, and in an orderly procession, spread out. Some were picked up by nearby vehicles, some went randomly into the darkness and some walked toward the distant twinkling lamppost. We were hesitant: to stick with the bus, now empty and with its lights off, or to follow the crowd walking toward dark empty field, in the middle of nowhere. That was the question.

A few days earlier, in Istanbul, Morning Prayer had echoed from the speakers as two of us, lazily, turned in our beds. It had been an exotic experience, to be awoken in such a way, in that nice, cozy, downtown hotel. Still groggy and half-asleep, I realized that my arm was itchy.

Whoa! Look at my arm man. I screamed.

O boy, you look like Popeye. He laughed.

The bedbugs had bit me so hard that my forearm swelled and indeed I look like the aforementioned sailor. And he couldn't stop laughing. It was quite annoying, and so itchy, but he laughed so full-heartedly that I had to join.

Fuck man, yesterday that bizarre crossing and now this. Turkey does not like us. I have a funny feeling about this.

Ha, ha, ha, don't worry, we'll get you some spinach soon, he replied.

But I was right. Turkey did not like us. And the whole thing did not look right. The night before, on the Greek border, we encountered true Ottomans. They separated all the westerners, two dozen of us, drove our train car to the far end, took all our passports and then disappeared. With their stern faces, thick mustaches and no explanation or comments, they posted an armed guard and left. We stayed like that, locked in, for hours, in the middle of the night, waiting. Later in the wee hours, a grouchy, eerie looking Ottoman came back with our passports, reading our names, one at the time, he would stare at our eyes and then handed out the passports. Never bothered to explain why it took hours to process us. For sure, things did not look right.

Undeterred, with my Popeye arms, him laughing all the way, we marched on. First we feasted on local cuisine: meat borek, shish kebabs and melons. Then we looked for a bus to India. Except, nobody knew of such a bus. This we anticipated, so we settled for Iran. That did not work either. No buses went to Iran. In the Orient, one learns not to give up, one tries and tries and bribes and questions and then tries again. And it always works. Almost always. Through the day, among the numerous: "*No, no bus to Iran*", a phrase *topkapi*, surfaced. Every now and then, and mainly among the folk with broken English, this word would appear. So, we went there. And indeed, at topkapi, one could find busses, a whole bunch of buses, a field full of buses. This was no regular bus station with kiosks and information booths, but rather an enormous, dusty, unpaved parking lot, with hundreds of randomly scattered buses of various shapes and sizes, some parked and some driving around in circles, calling for passengers, all going somewhere. Apparently. It was impossible to deduce where, for nobody spoke any English. Finally, one of the hustlers, a short, stocky fellow, who spoke some English, he understood what we wanted.

Bus to Iran? Yes, come, no problem. Iran no problem.

So he quickly went around, inquiring, asking, talking to various drivers, two of us following behind, making sure not to lose him in the crowd. Finally he found one.

Yes, this one, go Iran. Iran? Right?

We knew that our hustler was getting a commission for each sold bus ticket regardless of where the bus went, so we were suspicious, to say the least. We knew that the bus was going somewhere, and we knew that with Khomeini and Iran-Iraq war going on, it was unlikely that the bus actually went to Iran. We checked with the driver:

Going to Iran?
Not knowing any English, but understanding the word Iran and our hand gesture he replied:

No, no Iran.

34

What the fuck? We looked at our guide.

Then he said something to the driver, who smiled and nodded his head, and kept repeating *Iran, Iran* waving his hand as if he were going there. True, he was pointing toward the east, where Iran was, but all this was not very reassuring. One way or the other, after two days in Istanbul, this was the closest we got to a bus for Iran. We figured, how bad it could be. Worst comes to worst we would end up somewhere in east Turkey and then we would find a way out. So we bought the tickets.

But then, there was one other thing on our mind: the Kurds. Yuri had been in Iraq, a year earlier, and he told me the stories, the lawlessness of Kurdistan, the semi-autonomous region covering Iraq and east Turkey, where bands of Kurds harass, rob and sometimes kidnap people, foreigners in particular. We asked our hustler:

Kurds? Any problems there?

Now that we had paid for our tickets, confident that his commission was secured, his demeanor changed completely. His face pale, and sincerely worried, he stared at us and said:

Kurds? Problem, big problem.
Fuck, you are telling me now?

It was there, and only there, during the whole journey of ours, that we nearly chickened out. We made many tough decisions later on, we entered Iran and Afghanistan, we illegally crossed into Pakistan, smuggled along the Mujahedeen, but all that was done while on the move. We had to do it because we had decided to go, and once you are on the move, you just move. But it was at that moment, at topkapi, that we have to make a crucial decision: do we go or do we not go? For you see, at topkapi, we had the choice: we could have gone back home.

There was some good news. The hustler's warning meant that the bus was going in a right direction, east, toward Iran. But where exactly, that we did not know. We did not have any dictionaries or maps. We never carried those. To confirm the story, we would had to go back downtown, and after two days of dead ends, we were fed up with endless inquires. The decision had to be made. It was frightening, the very idea of being dumped in a middle of Kurdistan with no contacts or plans, but we rationalized:

Nhai, he is a Turk, he is scared of Kurds, probably it is not that bad.
It is bad man, I saw them, on their horses raiding the workers' camp, Yuri said.
C'mon, this bus will probably go to some city, there will be a hotel a police station. We'll be OK, I reasoned.

We knew, all too well, that once we steped into that bus, we would not quit half-way, we would go to the last stop, whatever that was. Silently, we stood there, and then walked around, deep in our thoughts, weighing the pros and the cons, glancing at our hustler, who, surprisingly, stuck around, clearly very worried for us. Then Yuri said:

Fuck it, let's go.

So we went. For thirty six hours, two nights and countless rest stops, drinking local black tea and staying away from any food, for who would risk diarrhea in a Turkish bus in the middle of nowhere, we managed. Every ten hours or so, a new driver would replace the worn-out old one. Passengers too were replenished along the way, for this bus served both as a long distance as well as a local transport. As we went deeper into Asia the landscape changed as well, from forests and hills to menacing mountains, green, yet without any trees or bushes even. Road often followed a canyon, with a fast-flowing river nearby, rushing from formidable heights, not visible, high above. This would then change into endless prairies with distant mountains on a horizon. The perpetual change. We would nap, for what else were we to do, only to realize, that while we slept, the whole landscape had changed, as well as the passengers, now belonging to a different ethnic group. Everything was slowly changing, the landscape, the locals, even the drivers. Only the two of us remained.

And yet, after a day or so, we noticed that we were not quite alone. There were others. The few isolated souls, who like us, seemed impervious to this change. A gentleman here, an old man over there, a young couple at the back, they all appeared to be in for a long ride. And they looked different. Better dressed than the local gangs, but also quieter and more reserved. They, like us, did not mingle much with the locals and they, like us, kept mostly to themselves. Clearly, they were going to the end of this voyage, to the bus's final destination, but unlike us, they knew where it was. We, on the other hand, could only tell that bus was on the right track. We were traveling east. We knew that by the position of the sun. And east was good, closer to Iran.

It might have seemed logical to ask, to inquire about the destination of our bus, but we knew better. Such a request would have exposed us, would have shown our vulnerability. For unlike the popular TV documentaries with friendly locals, smiling and eager to help, real life locals, by far and large, are quiet, reserved and suspicious folk. And the talkative ones, the ones that seem so eager to help, they are often there to get you. Such is life, here at the steppes of Central Asia, far from living-rooms and coffee-table National Geographic magazines. To advertise the fact that we did not know where we were going, that once we arrive at the final destination we would have no idea what to do and no friends and family to help, to do so was out of the question. One does not communicate such a weakness to a random stranger. Not in the middle of Turkish highlands.

But now, it was too late. The two of us, we stood alone, in the middle of the night at the open steppe, somewhere in east Turkey. The bus was gone and we looked around and saw nothing but an empty field stretching forever in all directions. The driver had chased us out, and disappeared somewhere, along with his bus. We stayed nearby, dazed and confused, instinctively wary of leaving that very spot, afraid of making an error and walking in wrong direction. Our eyes, now more accustomed to the darkness, with some help from the moonlight hiding beyond the horizon, we could see more, but what we saw was not good. The plateau was enormous. For miles, if not hundreds of miles, there was nothing. There were no lights coming from distant cities or buildings or bus outposts. Nothing. A good portion of our passengers spread out, somewhat haphazardly, walking in the direction of a small cluster of lights, somewhere far, too far, in a distance. The other group walked in an orderly procession, toward that remote lamp post.

We had to blow our cover and ask someone, before it was too late, before everybody left. We confronted the well-dressed gentleman, one of those few souls that we identified as a likely Iranian:

Iran? I asked.
Iran, Iran, he responded, nodding his head, packing his luggage and leaving in a hurry. So we asked again:

Where is Iran?
There, he pointed out toward the distant lamp post.
So, we are to just walk a mile, and then enter Iran on foot?

Yes, yes, we walk there, he replied.
What the fuck? I looked at Yuri. *There is nothing there. What should we do when we cross?*

He was as puzzled as I was. There were no buses or hotels over there. Just an isolated lamp and probably a small army barrack, an outpost. These locals have probably arranged for a pickup, once they have crossed the border, but what the hack were we to do? Spend a night among the Iranian military guard? Sleeping where? Eating what? But, the alternative, to spend a night, in the middle of this highland, near Turkey-Iran border, among the Kurds, alone, was not an option.

With our heads bowed down, deep in our thoughts, trying to suppress our fear, we marched on. Our silent companions nearby, stretched out in a long line, we paced ourselves. Neither of us spoke a word, for what could we say? We just walked along and hoped for the best. *It will be whatever was meant to be.* The moon slowly came out and the full scale of the landscape presented itself. It is then when we saw it. The dark impenetrable mass, the one we faced just moments ago, it was not an endless mysterious steppe, but rather the foot of a mountain. And what a mountain! Three miles high cone, towering alone in this flat highland, like a sacred temple, guarding this endless steppe, Mount Ararat stood there. Like a custodian of life itself, his peak so high up, and yet right in front of us, so close that one had to lean backward in order to see the huge snow cap on the top, and the moonlight shining on it. It was an omen, a good one, and we both knew it. As usual, reading each other's thoughts, ever since childhood, we did not need to say a word. Just a smile, a nod, and a jolt to our pace, were all that we needed. So, we marched on, toward Iran, assured that the gods were with us and that we had shaken off the Turkish curse.

Istanbul bus station.

Our Street

It was rather short street, from that crossroad and rickshaws stop, up to our hotel. Further down we never ventured. A bit shy of half a mile, it was. There were many shops and small restaurants, tea shops and eateries, but for a while, we stayed away from any meals, meat in particular. And water, of course. Partly because we were worried about some unknown strange diseases, but mainly to avoid, or rather to postpone, the inevitable diarrhea. So we ate fruits. There were many vendors, almost at every corner, and getting a fresh fruit, costing us next to nothing, it was easy. Most of those tropical delights we did not recognize, so, at first, we picked the things we knew, mainly oranges, bananas and some mangos. Coconuts were the best. One could eat them and one could drink them. In fact one could live on coconuts alone, except, we could not open the damn thing.

We brought them back to our room, and we tried hitting them, crushing them, but it did not work. Even just poking a hole was impossible. We had some menacing knives with us, but the damn thing would not crack. We almost cut ourselves in the process, which there, with all the germs and dirt, was a scary proposition. But, as we quickly learned, our vendor, all too happy to see us again, was willing to help. Holding the nut in his left hand and a huge machete in his right, with two, simple, precise blows, he would crack the nut for us. It was a pleasure to watch, the man and his knife, working so gracefully. Later, in the room, we would enlarge the crack. We had to do this upstairs, in our hotel. We did not want to freak out the locals, for our knives did not belong to these streets. In Afghanistan and Turkey, we would freely flash them out and often use them as utensils, for they were handy and they kept the locals in check. But not here, in this peaceful, cacophonic Nirvana. Here, they were unnecessary, embarrassing even. So we kept them upstairs.

We knew that the hotel owner, once we were out the room, would sneak in, just to check us out and maybe snatch a thing or two, later claiming his ignorance. A trick we had seen so many times in so many places, from Agadir to Quetta. So we kept all our money and passports with us, but we left the knives, although quite expensive, on our beds, in plain sight. And it worked, for nobody took the cassette player or sleeping bags or vitamin bottle or sun glasses or gas burner. It was all there, untouched, for days. Two large foreigners, and the menacing knives, so openly displayed, was a message loud enough. Back home, we were of average height and built, but here, we were giants. We did not ask for it, it just happened that way. In some other place, we would have been the puny ones, and we would have played our parts accordingly.

The hotel itself, as well as the room, was cheap, shabby and sparsely furnished, but there was a ceiling fan, a sink with running water in a corner, our own toilet, and a very nice, shared terrace, some twenty feet across, with a large shady tree in the middle. One could lean over the terrace and observe life below, the endless procession of people, cows, and motorized tricycle rickshaws that slowly maneuvered among the shops and the cows and the people. So many people. They were everywhere. There were people sitting on the floor, in the small hallway of our hotel which extended to the street, there were people sitting on the sidewalks, in the shade of the trees across the hotel, there were young rickshaw boys, sleeping and resting on their bikes, obviously their sole possession, their home and their source of income. At night, the whole street, or at least our corner of the street, would transform into sleeping quarters. People would make their beds, mostly out of newspapers, but some had makeshift

42

bedding, a dirty cloth and slim pillow. They would lie down, in orderly ways, some positioned in the corner, sleeping on their sides, with their backs leaning on the buildings. Those were prime locations, and I must say, with the warm asphalt below, and tropical night above, anchored against the wall, with the gentle cacophony of sounds now toned down a notch, they looked quite comfortable. Almost inviting.

But the most of them were not so lucky and had to sleep on the floor, all around. There were so many of them, around our hotel in particular. They covered the ground, like sardines. So much so, that we had to be careful how we walked, in and out of our room, making sure not to step on someone, our hallway being another prime location. This was easier said than done, for we would inevitably step on an arm or a leg. But these were gentle folk. They would never complain, just quiet grunt or shift of their body was all that we would get from them. These people did not seem sad, or starving but quite the opposite. They were not aggressive, not intruding, barely ever making eye contact, so after a while one would just get used to them. One did not ignore them or pretended not to see them, for one couldn't help but see them. Instead, they just blended into the whole scene, become part of the painting, like another oddity, a peculiarity of this place, like the unusual plants or cows on the street.

And there were many cows on our street. They were the very reason for the slow, mainly pedestrian traffic, which in turn made the street so appealing. There were barely any cars or trucks and even the small motorized rickshaws - the yellow devils that so freely rushed through Delhi's never ending traffic jam- there, in our street, had to slow to a crawl. In order to negotiate the cows. Pedestrians, ourselves included, we had to navigate the cows too. They were large, well fed, constantly mulching on lettuce, cabbage and other produce that was thrown on the street by the vendors. This maneuvering around the cows was not that simple, for one needed some time to get used to it and learn how to read their minds. One couldn't just avoid them for they moved in random directions, but then again, one couldn't just press forward and expect that the five hundred pound cow would step aside. One could, as the locals often did, shoo them away and sometimes gently slap them on their backs to make room, but that too had to be done with a care, for some of them would fight back. A delicate balance, a give and take, between the cow and the man, was required. And for the first few days, we looked quite ridiculous. We had been either chased by a cow or stopped to a halt, in the middle of the street, by one that just decided to stop, there, in front of us. Elephants, on the other hand, they were completely different story.

We liked Delhi, and we planned to stay longer and learn the city, the same way we did in Barcelona and Valletta, but one does not do that by rushing through museums, parks, and castles, with a map and a tour guide. Instead, we learned to play it low, to stay local, and to take it easy. As days passed by, and as we become more comfortable with the locals, restaurants and shop owners, we enlarged our circle. There was no need to rush and instead we just savored the moment, the ambiance, and we blended in. Typically, we would pick a nice tea-shop, a restaurant, a fruit vendor, and then we would visit them, repeatedly. As we did so, we created an interesting bond. The vendor became our vendor, the tea-shop waiter became our waiter. They would greet us when we passed by, they would serve us earnestly when we stopped by. Later, as we slowly switched from our all-fruit-diet, we would order some tea, strong, black Indian tea with milk and some food as well, mainly vegetarian dishes and some fried eggs, still wary of meat products. Eventually, I

44

managed to stay away from diarrhea, but Yuri did not do as well.

We took it one day at a time, sipping tea, smoking hashish, and reading our books, a cacophony of sounds and people and fragrances for us to relish. Now and then, we would venture out, up to the mouth of our street, where it spilled out into the river of rickshaws, people and motorbikes, where the noise and the echo of this megalopolis magnified itself. At first, these were short trips, like children going up to the ocean shore, just to wet their feet, just a glance, a short stroll into the chaos, and then back to the safety of our street. Later, we discovered that a short walk down this chaos would lead to another, more prominent, and interesting city block. But mainly, we hung around the tea shops, and with our waiter or restaurant owner, we would just observe the scene and soak in this marvelous city. Occasionally, a holy man would pass by. Sometimes he would look like a Buddhist monk, all dressed in red and some yellow, but with a beard, so not quite a Buddhist, and then other times, he would be painted blue, with a gray beard, and a walking stick. They were dignified, these holy men. They walked calmly, always alone. They would never beg, but sometimes, they would just stop in front of a fruit vendor, and he would offer an orange or a mango. No word was spoken, just a fruit in a hand and a nod from a holy man.

There were westerners in Delhi, of course, and two of us, never too eager to interact with them, we kept our distance. Tourists annoyed us, too loud and too intrusive, and the fakers were just boring. No tourist would come to our street, not with all the cows and elephant dung and people sleeping on the floor. Though, we had to admit that the westerners in our street, they were the real deal. They too kept a distance from us, and from each other, spending their time among the locals. We knew that we had to prove ourselves, to earn their respect, before the first contact was made. So we had to wait, do our thing, ignore them, and not ask for any directions or advice. In our tea shop, we would meet some of them, the regulars, and after a while we would acknowledge them, and they would nod back. We actually did not need any pressing advice nor were we eager to talk to anybody, but then again, a conversation with a real traveler, could be worth the trouble.

But it was not that easy to identify them. The westerners, who were eager to talk and bore you to death with their journeys and their achievements, they were mostly the fakers, and the real ones, the true outlanders, the ones that could provide some notable tales, would not go around advertising. It was a Catch 22 actually. And then there were the junkies. They were real, all right, for they did blend with the city and they were as authentic as one could get, but who wants to talk to a junky? They were quite easy to spot, never wasting their money on food or drink. They were seldom in tea shops and restaurants and they were skinny. Dirty heroin, or Brown Sugar as they called it, was cheap and available, but they could not keep it in check and some of them were too deep in the hole, so much that they could not provide any source of income, and for a western junky in India that meant only one thing: smooching out of the other westerners. Begging from Indians would have been pointless, and they knew it. Tourists were scared of them and the real outlanders would ignore them. Which meant that they were on a hunt for the fakers, the only westerners that would listen. We learned how to spot them from a distance, and our postures, eye contacts, or gestures, were enough to keep them at distance. Although, I must say, they could be crafty and smooch a rupee out of you in a most cunning of ways, as did that French bustard, scamming the hundred rupees from me.

Beggars were part of a daily life over there, western junkies and cripples on the street corners. Eventually, one got used to them. Even to children beggars. In small groups, bands of four or so, they roamed the streets, stocking the more touristic places and better restaurants. The really fancy places, like big western hotels or popular touristic attractions, were off limits. The authorities would chase these little buggers with bamboo sticks. But there were plenty of places in the middle, more sophisticated than our street and yet not as glamorous as Hilton hotel or Taj Mahal. They would prey on train stations, better shops and restaurants, they would run after you, surrounding you as you walked, not more than six or eight years old, calling: *A rupee mister, rupee please.* It was hard to tell if they actually lived on the streets or if they were sent by someone to do the work. At night, most of them would disappear, but then again, some of them would hang around, sleeping on train stations and busier city corners, protected, somewhat, by the crowd, hiding in a plain sight. I remember, one especially cute little girl, no more than eight years old, running after us, begging for money, claiming to be hungry. So I gave her a banana. She ate it, but she did not peel it, she bit the whole thing. She took the whole banana, stuck it in her mouth and ate it. She sucked the sweet part and spit out the bitter banana skin. I thought that even monkeys knew how to peel a banana. But this was India, the crazy place that never ceases to surprise.

The Law

Shit,
What?
The fucker just pulled my pony-tail.

As if we did not have enough trouble, crammed for days, in this bus, that went forever, through the endless Turkish Steppe, now we had to deal with these idiots. The locals, the various ethnic groups that seemed to endlessly replenish themselves, through this saga, they were seldom friendly, at best tolerable, but this particular bunch, these morons, they were something else. Not used to seeing actual westerners, this far east, and now sitting next to them in a bus, apparently, it was exhilarating. They giggled and they stared. At one point, they yelled something to another guy, way up in the front. He stood up, looked at us, and laughingly he came down to our seat, right next to me, and just stared. His face, inches away from mine, he gazed at me, then he turned toward the guys behind us, and hysterically laughed. It was annoying, to no ends. And now this. They crossed the line.

There is this law, an unwritten universal law, one that works in the jungles of South America as well as in the desert of Morocco: you do not touch. For you see, staring, laughing and gesticulating, as intimidating and annoying as it could be, belongs to a separate category. But to touch someone, and in such a matter, by deliberating pulling his hair, well, that is a completely different ball game. I knew it, Yuri knew it, and they knew it. There was not much I could do at that point. I had to ignore it, and hope that it would not happen again, which I knew it would.

There again, I jolted from my seat, *they pulled it again.*

I looked at Yuri, and he said nothing, but his face, boy, his face, I knew that face. It meant that his cool was over and that, sooner or later, he was gonna do something, and it wasn't gonna be pretty. My face was not less resolute, but deep inside, I was still hoping that the predicament would resolve itself, that if we only stayed put, all would just go away. He knew better, which made me even more worried. Who the hell knew what this son-of-gun was gonna do? We were not really scared, just pissed. The folk, in these parts, are skinny and frail. These were small people, and we could have easily taken them down in a real fight. But this was not a fight. It was a game. We knew what they were up to. An old trick. One uses a kid to irritate, to provoke, and to put you off balance. For you see, the law, it does not apply to a kid. For a kid is just a kid, one cannot beat up a kid. But of course, it was them all the way, and of course they knew that, and you knew that, and you couldn't do anything. They just intimidate you and they humiliate you, and it was all fun, for them.

I had to act, to cut this crap. I stood up and turned around. I decided to stare them down. Towering over these small bus seats, a foot taller than the tallest of them, with my face, as firm as I could muster, I glared at them. Slowly turning my head, and checking them out, trying to find the kid who did it and scare the shit out of him.

It's not the kid.
You are kidding me, Yuri said.
Nope, it is an old man.
Fuckers.

Not only did my showdown not work, it backfired. Yes, I stood up and yes, I showed them how big and how pissed off I was, but they just giggled and stared back at me. As if saying: *we dare you, what you gonna do?* The jerks raised the stakes. They had not even bothered with a kid, they pulled my hair on their own. And now, I saw it, and they knew that I knew it, and they knew that I could not do anything about it. They fixed their eyes on me, never lowering their gaze. I sat back, them chuckling behind us, clearly enjoying our predicament.

Just smack the fucker, Yuri said.
No.
Just grab the fucker by the throat and shake him down.
No, there are too many of them.
You sissy.

I had no doubt that he would have done it, had they messed with him. He would have dealt with them the way he had in Barcelona. Over there, he picked the strongest of the three buggers, grabbed him by his throat. His arm straight, pressing the fucker to the wall. Yuri's fist, as big as the guy's head, clutched his throat, the sucker's body pressed to the building's wall, unable to kick, his arms, much shorter, could not reach Yuri's face. Yuri held him like that, staring at him, not saying a word. The guy's face turned blue, the two buddies, the bugger's friends, speechless, just looked at the whole scene. After ten seconds he let go of him, turned around and nonchalantly left. Did not even bother looking and the bums. And the three, they just melted away.

But, that feat, I could not repeat. There were too many of them. They felt secure, in their numbers and in their bus. For this was their bus. It was too risky for us. Any skirmish would have resulted with the driver's intervention, and he would have sided with them. The problems with local authorities at the next bus stop would have likely followed. All this was on my mind. And the buggers, they felt it too. They smelled weakness which was why they were so cocky and confident. They escalated. They become louder, calling each other, across the bus, for apparently, there were a few others, of the same ethnic group, all over the bus. We could not understand what were they saying, but we could tell, by the concerned looks coming from the other passengers, that it did not look good.

Yuri had had enough. He stood up, and move toward the aisle, between the bus seats. Him, being at window seat meant that I had to get up as well. Yuri was taller than I, and his shaved head, mustache and his darker complexion, stunned them a bit, for he looked like a menacing, angry Turk. And to that, they could relate. Not fully understanding what he was up to, and quite concerned that he was about to beat the crap out of their ringleader, I flinched.

What's up?
Pass me the bag, he said.

He pointed toward the rucksack, at the compartment above our heads. I knew what was he up to.

Ooh, that, I get it.

The locals, they gazed at us, their giggling absent, their faces concerned, wondering: *Are these guys crazy enough to start a fight? Here in our bus?* Instead, Yuri took his bag, and pulled out an apple and his knife. That was our Tangier trick. I too, picked my bag and my knife, as if for peeling the apple. But these were not eating knifes. Yuri had this beautiful, gold bladed, folding Bowie knife, its huge blade shimmering in his hand. My knife was an ugly monstrosity, black, ten inch blade, the army surplus bayonet. It had a pollster, which produced a loud click, when knife was pulled out. A stunning effect this was, a click, and then the horrific blade appeared in my hand. Yuri, peeling the apple, his face now smiling, not angry

51

but more cynical, he addressed the puny buggers in our language:

You wanna raise the stakes? Here is my raise, you fuckers.

They did not understand a word he said. But they understood, nevertheless. One could see the fear in their eyes, and one could see an older guy, probably the ring leader, clinching his fist, holding a younger fellow next to him down, as if saying: *shut up, stay quiet, these guys are crazy son-of-bitches.* But of course, this was a bluff, a showdown. They raised the stake by ignoring the law, so we raised it even more by ignoring another one: do not pull out a weapon. We never intended a knife fight. At least I didn't. As for Yuri, who the heck knows? Crazy son-of-bitch.

Zahedan

Bus to India? Nope, no way, he said.
What about Pakistan? Can we get to Pakistan?
Pakistan? Bus to Pakistan? Forget buses, there are no roads over there.
What about Afghanistan? Surely we can get into Afghanistan?
Are you crazy? Who wants to go to Afghanistan? There are Mujahedeen over there, they kill you over there.
How close to Pakistan can we get?
Zahedan, he said.
What is Zahedan? Where is it?

But he could not explain. We did not have any maps, so on a napkin we outlined the potato shape contours of Iran. We placed two dots: the first in the upper left, north-west corner:

Tabriz, here, we said, he nodded his head. Than we placed another dot, more or less in the center:

Teheran here, we said. He nodded again.

Zahedan where? we said.

He understood, he nodded his head, took the pencil and placed a dot somewhere in the lower right corner. South-East, close to Pakistan and Afghanistan.

So, Zahedan it is.

That was a relief. We, of course, did not know where to get the bus for Zahedan, or how often the buses went there or how long the journey was, but that did not matter. Those were details. We would figure them later. We did not worry. After all, Iran was a pleasant surprise, Teheran in particular. It was well organized and orderly. We knew that there would be a bus station and that, unlike the Turkish topkapi, there would be a proper bus terminal, with kiosks and schedules. And although nobody would speak much English, some kind of help would be provided. People were polite, civilized, clean and well-dressed. It felt like the Switzerland of the Asian Steppe, an oasis of civilization, here in the middle of a God forsaken land, squeezed among wretched Arabs, Turks and Afghanis. For indeed, it was Alexander who chased them away from the cultured shores of Mediterranean, some twenty-five centuries ago. And now, these descendants of Darius, they endure in this miserable place, the best they can.

The ever-present posters of Ayatollah were there, all right, but one got used to them and the everyday life went on, quite pleasantly. Persian princesses went on smiling at us and checking us out, which frankly, never got old. How could it? There were the inevitable frustrations with the locals, with transportations or directions. We would lose hours walking toward a park that turn out to be closed, but along the way, a princess or two would approach, with her elegant figure, hidden, yet well recognized under her chador, her feet immaculately manicured, in high heels, her perfect hands, and those dark eyes, on pale face. Without any hesitation, she would approach, our eyes locked together, she would smile and we would smile back. And all would be well again. We figured out the taxis, which were like communal shuttles, stopping and picking up passengers along the way. The passengers would squeeze in the back seat of a giant, antique, American limousine. We would just stay on a curb, for mere few minutes with our hands raised, a taxi would stop, the door would open, and more often than not, few girls, sometimes even older women, would open the back door and say: *Come, come in.* The driver would occasionally object, two guys, westerners, squeezed with girls in a back of Teheran taxi, but they would shush him off, them being of a wealthier and more educated class.

We loved Teheran. The food was good and our money went a long way. We met quite a few shop owners, businessman and students. They loved talking to us, our country being well respected in these parts. Especially, this one student, so eager to show us the ropes, the city, their political system, their democracy, parliament, elections and such.

You have elections?
Yes, yes elections.
No way. This is the axis of evil, I said
Ha , ha, no really, there is a parliament and anybody can come and raise an issue for a debate.
What do you mean anybody? So, you and I can come and try to debate the lawmakers?
Yes, yes. Do you want to come? I go all the time. There will be a session tomorrow.
I don't think so.

Was he lying or not, I had no idea, but we could not shake the feeling that the west demonized the wrong country. We clearly remembered the news stories, back home, the horrific accounts, about people disappearing, and prosecutions and tortures, here in Iran. Apparently, the whole country was supposed to be in lockdown mode, people horrified, oppressed, by crazy Mullahs. We expected to see a bizarre society, *stuck in twelfth century modus operands* (an actual quote from well-known newspaper). We believed these stories, and we planned to just sail through Iran, as fast as we could. Instead, we encountered a country and society infinitely more civilized and orderly than Turkey or Morocco or Egypt. We could not feel but being tricked by the media and politicians. And it was a strange feeling, your mind, your brainwashed mind expecting one thing, but your eyes and your senses telling you otherwise. We did not care much about politics, but we truly wished, hoped, that one could somehow arrange to take those false journalists, those politicians who claimed that Turkey and Morocco are wonderful countries while Iran is terrible, and then station them a few weeks, down in Turkish Erzurum, or Moroccan Agadir. We even imagined the conversation:

You think Turkey is great? Well, here is your Turkey, you punk.

For we had been there, in Erzurum and Agadir, and we knew that no way on earth, not in million years, would someone praise Turkey, and criticize Iran. If only one would actually visit these countries. Forget politics, just plain common sense, just a few days among the locals, down the street, away from airports and fancy hotels, would quickly reveal the truth. The lazy lying punks, they mingled with dignitaries in convention halls, spent a few hours sipping cold beer, and then wrote their eloquent rapports, demonizing the wrong country. That was why we had such beef with the false travelers, the fake adventurers, and journeyers, who covered the world, between airports and Hilton hotels. The sterile National Geographic imposters, who never seemed to encounter lies and deceits, con artists and robbers, crooks and scoundrels, and killers. No, apparently, the world was entirely populated with nice and gentle folk, smiling for their ever so perfect cameras.

But it was time for us to leave, for the goal was India and not Persia. We hailed a taxi and asked for the bus station. He answered in Farsi, so we repeated: *Bus, bus station.* The locals, the uneducated locals, spoke no English, so this struggle was not unexpected. We were quite

56

confident that he knew the word bus, so we yelled back *Bus, bus station.* He clearly understood, for he repeated it back, irritated and quite annoyed. It went on like that for a while, us yelling *bus station* and him gesticulating and saying something back, until he gave up and let us in. That was odd, but then again, not the only odd thing in Iran. Their numbers, for example. Iranians do not use the Arabic numerals. Things like 1,2,3,4, were nowhere to be seen. This might have seemed like a small oddity, but it was rather irritating. One could cope with non-English speaking nations, even with strange alphabets. After all, what is the use of recognizing the alphabet if it says: *mennyit, hogy a hús.* But numbers? Not recognizing numerals created some bizarre situations. The street numbers, bus schedules, currency values, things that one takes for granted, were impossible to decipher in Iran. A vendor would give you a few bills and you could not tell them apart. Were they worth twenty Rials or fifty? Did he cheat or not? In a restaurant, the menu would have prices, but you could not tell how much was the meal, you would just hand the bills, hoping for the best. You asked someone when the park closed, and he would write down the time, but you could not decipher the numbers. Very odd indeed.

In the taxi, we were quiet, contemplating, sorting out our feelings and emotions, this odd country, this forgotten civilization, with gorgeous women and friendly people, this wrongly ostracized society. In some sense we were both happy and sad. We wanted to stay longer, a few weeks maybe, but then again, knowing that we were about to board a bus that would bring us to the doorstep of our goal, it was exhilarating. Neither of us talked much, each of us sitting on his own side of the car, looking through the window. The bus station was apparently far away. The taxi had been going for a while, now in the outskirts of the city. The scenery changed, it was much flatter, the roads much wider, three or four lanes wide, with no tall buildings in sight. There was an open field, more like a desert, stretching all around us and we could see the sunset, which here, was nothing short of spectacular.

Still hanging quite far above horizon, the sun, which should have been too strong to look at, was transformed by desert dust into a gentle, perfectly circular orange disk. It rolled over the horizon, following us as we sped through the desert and toward the bus station. In the distance, through the haze, one could see the mosques and their minarets standing tall. The highway itself was an oddity. There were no overpasses or bridges, and instead, several highways would intercept, confronting each other in a gigantic, circular roundabout. One could only imagine the chaos, highways merging into this circular entity, as big as a football field, four lines wide, with thousands, literally thousands of vehicles, of all kinds, moving counter-clockwise. Nobody followed any traffic lights or rules, and the four designated highway lanes disintegrated into a colossal whirlpool, engulfing the thousands of drivers, all yelling and cursing at each other, slowly disentangling themselves out of the grip of this vortex, and into an adjacent, designated highway exit.

Finally, we arrived. We paid the driver and entered the bus station, which, by all accounts was the biggest and most stupendous we had ever seen. As big as an airport and equally well organized, cleaned and maintained, this was a hall, some hundred feet high and who knew how long, with dozens of kiosks and information booths, and restaurants and tea shops. With the white marble floor, this was New York's Grand Central Station in the middle of Asian desert. We were overwhelmed, for how were we to find a booth that would sell us a ticket to Zahedan, and how on earth would we to figure out when the bus was to depart, us not knowing how to read their numbers and bus schedules, and no English speaking folk in sight. But, by then, we had learned the ropes: If confused in Iran, just stand there, in the middle of a crowded place and wait. Sooner or later, a friendly fellow will approach and offer some help. Most likely he, and it was always he, will not speak any English, but that too will fix itself, since inevitably, a few others will approach, and an English speaking fellow will emerge. It worked like charm, every single time.

Where to? He asked
Zahedan, we replied
No Zahedan, cannot go Zahedan.
What do you mean? There are no buses to Zahedan?
No buses for Zahedan.
What! Wait, they told us buses go to Zahedan every day!
Yes, yes, but not from this station.

Now we understood. This was just one of the many bus stations, strategically located in the outskirts of this great city. We also understood the driver's frustration. We insisted on a bus station, but the poor fellow could not figure out which one we meant. It was as if one forced a Manhattan cabby to drive to an airport, without specifying JFK, or LaGuardia or Newark. No wander he was frustrated, and insulted by our yelling. That is why he drove us to the furthest one possible, making a few extra bucks, capitalizing on our rudeness. We did not mind, the ride itself was pleasant and scenery beautiful, and we were in no hurry. The friendly locals helped us with a new taxi and precise instructions, and due to a favorable, black market dollar exchange, it cost us little, to repeat this phenomenal ride, now driving in a huge semicircle, around Teheran.

It was a warm night, the bus was gently rolling through the desert, the seats were comfortable, and the bus was clean and new. There was no air conditioning, of course, but a fast going bus, its windows open, and the night outside made it very pleasant, cozy in fact. Unlike the rest of Asia, here, our seats were actually assigned, so we did not have to fight for them. In Turkey and elsewhere, at the bus stop, you would go out to the restroom, only to find some local sitting in your seat, and he would be quite surprised, *why are you angry and why does he need to vacate your seat, after all, you just left, didn't you.* Not in Iran. In Iran, they do not sell more tickets than there are seats, so there were no people standing in the aisle, leaning on you or sitting on your seat handle. Every hour or so, the bus would stop for us to rest, the driver would open the door, and then greet, each and every passenger on their way out. He would say *Salam*, and nod his head and you would say, *Salam* and nod back. After a few snacks, some honey roasted pistachios and cold sodas, we would go back to our seats, and the whole ritual would repeat itself. Now we were entering the bus, and the driver would greet, each of us, with *Salam* and we would greet him back: *Salam*. Once seated, he would make some announcement in Farsi, and then offer a gentle prayer to Allah, which most of the passengers would repeat. This prayer thing looked bizarre, and bit scary at first, but after a while, not only that we did not mind, but in many ways, it made the whole trip more interesting and the whole ritual more pleasant.

By the time we woke up, late in the morning, the scenery had changed dramatically. The desert, looked much harsher now, the ominous, rugged looking rocky landscape, strange black boulders, some kind of basalt rock with a crystal structure within, shimmered in the sun as we passed by. The sun was menacing, and the dust devils, like miniature sand tornados, were forming. The terrain was not completely flat, there were some rolling hills, and once on the top, we could see forever. The air was clear, not a cloud in the sky, and the well-maintained highway stretched endlessly. There were no trees or even bushes to be seen, and as far as our eyes could tell there were no signs of civilization, no houses, no power lines or outposts. Nothing. And the bus itself now looked ominous. It was practically empty. Through the night, while we slept, it emptied and a different ethnic group entered, which was not uncommon in these parts. But these were unusual people. They looked sinister, much more rugged than the Turks or Kurds. There were only few of them, the bus being basically empty, and they looked frightening. Their faces, burned by the sun, their eyes, more Asian looking. And their scars. They had turbans, which did not help. Two of us, just looked at each other, exchanging the worrying glances. We said nothing. We did not have to.

Finally, after a few hours of this strange landscape with no towns or bus stops, and a highway with no cars, we entered a town, at high noon, in the middle of a desert. And it was a strange looking town. As the bus rolled through, we looked out, trying to get a sense of this city, but what we saw was just dusty dirt roads, empty city squares and a town with almost no cars or pedestrians. A ghost town of sorts. Here and there, we would spot a women walking by, but these were no Persian princesses of Teheran. Here, they were under burka, a black blanket, which covered them from head to toe. Finally, the bus stopped, at the corner of a dusty street. All the passengers got out and so did we. Hoping that this was not the final stop we asked the driver:

Zahedan? And we pointed further out, toward the road.
No, no, Zahedan! He replied pointing toward the dusty street corner we were standing at.

Fuck, I said looking at Yuri. *It looks like we have arrived.*

This was no orderly bus station, nothing like the stations we had seen in Iran. This was just a corner in a ghost town. There were no cars or people around, and judging by what we had seen through the window, we did not expect much of a crowd. How to find a hotel or transportation to Afghanistan, we had no idea. The bus driver, after saying his Salam, looked at us from his seat, through the bus door. He was clearly worried for us, but there was nothing much he could have done, and one could tell that he too was not very comfortable here in this place, in Zahedan. He closed the bus doors and drove away. Alone, with our bags, we stood there, utterly confused and somewhat scared. We saw a few fellows from our bus heading toward a tea shop behind the corner, so we followed them there. The establishment was plain, a few plastic tables with some plastic chairs, plain white walls and small dirty windows, a ceiling fan, a cheap windowed fridge with some sweets displayed in there, a shop owner, with a thick mustache, a few Mujahedeen sitting in the corner, and two us, sipping our tea. Having no clue what to do, we just sat there. And waited.

Bombay

Jesus, this is spicy.
You're telling me. Whoa. I cannot eat this. I'll just eat the
rice and you take the meat if you want.
What meat? There is no meat here. Is there any meat? I
cannot tell the difference. I cannot taste anything.

It smelled fantastic and it looked great, some kind of
Basmati rice and a scoop of a sauce on the side, meat or
vegetable I couldn't tell. We were hungry after day and a
half on a train, us not eating while traveling, we were like
wolfs, and would have eaten a greasy blanket if needed.
But it was hard to eat the damn thing. I could tolerate
spicy food, much better the Yuri could, but this was above
my calibration. He stood up, in this small, two-plastic-
table-eatery, on the corner of a muddy road, the dark
noisy night outside, he looked around the shop, at the
food, displayed on the aisle, wondering:

Is this one spicy too? He asked the vendor.

No, no spicy. This one good.

He ordered it, some kind of vegetable samosa.

Fuck, this is spicy too. Try this, can you eat it? You pig,
you can eat anything.

Indeed, I could eat it, but boy it was a struggle, my tongue
was burning, but the texture and the flavor and the aroma
was wonderful, so I plowed through. With my eyes
tearing, and him laughing at me, I munched, giggled, with
my mouth full, almost choking on my laughter as well as
on the fiery food. He was hungry:

Look at him, what a fucking pig. How could you eat that stuff? You gonna chock to death you moron.

You are jealous, you sissy, give me that Limca, I need to wash this stuff out.

He passed me the Indian soda drink, lemon flavored. This was fifth one so far. I needed it to wash the heat out of my mouth. He was hungry and restless, so he ventured outside, to buy some candy. I stayed inside, working hard on my meal.

Fuck it, it is wet outside, he came back with some western-type candy he bought in the shop next door. *We have to find a place soon.*

I know I know. Let me finish with this first. Pass me that Limca.

The streets were muddy and the rain was relentless, on and off for who knows how long, now at the end of the dying monsoon, the water puddles everywhere, garbage and filth floating around and the humidity. The air was saturated with moisture, so much so that fishes were swimming through the windows, so to speak. We were completely wet, even though we carefully avoided the downpours and ventured on the streets only during the breaks in the rain. It did not help. It was dark and wet and warm, like a bathroom after taking a long hot shower with the lights shut off. The chaos on the streets, the scents and the noise and the commotion, did not subside, not by a long shot. The cows were on the streets, munching on the produce, now floating gently on the little rivulets that formed outside. The ocean of people and the rickshaws and the occasional elephant were there all right, but this was a different India. This was not Delhi.

We arrived in Bombay earlier that day, and with no help from a friend or any information, we wandered the streets looking for lodging. We had stayed in Delhi for quite some time and felt comfortable with India. We were certain that after few hours of strolling around we would be able to find a place, a nice, cozy, cheap hotel, in an area not too westernized and yet not exactly a shithole. The problem was they were all shitholes. And how could they not be, with rivers of actual filth floating around. Even just sitting outside, under the cover, far from the raindrops, was enough to make you wet, our shirts sticky, peeling off our wet skin, our pants, soaking wet, underwear too. The hour was getting late, and although we had no idea where to sleep, we did not worry, not for a second. We were in India. You never worry in India.

Should we go out? Check more places?
Nah, I am sick of this hunt. Let's get us a nice place.
Nice place?
Yeah, a real hotel for a change. C'mon, we deserve it.

And we did deserve it, after three weeks on the road, through Turkey, Iran and Afghanistan, sleeping on the streets and who the heck knows where not, we were finally in India. We made it, through lawless Kurdistan, war-torn Iran and Mujahedeen infested Afghanistan, we plowed. We said we will reach India, like true travelers, by bus, among locals, and we did, against the odds. So, of course we deserved the break, we were entitled to a short break. We rationalized this way, but we knew, all too well, that this was a sign of weakness, for one does not run a marathon, and then, somewhere, close to the end, decides to take a short nap; just because one deserves it.

Yeah, let's find a nice hotel, so we can watch the race. It is tonight?
No, tomorrow morning.

65

We got ourselves a nice hotel. In fact, it was the nicest hotel we had ever been in, us, not used to traveling fancy. It was all in white marble, the reception room was, the salon with deep dark leather sofas and flower arrangements on exquisite glass coffee tables. The whole nine yards, it was. It burned a hole in our budget, fifteen dollars, which might not seem much, but that was more than we paid for a week back in Delhi. Simpletons, as we were, we did not know what to do with the service boys: *Hey, you, get your dirty hands out of my luggage*, we yelled, and did the same with a lift boy, never seeing one before, or since.

Should we pay him a tip?
I guess so.
Every time we use the elevator?

No fucking way.
We ignored the service boys and decided not to tip anybody. Screw the tip, we said. The bathroom too was all in white marble, as were the floors of our room. The hot showers, the clean sheets, the soft pillows, the first in three weeks. At least three weeks. We felt like kings.

Hey! They have these little soaps, and shampoos,...,what the fuck is this?

He was narrating from the bathroom, while I surfed the channels on TV, looking for the Olympics.

Helloo! , He announced coming out of the bathroom, all showered and in a white robe.

You faggot, get the fuck out of here, I cannot find the Olympics.
Boy, I can get used to this. This is the fucking way to travel. You dumbass.

The Swimming preliminaries were on that week, and a kid from our club was in a race. A daughter of our coach, herself an Olympic gold medalist, she had a chance to repeat her mother's triumph. It was a big deal for all of us, and we used it as an excuse for this fancy treat, to watch the Seoul Olympics. India, her majesty, this land frozen in time, in some parallel universe of her own, she could not care less for such a worldly trifle like the Olympic Games. Only fancy hotels would carry an English channel that would cover it on TV. We specifically asked for it. The clerk said:

Yes sir, most certainly sir. We have it on our television sir.

But I could not find it now.

Fucking Indian. Fucking liar. I was cursing aloud.

Yuri, himself not exactly a timid one, joined me downstairs for a confrontation with the receptionist. Down we went, two Balkan savages, letting the moron know what he did to us. We were quite clear, and quite loud. But, he calmly explained that it was two in the morning, now in Korea, and that clearly there were no games right now, and that tomorrow morning, at such and such time, there will be swimming on TV. He even gave us the Times of India to check the schedule and the necessary details. We felt stupid, of course, but the brutes as we were, we did not apologize, instead we just mumbled something and left, our tails between our legs.

A bit embarrassed, but unfazed by this incident, we ventured out, now on a spending spree, and hungry. The rained stopped and we scouted a Chinese restaurant in the neighborhood. It was splendid looking one, with dragon sculptures, a pagoda roof, and a water lily pond around it.

Two of us, having never eaten Chinese food before, we figured, *what a heck, this is as good time as any.* The last time we had seen such food, in London's China town, the roasted ducks, and other delicatessen, hanging on the windows, teasing us, all that was way out of our price range. In India, we could afford it, so we did. We put our best foot forward, cleaned, showered, and with our western clothes on, the Indian attire drying in our hotel room, brash and self confident, we entered.

Right from the doorsteps we felt uneasy. It was all so fancy inside, with well-off Indians as well as pale Anglos, all nicely dressed, and all measuring us up. Hesitant, we marched in, to a nearby table. That did not go well. A well-dressed fellow, a head waiter of sorts came to us:

Sir, sir, please, you need to be seated.
Yes, we are seated. The table is free. Isn't it?
Yes, it is, but that is not the point.
So what is the point?
Sir, please could you please keep your voice down, sir.
Yeah, bozo, keep your voice down, you are embarrassing me.
Please, again, both of you, could you keep your voices down and could you please follow me?

So, we stood up, and then he paraded us to the front desk, the tiny little fellow and two clumsy, large, hairy foreigners. He checked something in his book, and then he paraded us back to another table. Just to show us who was in charge. Two of us, now realizing that our attire, dirty jeans, t-shirts and flip flops, still with Afghan dust on it, was too much for this crowd. We felt uncomfortable. But, we were hungry, and we were determined. The waiter came:

Please, sir, what would you like to drink?
Now we are talking, Taj beer, large, one for each.

Sorry sir. We do not serve beer, here.
What the fuck? No beer? Then just give me water.
Are you crazy? Water in this shithole? This is still India you know.
Oops, you are right, Limca, give us two Limcas.
Sir, can I please ask you to keep your voice down.
See, you moron, you are too loud again.

But this time, my teasing felt empty. We both knew that we had been humiliated and neither of us knew what to do. This crowd was too much for us. We could deal with the Turks and with the Mujahedeen, but here it all felt like the world was crushing us. Whatever we tried backfired. Being serious and tough resulted with shushing and scorching looks, and our jokes and sarcastic remarks, our shenanigans, made it only worse. We would ask something, often something stupid, or just too loud, and then the neighboring Anglo couple with that cute little blond girl, who could not stop giggling and staring at us, would give us a look. You know the look. Or the waiter would come to shush us. When the meal finally came, the show continued, for we ordered a lot, a mountain of food. Two of us, not having eaten for two days, we devoured the meal, ordered and reordered more and the empty plates piled out. But unlike the Afghan crowd, which would have looked at us approvingly, as if saying, *look how good is our food, these foreign devils enjoy it so much,* here they observed the spectacle as if we were circus freaks.

We finished the meal and left the establishment as fast as we could. We even paid the tip, clumsily. Confused and humiliated, angry and embarrassed, we walked back to hotel. A bunch of kids, beggars scouting the well-off establishments, hurled toward us, and then, noticing that we did not look like the regular costumers, they flinched.

But, one of the boys, braver then the rest, approached and I encouraged him:

C' mon, here, little fucker, here is a rupee for you,

More of them came, and us, happy to be with the real people, back on the streets again, we gave rupees, left and right, until we were out of coins. But they still came, and they begged and they followed us, now walking toward the hotel, like little ducklings, not believing that we were out of money.

Shoo, shoo, I said, *with a smile on my face*

They smile back, with their hands extended:

One more rupee please, mister please.
No, more you rascal, I do not have any.

I even stopped and turned out my pockets. There were no coins in there, just a few bills. Little girl, maybe ten years old, gave me that cute seductive look, pointing toward the bills:

Maybe that, she said.
Ha, ha, you wish, I said. *Off, off you go you little fuckers,*

We laughed, and with rolled newspapers in our hand, we started gently tapping them on their heads, shooing them off. They laughed back, but when our tapping become a bit harsher, like gentle smacks on their foreheads, with the rolled Times of India, they got the message, and ran back to the restaurants, laughing all the way, and counting the coins. Next morning, before we left the splendor of clean sheets and soft pillows, and left it for good, we watched the Olympics. Our swimmer, she did not make it.

A Sleepless Night in Taftan

Boom, boom. Someone was banging at our door. We woke up, but not from a deep sleep. That whole night we barely slept, going back and forth between our dreams and our fears, sleeping for a few minutes, only to wake up, not sure if this was all a bad dream or if this was for real. Our mind was racing, trying to figure out what the heck was going on, and while we did so, we would doze off again, only to awake, a few moments later. And now this *boom, boom boom*, slamming at our door. We were on the floor, in our sleeping bags. The room was actually some kind of storage place, ten feet across, with cinderblock walls, unpainted naked cinderblocks. The storage was completely empty, save for the two of us. The floor was hard-pressed earth, not very flat, bumpy and uneven. It was a hell to sleep on but sleeping was not our concern. How to survive till morning was on our minds. This storage place had a door, of sorts. Not a regular door, just heavy sheet of metal, with some improvised hinges that attached it to a wall. There was no doorknob or lock or anything else that would indicate that this was an actual door. In order to open it, all one needed was to lift it a bit, off the ground, and then push it inwards. Luckily, it opened inward. With our bags, as pillows, we slept on the floor, our legs pressing at the door. We anticipated some trouble, after the sunset, in this lawless place. It would have been foolish not to. Anchored like that, our legs, high up against the door, at forty five degrees angle, our backs firmly pitted on the ground, we kept quiet.

Boom, boom, he kept hitting and yelling; *Abulakhem, abulludu abuluda,,..,* or something of that sort. Clearly we could not understand a word that the Mujahedeen was shouting, but he stopped banging the door and tried pushing it in. The door, it did not have any locks, so once he leaned on it, it did give a way, an inch or so, but we

71

stopped it with our legs. This encouraged him, for he pushed harder, but quietly. We could only hear his panting, his body, hard at work, trying to shove his way in. But the door was heavy, several hundred pounds of crude steel. It was very hard to open even without us pressing from behind. And boy did we press. With all our might, and desperation, we pressed. We managed to push it back and regain that inch, the one he conquered on his first try. We could see that he was giving up, realizing that he was no match for us, anchored like that, and against such a heavy door. And we were thankful for that solid sheet of metal, strong enough to stop a bullet. Although we were quite certain that no bullets would be used that night. This was more of a knife crowd.

The two of us, in this dark room, some faint light coming in from outside and through the cracks in between the makeshift door and the wall, we saw each other, and what we saw, we liked. There was no panic on our faces, just cold determination. We knew that the only thing we could do was to stay put and to stay quiet and that, sooner or later, the intruder would leave. For what else was he to do? He was alone, which was a good sign. Al Mashir, the cleric whom we befriended that day, was nowhere in sight and we did not expect any help. We knew that he, too, was hiding somewhere, probably better protected than us. At least he arranged this hideout for us, and for that, we were thankful. We had to fend for ourselves. We had knives in our hands. We slept with them, rested on our stomachs, us on the floor, facing the entrance, with our legs, way up against the door. We waited. *What if he comes back with more of his buddies?*

Robbing two foreigners in this makeshift shanty town, was a logical thing to try. The place was filled up with Mujahedeen and other poor Afghans, trying to smuggle their way into Pakistan and they knew that we had money.

We had to. It would have been foolish of them not to try to rob us. There were no authorities of any kind here, no police or soldiers. The town itself did not formally exist, so robbing two foreign devils carried very little risk. Even if the foreigners were to be slaughtered. Probably even better if they were slaughtered, for that would have eliminated any witnesses. But if they were to rob us and kill us, they had to do it fast, and quietly. For even there, among the scoundrels of Afghanistan, there were some rules. One cannot just slaughter someone in plain sight with lots of noise and witnesses and expect zero consequences. We reasoned like that, for what else could have we done? We just had to survive till morning.

He came back, now not alone. They pushed the door, with all their might, two, probably three of them. That was a bad sign. And they were quiet this time. There was no yelling and no banging on the doors, just muffled noises, them huffing and puffing, leaning on the door and trying to push their way in. That was a good sign. That meant that they had to take us quietly, which meant that they were scared of someone. We had no idea what could have been the reason for their caution, but we knew, o boy we knew, that was a good sign. Maybe some local warlord did not want any extra heat from authorities, or maybe they did not want to deal with awakened witnesses and inevitable blackmail that would have followed. We had no clue as for their reasons, but we welcomed them. They pushed and they tried to shove their way in, they would gain an inch only to be pushed back by us. It went on like this, for good ten maybe twenty minutes, but the heavy metal door, with our bodies anchored against it, proved too much for our fellow Mujahedeen. So they gave up. That was another thing about the folk in these parts, they give up easily.

After that it was quiet. For who knows how long. My watch did not have the night light and it was too dark to see. But gradually, the whole place become quiet and a heavy cloth of silence engulfed this town. Taftan. A makeshift, shanty town, just on the other side of the fence, on the Afghanistan side of the border. Iran was just few hundred yards away, and it never looked so good, so beautiful and so pleasant, as it did that night. There was nothing over there now, on the Iranian side, no policeman, no town, no traces of human existence, for some eighty miles or so. However, we knew that over there, across the wire fence, there was a real country, a civilization with proper authorities, police, soldiers and judges. A place where one did not have to sleep with his knife in his hand and a place where one did not have to fight, for his life, over a few hundred dollars.

We slept with our legs up on the door, so if anybody tried again, we would know. But nobody tried anything. I woke up a few hours later. I had to go to the toilet. It was an emergency.

What the fuck is with you?
Man, I have to take a dump.
Don't go outside. Can you hold it?
No. Jesus. Do you think I would make such a fuss if I could hold it?
Can you do it here in the corner?
Fuck no, I ain't shitting here while you watching.
I won't look. You moron. What's the big deal?

I had to go out. In any other situation he would have made fun of me. I was about to risk my life in order to take a dump, and how is one to pass on such an opportunity? But he was worried. He did not feel like joking. Not that time. A bit angry, for putting his life in danger, he moved away from the door and let me venture outside.

74

It was rather chilly, the wee hours of morning, eerily quiet, in the middle of desert. There was one, only one, naked light bulb, a few hundred feet away to my right. Our sleeping hole, the storage place, was at the outskirts of this town, facing the dark, impenetrable landscape. Moonless night, myself alone, searching horizon, looking for a bush or a rock, where I could do my business. I knew I had to go far out and yet, I did not feel comfortable venturing too far. A few hundred feet away, a bit to the left, towards the desert, in the dark, I saw a small structure, a barrack of sorts. Then I saw an Afghan, leaving that place, in his baggy pants and turban, he quickly rushed back to the town and the illusive safety it provided. He walked fast, almost running, diagonally, going away from me, toward that light bulb on my right. I did not think he saw me, for he never looked at my direction.

So, *this is it*, I thought. This was the public restroom. I walked toward it. There was no door, just three sheets of tin, some four feet across and some eight feet high, and another piece stuck on the top, forming a shed. It was completely dark so I could not see anything inside. But it smelled like hell, so I knew it had to be the toilet. I stuck my head inside, and stared for a few moments, trying to accustom my eyes to the darkness, but it did not help much. I saw some black stain-like thing on the floor and could hear some gentle shushing noise, probably some insects or bats, and hopefully not a snake. I did not use my hands, for I did not want to touch anything in there. I stared inside for a while and, as my eyes adjusted, I managed to resemble some contours. There was a hole on the floor, and one was suppose to squat over it and do the business. Except, I was not sure how big was the hole. The floor was so dark, and black, and it was hard to tell were the hole started and where the floor ended. I used my foot to gently tap around, and figure out the contours and the size of the shithole. As I did that, I heard more of that *Sh-sh-sh* sound. Nevertheless, I had to go, so I squatted down and did what I had to do.

In this rather compromising position, for there were no handles to grip on, unsure where to step and not to fall into this abyss of filth, I looked around, examining the place. I could see the tin walls and the dark rusty coloration as well as some other parts of the structure that were black, probably painted that way. This black structure was at my left, the whole wall as well as the roof. On the right, this paint was faded and I could see the slightly lighter, brownish color. My eyes, now better adapted to the darkness, could detect the faint light, coming through the cracks, from that distant light bulb. I shifted my position a bit and that sloshing noise, *Sh-sh-sh* , now increased. I was worried, maybe there were some snakes in there. I finished as fast as I could, pulled up my pants and went out of the toilet. But I was still puzzled and wanted to investigate. I bent down, closer to the floor, gazing into the darkness. I still could not fully distinguish the shithole from the black floor. I could see the contours, closer to me where the dark hole contrasted the gray desert sand, but the rest of it, further in the shed, was all black. I looked up, at this black stain, covering the whole left wall and parts of the ceiling, and as I leaned closer to examine it, it moved.

Terrified, as well as mesmerized, like a little child, I extended my hand, a bit closer toward this mass that covered the whole wall. Now it shifted faster, and toward the lighter parts of the shed. With the light coming through the cracks and with my eyes, now completely adjusted to the darkness, I finally realized what it was. Cockroaches. Thousands and thousands of cockroaches, large, some two inches long, clustered together, they formed the black, movable mass. Chills went through my spine: I was in there, squatted, completely exposed, just moments ago. These cockroaches, in panic, coalesced into this black mass. I raised my head, and saw them up there, now very clearly, above my head, on a ceiling, hundreds of cockroaches, clutching up there. I ran out, as fast as I could.

Fuck, you won't believe what shit I just saw, I said entering the safety of our room.
Go to sleep, you shit maker, I am tired, he replied.

Torpedo man

Two days earlier we boarded the train from Delhi, but we made a rooky mistake. We bought the cheapest tickets for Bombay; third class. Not because the train was expensive but because when we travel, two us, we travel with the people. And the common folk, they do not use fancy planes and automobiles. The problem was that in India one does not just go and mingle with the people. There are so many different people. Myriads of people, of different classes and hierarchies. We knew all that but we decided to ignore it. We were big shots we could endure anything, for how bad could it be? Well, it was bad. Really bad. We entered the train and the filth, and the crowd, the skinny, almost skeleton-like people, they overwhelmed us. Their faces emotionless, their eyes deep in their sockets, they stared at us. It looked like Auschwitz in there. Literally, it looked like a concentration camp, with hundreds of people jammed on the seats, pilling up two, even three high, the bone skinny, half-naked fellows hanging from the compartment where one usually puts luggage, the naked children mingling around, the hallway filled with people and animals. The smell was indescribable; it was the human sewage on wheels. The buses of Afghanistan, compared to that mess, were limousines.

No fucking way, no way I gonna spend the next 20 hours in this shithole.

Yuri, looked at me, with a smirk on his face, realizing that we made a mistake:

Second class. We need second class, maybe even first, this shit is intolerable.

So we did that, we got second class tickets, but by that time, the crowd swelled and a stampede of passengers rushed toward the train. There were thousands of them, and we were not sure if our assigned seats were of any value once in there. But, we were in India, and there is always a solution in India. Apparently, there was a service for exactly this type of predicament: to secure a seat on a train. As we were informed by a funny looking fellow, who hustled us, while we stood there, wondering if we should board the train or try with first class.

I help, he said.
How?
You have ticket?
Yes, we have ticket?
No worry, ten rupees, I get seat for you.
OK, ten rupees, let see what you got.

The fellow looked very determined, and he looked as he could back up his claim. He was a barrel of a man. Literally. Less than five feet tall, but built as a bulldog, probably hundred fifty pounds of muscles, his torso, two feet wide and his large arms like cannons, hanging down, almost touching his knees. He looked like a wrestler or a jester from some kind of court a maharaja would have. His head was huge, stuck on top of his strange frame, with no neck to support it, just a head on top of torso. He never smiled, never offered the usual submissive Indian: *Sir, yes sir, come here sir*. No, he just took our tickets, put them in his pocket, he picked our bags, one in each hand, and these were heavy bags, and then he charged. Like a bull of Pamplona he charged the crowd. It was a funny scene. Skinny Indians, now better dressed than the third class passengers, although equally numerous, formed a large barely moving barrier in front of us. But this torpedo of a man, with two bags, one in each hand, he just plowed through this crowd, and the two giant westerners, we followed behind.

Technically, we could have done it ourselves, rush through the crowd and force our way in, but that would not have been appropriate. To hire a local bulldog to do that for us, well that seemed OK. The locals did not object much. The torpedo man just pushed forward, forced his way through, and people stepped away, giving him a disapproving look but then they would see two tall foreigners following behind, and they would accept the deal. We felt uneasy. These people bought the same tickets as we did, so why would we have the right to just push through, ahead of them? So we slowed down. Torpedo man did not care. He went ahead, entered the train and just kept going, like the true warrior that he was. We lost sight of him, and for a few moments we did not worry, we knew we can catch up. Then it hit us. *Was this an elaborate scheme to steal our luggage?* We both sensed the danger and we both rushed forward.

Fuck, fuck, I do not see him, where is he, Yuri was cursing.
Stop looking and hurry, we must catch up with him. He has all our stuff.

We were furious, we forgot all the ethic and morality, and like two rhinos we just tossed the poor Indians left and right, not caring for their cries and pleadings and yelling. Yuri even punched a few of them, as if this was their fault.

Fuck this, if I get him I'll kill him.
Forget about him, I said. *They have probably trashed the luggage already, just look for the bags.*

We climbed the train and in the hallway, now completely blocked by passengers, we slowed our progress. We were much taller and above their heads we could clearly see the whole aisle, and he was not there. So we pushed through, and checked, one cabin at the time, looking for him. We would wrestle our way through, and then force open the adjacent doors of a cabin, and then search for our fellow. This was not an easy task. Tossing little Indian fellows, outside in an open field was one thing. Here in the narrow corridor, jammed with their bodies, it was much more difficult. They could tell that we were infuriated and they had no intention of confronting us, but there was not much room for them to move away.

Fuck, fuck, do you see him?
Nope, not here, keep going.
Open the doors, open the doors, don't just look through window he might be hiding in there.

Somehow we pushed through, now certain that we had been robbed. He probably had an accomplice or two, they waited inside, took our luggage and then they split. That was certain. We were hoping that since the bags were bulky and heavy, they did not take everything, but rather opened it and picked the few valuables. The cassette player, the sunglasses, the knives and such. At least, our clothes should still be there, somewhere on the floor. The money and the passports, we always had on us, so it was not a complete disaster. We continued like that, for good ten minutes, but could not find the bags, and of course there was no trace of our torpedo man. And then, somewhere, three quarters down the aisle, in one of the cabins, there he was. We saw him through the window, but he did not see us.

He was lying sideways, occupying two seats, holding onto our bags, while the locals yelled at him. They were screaming, for here was a train, so filled up that even the hallways were impenetrable, and this crazy fellow was blocking not one, but two seats. And god knows how many people he had to toss out before he got these seats. But he just lay there. His short frame, just long enough to cover the two seats, his head pressing on the window side of the train and his feet pushing the handle of the second seat, his stocky body anchored there, determined not to move. He was saving the seats for us. Locals tried to push him aside and they yelled at him, and they pleaded, but to no avail, our bulldog would not budge. We saw all that developing in front of our eyes, while we were pushing forward through the crowded hallways. Then he saw us. His face now much more confident, a bit angry with us:

You late. Come fast.

The other passengers, and there were half a dozen of them, standing in the small cabin, realized what just happened and quickly backed off. We moved in, impressed by our little fellow. We gave him an extra five rupees, happy to have an actual seat and happy to avoid the twenty-hour stay in hallways. But we felt a bit uneasy. Taking the seats, by force like this, it did not feel right. He was grateful for the tip and he helped us with the luggage, now that cabin had emptied and only the sitting passengers were inside. He also handed back our ticket to us, and he pointed to the seats. And, what do you know? The two seats, the ones he fought for, were the seats assigned to us on the ticket. Funny place, this India.

On the border

Jesus! Are you kidding me? There are thousands of them!

We walked through Turkish side of the border. It was that easy. The fact that we had to actually walk a mile to reach the post was bizarre, but overall, the Ottomans just looked at our passports, did not ask any questions and let us through. The line was small, a dozen or so people and it moved quickly. That Albanian bummed me out, though. He spoke in our language:

Brother? You go in like that, brother?
Yeah, what's wrong?
Your hair, your earring. He reached and pulled my pony tail and my earring, behaving like a true Albanian would.
You crazy. They arrest you there.

Stupid Albanian, what the hell does he know? I tried calming myself. The Armenian fellow, who stayed with us since we left the bus, observed this exchange. He did not say anything, did not understand what was said, but I could tell that he agreed. He had a pleasant demeanor and business-like attire and his grey three-piece suit, among this bunch, spoke of a true gentleman. He projected certain respect and trust. So, when I saw his worried face, his lips tight, his head shaking from left to right, I froze. He looked at me as if saying: *Son, you have no idea where you are going, do you?*

After that we walked out, to the open field and toward Iranian post, a few hundred yards down the hill. It was late night, dark and chilly outside, and we were nervous. This was Iran we were entering, and there was no way back. The evil empire, the kingdom of Mullahs, was over there and we were in no hurry to proceed. The people around us, on the other hand, they were walking very fast,

83

almost running. Carrying suitcases, they rushed toward Iran. We were a bit confused, *Why are they so eager? What is the point of running these last few hundred yards?*

As soon as we reached the Iranian post we realized why they rushed. It was a colossal mess. The hall, a rather large room, some hundred feet across, was filled with people. Hundreds and hundreds of them, waiting to be processed before entering Iran. One could only guess how many hours they had been there already.

Fuck, this is gonna take forever. We'll be here till dawn.

The people, they were fairly quiet. There was no usual yelling, gesticulating and pushing around, things one would expect for such a large crowd, here in Asian steppe. But, even this subdued and discipline crowd was noisy. With several hundred people, crammed like that, regular talk, or even a whisper, amplified itself and the whole place was echoing with murmurs, a very distinct and rather loud sound: *mrum-mrum-mrum.*

Jesus! Are you kidding me? There are thousands of them!

Two of us stood there completely awestruck. What now? To wait? For how long? We were taller than the rest, so we could clearly see across the hall, over the hundreds, if not thousands of heads. And what we saw we could not believe. There were three, just three, small windows, some hundred feet down. Each window had iron bars across and a single clerk, a policeman, behind it processing the crowd. One person at time. Clearly in no hurry. The evil empire was not too eager to accept the people coming back from the western world. The clerks, they took their time, asking endless questions. We could see the poor people, most of them Iranians, producing the paperwork, work visas, documentations, and the clerk would ask for more. And it took forever.

We were frustrated, angry, but not dumb enough to actually vent out our anger. Not here. We took our passports out, and waited. The Armenian fellow, the one that was next to us all this time, looked at our hands and our passports:

Yugoslavia?
Yes, Yugoslavia.
Give me the passports. I help. Please.

We gave him the passports, and we kept a close eye on him, not letting him leave our sight. But that was not his intention. Instead, he raised the hand, now holding our two passports and on his tiptoes he started yelling something toward the distant clerk at the window down the hall:

*Abu, abhor, abduar,…*something like that.

Everybody turned around and started staring at him, and then at us. We froze. *What the heck? Is this guy for real?* Everybody was glaring at us. Yuri's face was as pale as a ghost. And the murmur, that was so prominent earlier, now died completely. Which only made the things worse:

Abu, abhor, abduar,… he kept yelling and pointing toward us and that policemen/clerk at the window.

The policeman finally noticed him. He was a tough-looking fellow, with a thick mustache and stern face. He stood up, behind that window, extended his hand through those iron bars, and he gesticulated the well known hand gesture for: *Come in, come in.*

The crowd went silent. The Armenian moved forward and we obediently followed. The people, the swarm of people, quickly made a room for us, and let us pass through, toward the policeman. We panicked. What was his play? Were they going to arrest us? Question us? Was he an agent? Those were our thoughts and we were scared to our bones. But, at that moment we did not have any option but to follow him. What else could have we done? Run back to Turkey? Then the Armenian said:

If he ask, you say I am your friend. OK?

Boy, what sweet words these were. At that moment we understood. For whatever reasons, our country, Yugoslavia, was highly revered in Iran, and this fellow, most likely convinced the policeman that we were his guests from this important country, and that we should not wait in line. And him, being our friend and host, he should be processed quickly as well. That was his play. He was not an agent. He just wanted to bypass the long wait. And it worked. The clerk never asked us anything. The Armenian handled our passports and the questioning. And we were done in no time.

After that, we entered a different room. A very different room. It resembled a European airport, much more than it did a police station in the middle of central Asia. It was well-lit, modern, with pleasant people, clean and well-furnished. This was the border custom. There was a table, and a person asked us to open our bags. It all looked very much like an airport security screening before one boards the plane, a detailed and careful inspection, but very professional and courteous. The guy was our age, twenty-something, and he spoke perfect English:

Where to? What brings you to Iran?
We decided to be completely honest.

We are just passing by, we plan to go to India.
India? You are taking a plane from Teheran?
No, we will try the bus.
Bus? No way. You guys are crazy. Cannot be done.

But he said so, not as a policeman, but as a twenty-year-old guy, envious of our adventure. He laughed, shaking his head, as if saying: *Boy I wish I could go with you.*

Good luck with that. He said, *do you have anything to declare?*
We have this gas burner, for tea, and these two knives.

He took the knives. And they were large knives. He held them in his hand, measuring them, and then he just put them back in our bags. Apparently, they were not a problem.

Any pornography? Playing cards? Just tell me now, I do not want you to have any problems later on.
No, nothing like that, we said.
OK, you guys are all set. Free to go.

Outside was pitch-dark, probably two o'clock in the morning. Through the glass doors, since the place indeed resembled a modern western airport, we could see the dark desert outside, and there were no taxis or busses or anything out there. Just darkness stretching for miles and miles. By that time our Armenian friend had disappeared, and we were alone. Not scared, but pretty confused.

Go where? We asked fellow custom officer.
Good point, he said, chuckling. *Everything is closed now. You have to wait till morning. Better get some sleep.*
Where should we sleep?

87

We asked in disbelief. Did he expect us to sleep there, at the Iranian border outpost? On the floor of a police station? He looked at us, then at those doors and then he said:

You know what? Take your sleeping bags and sleep there in the corner. Just be quiet and do not move around. This is a police station after all.

Thanks. Thanks man, very much.

So we did that. We unrolled our sleeping bags on the floor of Iranian police station. We made the bed, our little, yoga type madras on the tile floor to make it softer, our bags as pillows and the sleeping bag hood over our heads to shield us from the light. It was very cozy and we were very tired. We slept like babies. Contrary to the popular belief, the evil empire of Mullahs was rather pleasant and civilized. And courteous. At least, it was for the two of us.

The day we met her

"How did I meet her, I don't know, a messenger sent her in a tropical storm."

She saw us first, of that I am sure. We could tell, right on the spot, that she was real. Not a faker, just a genuine outlander, sincere and cheerful. Two of us, still a bit confused and insecure about this place, we strolled around, aimlessly. We were content, ready to slowly absorb the town, which looked promising, but, like two cats in a new home, we proceeded cautiously. The street was a dusty gravel road, fairly clean and sunny, with a few shops and some tourists in their sandals, sunhats and shorts. In this beach paradise, these tourists mingled around, window shopping, mixing with the locals. The road led directly downhill, toward the beach, white one-story cottages, mainly shops and some eateries, on each side of the road. The palm trees gently swayed in the wind and the ocean rolled, the waves softly washing on the beach sand, not exactly a swell more like choppy breakers. Menacing looking clouds were far at the horizon, a memento of a dying Monsoon and the aforementioned tropical storm.

We grew up on the beach, and whenever we traveled we tried to follow the ocean. We tried not to stray far from it. Except this time, we had to leave it behind and travel far from its shores. This was the first beach in weeks, after jungles and deserts. So many deserts. We missed the beach. Its warm waters and pleasing sand, and local fishermen and the kids, playing, swimming. It is hard to describe the feeling, but somehow, with a warm ocean in our sight, we felt secure. We felt at home, far from our actual home and yet within a familiar scene, foreign and unusual perhaps, but safe and welcoming. The beach was. We knew that the locals would have some fresh sea food to offer, we knew that there would be some nice shady and breezy place to sip our beer, we knew where to wash ourselves and we knew what to do once we get bored or hot. We have already tried the waves. That was the very first thing we did, after we checked in. We dropped everything and we rushed to the water. There was no surfing gear of any kind so we improvised, which did not work that well, but that did not matter. We played and horsed around, jumping over and under the waves, like we did as kids back home.

After we finished our beach play, we went to work. Diligently. We knew what to do, for that was our routine. We dressed ourselves, in full gear, jeans and shirts, and jumped back into the ocean. Afterwards, our clothes completely wet, we took our soaps, the heavy-duty industrial type soaps, and washed ourselves. It was probably funny and odd to see two fellows performing the usual, shower soap rub, but fully dressed on the beach sand. But that was what we did. With the soaps in our hands, and wet clothes, we washed our armpits and all the usual parts that one tends to rub with soap, the way we would have done in the shower. That was the soaking part. After that, with our wet clothes, now saturated with the soap, we went back to the ocean surf, we swam and jumped and continued our horsing around, which was the rinsing part of the washing cycle. The final stage, the drying, was easy. We just spread our jeans and shirts on a nearby bush for the tropical sun to do its magic. It worked like a charm, the soap took out all the dirt and the tropical sun, helped by leftover salt disinfected the clothes, perfectly.

When one travels the way we did, one travels light, with one pair of jeans and a few shirts, and on a dusty roads and stinky buses and trains, one gets dirty. The hotels we patronized, they seldom had soap and shower, let alone a washing service. So, like it or not, true journeyers, they stink. There is no way around it, for there are no laundromats in Baluchistan and no washers and driers in Lahore. Such is the life on the road. Washing the attire, by hand, in small sinks, and drying it in damp, dusty rooms has only limited effect. And it often backfires. The clothes, the jeans in particular, do not dry properly, and walking around, in a warm, humid climate, and with wet jeans, it does a number on you. Our ocean trick, on the other hand, worked perfectly. Not only did it clean the clothes, but a layer of salt stayed embedded in the fabric, which kept the germs out, salt being the ultimate disinfector. Now, I have to admit that the clothes treated this way were a bit stiff, and wearing them was an acquired taste. But for us, who grew up on the beach, and spent most of our childhood never taking showers, since there were none on our beach, having salty jeans and shirts was normal thing. We spent our summers running around in salty clothes, stiff and harsh. All said and done, the two of us, we smelled the way the beach smells, which, compared to the other outlanders was a great improvement.

Afterwards, we went back to our hotel, a nice beachside establishment, a bed and breakfast just a few hundred feet from the shore. It was a family-run business, and very affordable, some sixty rupees a night, about two dollars that was. The hotel and the whole town were much cleaner than the usual Indian places and the pictures on the walls were not of Hindi gods but Catholic saints. The girl at reception was dressed like a Portuguese girl, and she looked more Brazilian than Indian, in her white shirt and western clothes. The place had its own restaurant, and for the first time in weeks, we had western food. I still remember the exact meal we had: Portuguese rolls, with some roasted beef, mashed potato and gravy on a side. It was twelve rupees, less than fifty cents, in a nice seaside hotel, in a tropical paradise.

That was earlier that day. But that afternoon, we were window-shopping and hanging out with the locals and the tourists, strolling around, killing the time and savoring the late afternoon in this tropical gem.

Well, well, well, what do we have here?

She spoke in our language. She had this Slovenian accent, soft and charming.

First time here? Ay?

Before answering, for a good few seconds, we measured her, from head to toe. Literally. With smirks on our faces, but a friendly, approving type of smirk, which after a few moments turned into smiles, we looked at her. We could not figure her out. Was she making fun of us? Was she putting us down? Did we really look like tourists?

Yeah, just came in, from Bombay.

Ha, Bombay, must have enjoyed the ride, she said, with a smile on her face, or maybe it was a smirk, we could not tell.

So she knows! She ain't a tourist. I didn't think so. She knew about the bus ride, the treacherous, thirty-hour journey through potholes and bumps and who the hell knows what else, from Bombay to Goa. There were no trains to Goa, I guess since it used to be a Portuguese colony and not British, so one could only reach it via road, except, that was not a road, only in India that would be called a road. At the beginning, we assumed, we were just navigating the shanty towns of Bombay. The constant

92

bumps, the ride through and around the potholes, which were often as big as sinkholes, we assumed that was temporary, that all would end once we hit the high road. Except there were no high roads, just an endless procession of shanty towns and poor villages and the road, the wiggly road, as bumpy as if it was going across the fields and not around them. And she knew about that! No tourist here knew about it, they all flew in. We decided to play it cool:

Yeah, the ride. It was all right. And you? When did you arrive?

Oooh, we'v been here for a while.

We? So she was not alone. And clearly she was the real deal, so at ease with the shop owners and the locals. A true traveler, we could tell. But she was too pretty, too fragile and too clean and proper. Her feet were manicured as well as her hands, her delicate figure and her porcelain tan, and those beautiful green eyes and her black hair. Something did not add up. We had met some girls, true journeyers, traveling in pairs, like those two cute New Zealanders in Athens. But, they were much tougher looking, their hands were not soft and their feet not manicured, and their frames, built to carry the heavy rucksacks. They were pretty and we had some fun, but they were no princesses, more of tom-boys they were. But not her, she was a delicate flower, a green eyed geisha. None of that made any sense.

Yeah, we came from Afghanistan, via Quetta, I said.

We pulled the ace out of our sleeves, our macho card. We wanted to cut this crap and establish some base ground, some hierarchy. And the overland trip to India, via Afghanistan, was a way to do it. That card, whenever we

93

used it, made the desired impression. Even hardcore travelers flinched at that deed. And how could they not?

Oooh, I love Afghanistan. We stayed there for whole summer. In the mountains, it is much cooler there. Quetta? I did not care much for Quetta.

What the fuck? Is she for real? We felt stupid. Two clumsy showoffs, macho wannabes, stopped dead-cold. Completely disarmed, and by a little girl. A cute little girl. *But how could this be?* She was clearly not some rich, snobbish tourist. She was an outlander, that was clear, but how could she look the way she did? She must have had some help. There was no way she could exist alone here, and look like that, of that, we were sure.

Hey Ned, look what I found, she said in our language, *they came from Afghanistan.*

We could not see the person she was talking to, and we still could not tell if she was messing with us, or if she was genuinely nice.

Where? What? the giant said.

And there he was, seven feet tall if he was an inch. He approached us, with his friendly smile. His whole face was a smile. And one could not help but like him. The friendly, sincere face, the man behind the puzzle, for now we knew how this delicate flower could exist in this unforgiving place. He was the protector, the jolly good giant he was. His hand shook mine, except it was not a hand, more of a shovel, which could have crushed me in an instant, but instead, he gave me such friendly handshake, firm and strong but not crushing, the way my grandfather used to do, when I was just a little boy. Was it his eyes, or his body position, his posture or tone of his voice, or all that combined, I could not tell. For what is it in a man that makes you trust him? It is hard to tell, but once you see it, you instantly recognize it. You just know: *this is one hell of a guy. This is my new friend.*

Quetta

We arrived in Quetta that morning. Not too early, nine or ten o'clock, it was hard to tell, this place being off charts and in its own time and space. The sun was up, but hiding behind the mountains. The bluish-gray, menacing, majestic looking mountains. It was a chilly morning, with a misty fog still lingering in the air, not unlike a sunny November morning in New York. Except, we were in Baluchistan, mid-August. We disembarked, in a flat, open space, like a paved parking lot, a bus station of sorts, and the streets were busy, with some motorized rickshaws, pedestrians, and very few cars. The people were dressed in some bizarre, strange fashion, long baggy pants, sometimes white, but often more colorful and with stripes. They had loose, long sleeve shirts, almost like vests, long, up to their knees. Most of them carried a turban or a cap, the funny looking caps, which came in two styles depending on ethnicity we presumed: either an elaborate beret-looking cap or more like an Arabic fez, but shorter and often decorated with golden glitter. There were no women to be seen. Only men, and most of them, particularly the younger men, wore high-heeled sandals. With two inch heels, on their sandals, they tiptoed around, often in pairs, an older fellow and a younger one, holding hands and walking by.

Bizarre, it was. We felt like we have entered a Hollywood movie set, and that Conan the Barbarian would come out any second. The whole place, the people and the buildings, save for rickshaws, looked medieval, as if Ganges Khan have just left. But to us, it was heaven on Earth. We prided ourselves of being tough and self-reliant, but after these two days, and it had only been two days, among the jackals of Afghanistan, we had had enough. It is one thing fending off scoundrels, here and there, but we were among the killers constantly, with no authority of any kind. We had to count on ourselves only, not on any moral code or ethic, and certainly not the law. We did not leave each other's backs, not for a moment, save for that midnight toilet incident. And it was hard living like that. So when we saw, at the corner of our eye, a police officer in his shabby uniform directing the morning traffic, we rejoiced. We saw a soldier, sitting in a local tea shop, with his bamboo stick resting on his lap, and oh boy did we like the sight of that bamboo stick. Typically, we abhorred the police, of any kind and in any country, but after those two days, we welcomed them, with our arms open. Compared to a knife in your back, police misconduct, it just pales in comparison.

We walked like that, absorbing this odd place, happy to see civilization, a shabby and scruffy one, but a civilization nevertheless. This city would have a hotel, one that you could lock the door and not sleep with your knife in your hand. And there would be a train station and some kind of official would help us proceed. And, we would be able to eat something, finally. Something decent. With such happy thoughts on our minds, we slowly walked uphill, clearing this asphalt plateau, this bus station of sorts. We saw Al Mashir. He was not on the bus, and yet there he was, followed by his idiot servant or a pupil as he called him:

Ha, how was your trip? Rested I presume.

Rested my foot, the ride was terrible. Last night's cozy nap helped, but overall, the worst trip of our lives.

Not bad, not bad, and you?

How did he get here before us? He was not in the bus? Did he arrange for different transportation, one that did not have to hide overnight, in that gorge? We were puzzled. But he deflected our question:

Looking for a hotel, I presume? Al Mashir said.

Yes, you have one for us?

Just follow me.

Dressed all in white, clean with no visible stains, skinny and tall, as tall as we were, which in these parts was gigantic, with his long steps, he paced up hill. He had his white hat and small spectacles, and he looked quite distinguished, like a chief, followed by his servant, and two large westerners. The local youth would turn and smile, still holding hands with the older fellows, who, for the most parts just ignored us. At the top of this clearing, we entered the city, the Kasbah, with its small narrow alleys, just a few yards across, with three, four, even five story high buildings on the sides. It was as if someone opened a new page in a book, for inside, everything suddenly changed. There were no cars, just people, and numerous shops, restaurants, eateries and little makeshift workshops. Everything was in the open. The shoemaker would display his craftsmanship while sitting at his doorsteps, facing the alley, working, while the world passed by. The same was true with carpenters, them working inside, while the doors and windows were open, and anybody could see inside, their store and their skills on display. Fascinating, it was. Much of the economy was based on truck tires. They would use the reinforced rubber from the tires and shape it as soles for sandals, as jugs for water, as seats for chairs. Tires everywhere.

We reached the hotel very soon. Al Mashir, apparently, had his living quarters conveniently located near the bus station. It was not much of a hotel. Our room was

98

upstairs, on the first floor. Al Mashir arranged everything with the owner, who clearly was the subordinate one. Our benefactor apparently had quite a standing in this community. We walked upstairs and checked the room, which was shabby and very sparsely furnished. The floor was cement, as well as the walls. That type of polished cement, with some fine black and white grains embedded. It was smooth and dark, and although it looked like marble, to us it resembled the surfaces one often finds in restrooms and urinals in older establishments through Europe. There was a shared restroom on the floor, and two beds in a small room. Al Mashir entered the room, along with us, and proudly presented it:

What do you think? Ha! Much better that Taftan.

Well, it was better than Taftan, I granted him that, but it was one appalling room.

Yes, yes, much better. Thank you Al Mashir, what would we do without you?

This was sincere, for he had helped us, with the place in Taftan, with the bus ride, and now with this hotel. Worn out and cheap, perhaps, but we got it quickly, just minutes after we left the bus, and that was worth something. He left, and we were ready to crash, since last night's few-hour nap was not enough, not nearly enough, to compensate for that horrendous, twenty-four hour ride through the canyons and gorges of Baluchistan. However, his moron servant did not leave the room and decided to stay and have a chat with us. He asked many a question. Weird, strange questions. He was Pakistani, not an Afghani, and as such he spoke decent English, but he only asked about pornography, about sex, and he went into some bizarre details, about oral and anal sex, and kept pressing us about our experiences. We were tired, so we did not make much of it, not at the beginning. All we wanted was to shoo him out of the room and go to sleep. We were careful not to be too rude, since he was Al Mashir's protégé, but he would not shut up. Then he saw our cassette player. It was small, but rather fancy-looking, in particular for Quetta standards. He asked if he could borrow it for a while, his and Al Mashir's room was just across the hall. We said, *sure, what a heck, just get out of here at let us sleep.*

We woke up later, much later. It was already dark. The sun sinks behind the mountains quite early over there. There was no trace of Al Mashir or his idiot, and their room was locked. So we ventured outside to check the place. And what a place this was! Busy, bustling, the people were friendly and curious, little bit intrusive and inquisitive, but that was to be expected here in the Orient. They would greet us when we entered their shops, they would smile back at us, and would invite us to visit their place of business, all cordial and welcoming. We were hungry and we looked for something decent to eat. As was our custom, we ate rarely, often skipping a day or two between meals, so the last decent meal we had was in Teheran, some three days ago. And we were ready for a culinary carnage, the hungry beasts that we were. We scouted a few eateries and zoomed on a place nearby, not too big, not too small. It had a few tables and the owner seemed friendly enough:

Come in, come in, welcome to my place. Please sit.

The owner greeted us, before we even entered. He knew that we would pay in dollars and that he will make some decent profit. And, by the look of us, he expected that we could eat a lot. He had no idea. The feast started with lamb and more lamb, and some chicken. But mainly lamb. Some of the meat was roasted, like a gyro or a shish kabob, and some was sautéed, with an assortment of vegetables. Tomatoes, eggplants, spinach, onions, zucchini, peppers, some grilled and some pureed with spices. The spices were more prominent than in Arab or Iranian cuisine, but much less aggressive than in India. The cuisine was extraordinary, by far the best meal we had through the whole journey. We had no idea what we ordered or how much it was, and whatever Yuri could not finish, and that sissy boy could apparently eat only grilled meat and plain naan bread, was for me to take. So we ordered more grilled meat for my delicate friend, while I savored his leftovers. It is hard to comprehend how much we ate. There were easily six maybe seven different servings, plates of food, and a mound of naan bread piled up on our table, and we devoured it all. The locals laughed like crazy. They teased us and they praised their food.

Good good?
Yeah very good, man very good.
Ha ha ha, Baluchistan good food, yes? Ha ha ha.
You said it man.

It went on like that for good hour or two. By the time we were done, we were surrounded by a crowd of some dozen people, cheering, tapping us at our backs, as if we were some kind of champions. They pooled their chairs and sat nearby, and some of them bought a dish or two for us:

Try this, you like this.

When we finished, we asked for dessert. There was not much of selection, since in these parts the sweets are sold separately, so we ordered it from a shop next door. They sent a kid to bring some baklavas. They were good so we ordered a few more. And then few more after that. It is hard to believe, but I remember very clearly, two of us finished more than twenty baklavas that night. And this was after that colossal meal. The crowed went berserk. We were local heroes, for that night. Baluchistan food was the best in the world and these two foreign devils could testify to that. The owner couldn't be happier. He made a good profit and his place was known now. He orchestrated the whole spectacle, the cook, the servants, the help boy, he walked around, helped with the delivery his whole face rosy red, smiling, happy, and satisfied. We walked back to the hotel, the crowd cheering behind our backs.

The next day, we woke up early, refreshed and well-fed, we started our search for the train station and our journey toward her majesty, India. We checked on Al Mashir, knocked at his door, hoping to find him or his servant and recoup that cassette player, but nobody responded to our knocking. We found the train station easily and learned that although Karachi is indeed the biggest and well-know Pakistani city and that although it is fairly close to the Indian border, that part of the country is a wasteland, and there are none and have never been any direct roads or trains between Karachi and India. Lahore was the place we should have been going to, apparently. It was very close to the Indian border, just fifty miles or so. The only issue, as it was explained to us, was that train ride was very long. The train could not go straight, some mountains I guessed, thus it had to go south-east for a few hundred miles and then another thousand miles up north, north-east. Our faces darkened, for we were not in a mood to repeat the Taftan-Queata ride. But the clerk assured us the train ride would be quite comfortable and secure, nothing remotely close to what we experienced in the bus.

You came from Taftan?
Yes, we came in yesterday.

But how? There are no buses or trains from there?
Well we hitched a ride with some scumbags. Do not ask.
You crazy. But not to worry. The train is quite pleasant,
long journey but very comfortable, I assure you.

Well, we were skeptical with Orientals, and their praises
and assurances, but then again, this was a train he was
talking about. We bought our seat reservation, and we
reasoned that it had to be better than that Afghani bus. He
saw the skepticism in our eyes:

Look, let me show you the pictures. It is a nice train, your
own cabin, six people inside, each has a leather seat, very
comfortable. I assure you, you will be pleased.

The pictures looked good. Too good. A well dressed
gentleman, sipping tea in a nice train cabin, a mountain
range, prominently seen through the cabin's window:
rainbows and unicorns. It occurred to us, at that very
moment, that this clerk had probably never traveled to
Lahore and that he actually, sincerely, believed that the
ride was so splendid. Nevertheless, all this helped. It
made us feel better. It had to be better than what we had
endured the day before. We were ready to leave, the train
was departing in few hours, enough time to pick our stuff
and say a final hello to this extraordinary place. We went
back to the hotel, but yet again, Al Mashir's room was
locked, and apparently empty.

Hay! I need that cassette player. Yuri was pissed.
I know, but what should we do? Miss the train and stay an
extra day just to get the player?
I don't care. I am going to talk to the hotel owner.

He went downstairs to confront the owner of this
establishment. Never a diplomat, my friend, was angry
and pissed and I could hear him yelling something while I

walked down the stairs. Despite Yuri's temper, the owner kept his cool:

I cannot do anything. They are not in their rooms.
Where are they?
I do not know.
Did you see them leave?

But he did not answer, and we could see that he was a bit nervous. And we could tell that he was genuinely contemplating if he should help us. It was illegal for him to enter a guest's room and snatch some valuables from there. We were quite sure that he believed us, that he had the right to intervene, and that this was obviously some misunderstanding between us and Al Mashir. He understood all that, but there was something else in his eyes. He hesitated. He was worried.

Do not worry, the cleric is our friend.
Cleric? He replied.

And then he gave us that look, as if saying: *poor boys you have no idea do you?* We yanked for a second, caught by surprise. We stood there, quite confused, contemplating what the heck was going on. Should we just leave and forget about the cassette player, Al Mashir and this place? Or should we try a bit harder and press the owner? Our faces were still angry, which probably helped, but all said and done, it was his good heart that decided the matter:

Come, but quick, just look for the cassette player and out.
You have ten seconds.

He opened their door, and we did what he said. Nothing was strange inside, two messy beds and our cassette player on one of them. We grabbed it and left the room. We were very grateful, and by the look in his eyes, we could tell that he did us a great favor. He knew that there would be some consequences for him, and that Al Mashir would be angry, and that he would have some explaining to do. And he did all this, for no profit or spite, just out of pure kindness. We understood all that, and his eyes on ours, we knew that he appreciated our understanding. At that moment, all three of us, without any words spoken, we understood that this was more than a stupid cassette player. It was just a good men helping another. And that touches your heart.

Thank you, thank you very much.
You boys. Be careful.

We nodded our heads, not saying anything.

Al Mashir. He is not who you think he is.

And then he left. Two of us, now confused as hell, we just stood there. Our benefactor, the person who had helped us the last few days, he was not a good guy? Strange, baffling thoughts flooded our minds. We were duped? What were his real intentions? Was he behind that late night attack in Taftan? Dazed and confused we walked down the alley, to our restaurant, the place we made history, yesternight:

Hey, kid, two coffees please.
Ha, ha, they are back. No coffee. Tea? Want some tea?
OK, two teas.
Fuck Al Mashir, I said to Yuri, *we move one.*

Yuri sat there, quietly, unpacking the famed cassette player. He worked on it for a few seconds, and then he put it on table. With a smirk on his face, he let it play. It was Dylan, in his nasal voice:

On more cup of coffee for the road
One more cup of coffee, before I go,
To the valley bellow....

Fuck Al Mashir, he said

Restaurant crowed Quetta   High heels in Quetta

Bike in Goa

I like to spend some time in Mozambique
The sunny sky is aqua blue
And all the couples dancing cheek to cheek
It's very nice to stay a week or two
To give the special one you seek a chance
Or maybe say hello with just a glance

Dylan was playing, on his cassette player, for he never went out without it, even there, lying on the beach, he had to have it on. At first, I did not quite get it, *why on earth do I need music all the time?* But later, I understood.

We rented two bikes. They were not large Harley-type bikes. They were a Honda and Yamaha, some 200 cc each, which for India, was like a Harley. We negotiated a ridiculously low price, 150 rupees each, some 5 bucks per day. The two youths, who gave us the bikes, were ecstatic. This was good money for them, hundred and fifty rupees for a day, doing nothing. But they were worried. There was no insurance or collateral. The bikes were their prime possession and they pleaded:

Mister, be careful. Do not break it mister.

We did not worry about that, the two of us learned to ride well before we learned how to drive a car. We grew up on a beach and on bikes. In fact, at that moment, I did not even know how to drive a car. A bike, on the other hand, we had ridden since we were fourteen, since eighth grade. Riding was not an issue. Driving on the left side of the road was.

Do not worry, it is easy. Just stay on the left, they assured us.

107

But, obviously it was not that easy. One learns a few things growing up with a bike: there are no small, bumper-to-bumper crashes. Life is cheap when you are on a bike. And we were in India, of all places. So we proceeded carefully. Luckily in Goa there was not much traffic. We practiced, in small circles, around our town square, carefully, like the first timers. Our crew, they had a blast, they cheered and they made fun of us. Ned, Monica and the German guy were there. And Ali, of course.

Look at that skill!
You can tell they grew up on a bike, what a grace.
Hey, why are you stopping? Just turn left, ha ha ha.
Fuck you. It is not that easy. Everything is upside down here.

The mind works in mysterious ways, and in a case of danger, instinct takes over, and our instinct, it drove on the right side of the road. So we would stall, stop and go at random times, and they laughed like crazy. But after a while, and under their watchful eyes careful not to miss any humiliation on our parts, we got a handle on it and were ready to embark.

What about police? We asked Ned; him knowing all that is to know in these parts.
What do you mean?
We do not have any papers, driving licenses. No proof that this is our bike.
Neyh, don't worry. You are white. Just give him fifty rupees and leave. He will ask hundred but do not budge. Fifty is already too much for him.
Just like that? Give him the money?
Yeah, think about it. If he brings you to the station, he has to do paperwork and deal with a bike and all the hassle and for what? He gets nothing.

Makes sense.
Do not worry about police. Just do not break the bike.
These are nice kids.
Screw the bike, I worry about my neck.
Left side? Ha ha, you'll be all right.

Heavy monsoon clouds were rolling on the horizon, a warm breeze in our hair, a drop of rain, here and there, patches of aqua blue skies between the clouds, and a ray of sunshine, now and then. The winding road followed the beach and the rolling hills, as we negotiated the curves, the ocean at our right and the endless palm forest all around. The road was empty, save for an occasional truck and very seldom, a car. Every so often we would stop, next to a beach or on top of a hill, just to have a better look. The bikes performed well, and the road was smooth but the ride on the left side of the road, it took its toll, and we needed to rest. We would pick a spot, a desolate beach outpost, a palm tree shack or a tiki-bar, a few westerners, some locals, a beer, and sand and beach. And girls. There were always some girls around, mostly Australians, but other westerners as well. Mainly Anglos. *And we would say hello with just a glance.*

Occasionally we went for a swim, horsed around with the waves. The unsurfable waves. But mostly, we would just lie down, he would play his cassette player, and we would wait for India to come to us. There were always people over there. No beach was desolate in India. That was all right, us preferring it that way. A boy would come, and we could see him approaching, miles down the beach, his silhouette, just a dot in a distance, slowly coming closer. He would stop, here and there, dislodge his large basket, clearly visible even from a distance, and try to sell his goods. We would wait for our turn, him advancing slowly, his silhouette, getting bigger and bigger. He would have this sweet fried dough sprinkled with sugar, a

Portuguese dessert we assumed. Or not. Sometimes he would come with a basket filled up with Indian dishes, pakoras, samosas and such. Or he would carry cold Limcas. And it was not only food, for these boys would bring clothes and toys and jewelry, all kind of gizmos. All one needed is to lie down on a beach and wait for this movable feast to commence. *Magic in magical land.*

We went on like that for a better part of the day. We would drive and stop, at random places, have a snack, flirt with the girls, and with waves. We loved those bikes. After few hours we were in sync with the machines and the left side of the road did not bother us anymore. The road was winding, but on those few stretches that were straight we would let it rip. And on the curves we would challenge each other, who could cut the corner better, the way we had done it as kids, down on the S-curve, next to Hotel Park, our high school buddies watching and girls cheering.

Let's try Vasco?
Vasco? How far is it?
Ned said maybe an hour.
OK. I am in.

So we went to Vasco, Goa's biggest city. We had the time. And good bikes. As we got closer to the city, the roads got worse, and the traffic picked up. But this was all manageable, since for the most part we were still traveling through a country road in a tropical paradise. Except it had a few extra trucks around. Before the city, there was a river. Rather large river, or a bay, we couldn't tell. Some half a mile across and the traffic slowed to a crawl. Dozens of trucks and some cars were waiting to board the river ferry. This was not the regular ferry, just a barge that would open and people and vehicles would get in. But, this was India, so naturally there was no order, and instead, everybody just hurled toward the barge. The pedestrians had an obvious advantage, for they easily negotiated the cars. We were on bikes and we were white, which worked magically in India. We rode around the cars, and once we got closer, we disembarked, and just pushed the bikes, walking along the rest of the pedestrians. There was an official, an Indian policeman, directing the traffic. He did not object our intrusion, he actually helped us. With his bamboo stick he cleared the way and once we embarked, he looked at us, and he gave us a nod, as if saying, *see I help you guys.*

The ride over the river was magical. The barge was filled up, up to, and over the rims, and on it, just pedestrians and bikes and two trucks that squeezed in. There were kids and animals too. The kids were inquisitive and they looked at us, curiously. And they would talk to us occasionally. We would talk back. But mainly they were shy, hiding behind their mothers' skirts, their brown eyes sparkling, they would just stare. Two boys, a bit older, maybe ten or so, they gazed at our bikes, which, in comparison, looked huge. They would touch them and examine them and we let them play, even helped them mount the bikes, them so happy and cheerful. As we slowly traversed the river, we got lost in our thoughts, a gentle breeze in our hairs, a huge river softly rolling into the ocean, among the people and the lazy Indian afternoon and the seagulls flying above our heads and around the boat, squaking, *Skwaeee, skwaeeee,....*

Once we arrived in Vasco, the magic was gone. The dirty streets, the crowd and the impossible traffic, all these things that we liked in a big Indian city, here, they were irritation. We were part of that traffic, our big bikes unsuited for this mess. Our constant confusion regarding the left and the right side of the road and the absence of any traffic lights or even an attempt to control this chaos, it was killing us. So we disembarked, chained our bikes to a nearby post and strolled around. We hoped to spark some magic, to find something interesting, but we could not. We decided to eat something. We found a small joint and recognized some Indian dishes, some vegetarian sauce, a red and dark brown, curry type dish and rice. It smelled great, and we were hungry, having eaten only a few snacks, while spending the whole day on the beach and on the bikes. But it was Bombay all over again. My palate had adjusted, somewhat, so I could savor the hot and spicy dishes, but my delicate friend suffered. We ordered some Limcas to wash the fire from our mouths. Afterwards, we sat there quietly. Dazed and confused we were. Us not needing to talk too much, reading each other's mind.

You think what I think?
Yeah, I know, I know.
Yeah?
Yes. Fuck the travel, fuck Madras and Calcutta, we stay in Goa.
How long?
Forever man, forever.

On the way back, fairly close to our beach, we stopped by a large hill. It was protruding into the ocean, like a small peninsula, some half a mile long and a few hundred feet high. The top was flat, a plateau of sorts, so we rode our bikes over there. We had to go off the road for a mile or so to reach there but the view was worth it. It was late afternoon already, and the sun was strong but closer to the horizon, hiding behind the menacing Monsoon clouds, far, far away. The Indian Ocean reflected this light, and it was dark blue and reddish, almost purple in color. The wind swayed the branches of the palm trees, which were the only trees around. To our left, over the cliff, we could see the waves gently braking on the black volcanic rock.

Mainly the choppy leftovers of the monsoon but with some swell, visible, since every minute or so one could see the whole ocean, gently lifting up, some four or five feet high, and then this huge mass of water would just unleash itself on the rock. That was to our left.

To our right, there was a lagoon, hiding behind this peninsula we were standing on. It was rather large, almost a mile long, curved, going deep into the jungle. The water was shallow, incredibly shallow, maybe only a foot or two deep. This peninsula protected it from the outside waves, but it was a low tide, and every now and then, a swell would penetrate, creating this beautiful wavelet, one foot tall, a perfect breaker, which would stretch through the whole length of the lagoon, and traverse toward the sandy shore. And there, way deep inland, there was a mouth of a river. A small river, maybe twenty-thirty feet across. It emptied there, into the ocean, in the middle of a jungle. The palm tree jungle. Thousands, millions of palm trees, spreading through this valley. As far as the eye could see. Strangely, this was a desolate beach, for we did not see anybody over there.

Fuck man, this is marvelous.
Yes, take a picture, they won't' believe us back home.
No way, I cannot capture this with my camera. This is better than any tourist brochure.
Yeah, this is ,....,it's like we entered a postcard man.
That river down,......, is this the place Ned brought us to see the leopard?

Goa: Leopard was supposedly down there

Biking on the left side of the road

To Taftan

We had been sitting in there for quite some time now. The ceiling fan was flapping lazily above our heads as we sipped tea observing the customers in this shabby place in this God forsaken town. There were only few of them. The three Mujahedeen in the back, with their scarred, sunburned faces, and their turbans. And two other fellows, up front, harmless looking, probably locals. The Mujahedeen, we kept our eyes on. The owner sat behind the desk, himself bored to death. It was quiet. Through the open door we could see the empty dusty road, the street with no people, in this heat, in the desert. Nobody spoke. A fellow would come in, now and then, exchange a word with the vendor. They would gesticulate something, pointing at us, and then he would leave. Apparently, they have never seen a westerner, for who would be crazy enough to come to these parts.

The frequency of these short visits, just a peek inside the establishment to see the foreign devils, increased steadily. We felt like some exotic creatures but this did not bother us. We expected it. Calmly, we smoked our cigarettes, sipped our tea, and reminisced. There was nothing else to do but wait. Finally, he showed up. For there was always a fellow, here in Iran. One just had to wait, patiently, and let the word spread, and sooner or later, he would show up. A man who spoke some English and the man that could help. It was always a man, never a woman.

I help.
OK.
What you need? Hotel? Sleep?
No, we want a ride to the border.

We had already inquired with the owner, about the possible transportation to Afghanistan border. His English

115

was nonexistent, but he understood the word *bus* and *Afghanistan* and we understood his: *No bus, no.* So we waited. Here in Orient, there is always a solution. Almost always.

I give you ride. Eighty dollars, my car.
Eighty bucks, no way hombre. We paid twenty bucks from Teheran and it is thousand miles away. This is around corner.
No, no, border far, hundred kilometers far. Eighty dollars good price.
No way. Fifty and that is it.

He stuck to his price. Did not budge. But, he did not leave either. He sat next to us, ordered some tea, and started to chitchat. He was a rather pleasant fellow, and interesting, and funny too. He was an English teacher, here in Zahedan. Young, in his late twenties, or maybe early thirties, who could tell with these foreigners. We talked about our trip to India and he informed us that long ago, there had been buses going there. He remembered, when he was a kid, Hippies would pass by. Their buses, spray-painted and colorful, long haired, bearded, blond fellows. And those girls. His face lit up, a smile from ear-to-ear, he described those fairies, their pale faces, blue eyes. Half naked, careless with their bodies, they would walk around, their legs, upper thighs, stomachs, even breasts, would pop out, under those loose, funny looking clothes. *Where are they now?* He asked.

There is a town over there, once you cross the border. Taftan, it is called. I have seen buses leaving from there.
OK, let's go there. Fifty bucks?
Ha,ha. No, no, no. Eighty dollars. It is very far, I spend a lot of gas.

116

But we did not budge either. Instead, we talked and had quite a pleasant time with the guy. By now, the word had spread, and more and more people stopped by the establishment. The three Mujahedeen approached, with their rough and scarred faces, but with friendly smiles and pleasant demeanor. What impressed them were our cigarettes. The two of us did not smoke much, and had one pack of Camel that lasted us more than a week. But to smoke American cigarettes, that was a big deal for them. Marlboro, they had seen, and admired, but Camel, with the exotic looking package, with palm trees, desert and pyramids in the background; that was a pure magic for them. We offered them a few cigarettes and they were mesmerized. The owner joined and asked if he could keep the empty cigarette box, as a display at his place. We said sure, and we took the remaining few cigarettes, distributed them among the locals, and gave him the box. He was delighted. Everybody was delighted. He took the box and displayed it promptly, for everybody to see that in his shop, people smoked Camel. The atmosphere was friendly and amicable. The three Mujahedeen asked if they could take the picture with us, so we went outside, took my camera and ask our English teacher to take a photo. I still have that photo with me. Somewhere. We looked at him:

Fifty dollars?
Ha, ha, no way. Eighty, he said.

By the time we went back inside, the crowd increased considerably. There were a dozen people inside, and more people were coming in and out, quite frequently now. Finally another fellow showed up. There is always another fellow. His English was much worse and his demeanor much tougher, but he said:

I drive. Fifty dollar. OK?

We looked at our guy, the pleasant English teacher. He quickly grabbed my hand and shook it:

OK, OK, fifty dollars. Let's go.
Ha, ha, now it's not that far, is it.

We could have lowered the price, and we could have incited a bidding war between him and that other man, but we liked him better.

The ride was pleasant and quite long. It took more than hour, through scorching desert, in the middle of a day. The scene was surreal. A hilly, rock desert, reddish in color with many strange looking boulders, black and turquoise, thousands little crystals imbedded in them, and these dark crystals, they shimmered as we passed by. There was no air-conditioning in the car, of course, and in this heat he had all windows down. The hot dry air blew hard and it helped with the heat, but the car was noisy and it was not easy to communicate.
Look over there! He yelled and we could barely hear him with all that noise, windows open, car driving fast on the highway.

Look, what did I tell you? Ha! He pointed to the left.

And indeed, on distant white boulders one could see the reminisces of the good old Hippy days. One could see "Doors", "Pink Floyd", "Deep Purple", painted in bright red and blue and yellow. Colors, they faded, but still they were remarkably well preserved. For most parts we were silent, observing the bizarre landscape. The highway was well kept, straight and with no potholes. But there were no cars. Zilch. An hour drive and not a single car, in our or the opposite direction. We did not see any houses or telephone posts or anything man-made. This highway was the only sign of any human presence. Finally, we came to the end. And, if there is a place on this planet, where one can decisively state: *here is where civilization ends*; this would be such a place.

The highway ended abruptly. There was a long fence, with a razor wire on the top, stretching for miles in each direction and a huge tent-like structure in front of us. There were no people, no cars no nothing over there. That is where the highway ended.

Border? We asked.
Border. He said.
Taftan? We asked pointing to that God forsaken shanty town behind the fence.
Taftan, he said and then he started to laugh, *Ha, ha, you guys are crazy.*

Across the fence was this shithole of a town. Except, it was not a town, just a random collection of tin houses, barely any standing building, some few hundred of them. There were no roads, in or out of that settlement. Not even dirt roads or tire marks. Nothing. Just this shanty town in the middle of a desert. There was nothing that would indicate any trace of civilization, no telephone posts, no towers or any official looking buildings. There were a few people over there; we could barely see them, some quarter mile in a distance. And they did not look friendly.

Fuck. Where are the policemen? How do we cross the border?
The border is closed now. The officials come after 6 pm, when it is cooler, they stay for an hour, process the people, and then they come back to Zahedan.
Those are Iranians, what about Afghani?

Afghani? Ha, ha, you are funny. There are no officials over there. Once you cross the border, you are on your own my friend.

He continued laughing like that. Shaking his head from left to right:

Ha, ha, you guys are crazy.

We paid him and let him get the fuck out of there. He was bumming us out. We walked to that large tent and waited. The structure was several hundred feet long and some twenty feet wide. It had metal posts, every ten or twenty feet, with nothing in between, and a roof on top, some fifteen feet high. The roof was not cement or metal, but more like rough cloth. Some kind of military grade tent material. It did its job very well. It was completely open, so if there was any breeze, and there was some, it was felt inside, and the tent roof provided well received shade. The floor was nice, smooth cement, some two three feet off the ground. With some breeze, under this shade, it was quite pleasant. We sat down, opened our bags and I assembled our gas burner. We poured some water and made us tea. In the corner of our eyes, we noticed a few more groups, sitting together, in threes and twos, waiting for border to open. Some of them were women, under black burkas, making some tea as well. On the other side of this structure was a wall, some five feet tall and some thirty feet long. On it, it was written, in large letters and in English: *We do not want anything except to establish Islamic rule of law through the whole world.* We took picture of that statement, sipped our tea and waited for six pm and the border to open.

Taftan's welcoming committee

Tiger

You did what? The Dutch guy could not believe it.

You came down from Afghanistan? No way!

As he was admiring our feat, there in the tea shop sitting outside at our street, in the corner of our eyes we saw it coming. The Dutch was still babbling something in disbelief, but we were sitting right next to the street and we saw the giant animal approaching. Slowly but steadily. The colossus was some twenty feet away, getting bigger and bigger, he moved right toward my seat. He was five feet away, then just a foot. Right next to me, it stopped. The mountain of flesh, some ten, twelve feet high, standing right next to me. I was sitting and I had to squat down a bit, so not to touch it with my shoulders. I could feel its breath and even the heat coming out of it, and the stench. We tried to stay cool, but our faces, they gave us up. We froze. There was a freaking elephant, right next to us! The Dutch guy saw it:

Ha ha, don't worry. That is nothing. Just stay calm.
Screw you. You are on the other side. The monster is
breathing on my neck.

And indeed, its trunk was hanging there, breathing heavily, a foot away from my ear. They saw that and they laughed, which calmed me down, a bit. A skinny fellow came down, from somewhere high up, behind the elephant's head. The elephant lifted his left leg, the one facing the street not the one inches away from my shoulder, and the skinny Indian used it to climb down. Then he took the rope, the one that was tied around the beast's neck, and gently rolled the other side of this leash to a metal post near my shoulder. And that was it. That was supposed to keep the giant in check. He saw how

122

uneasy I was with the beast, parked like that next to me. He was a bit cocky, the Indian was, and he looked at me and said:

She a good girl. She no problem.

And the Dutch guy, he did not care much about this incident, he had seen his share of elephants, there at our street. He was much more fascinated by our tale:

I do not get it. How did you go through Iran?
No problem, we just crossed the border.
You had some special papers? Permits, visas?
Nope, nothing. Just our passports.
I cannot believe this, let me see it.

We show him our passports, and we watched him carefully. He seemed all right, but for us, and any outlander, the passports are the prime possessions. Cash and passports are what you keep at your side, at all the times. Everything else, you can replace. But if you lose your passport, far from home and fancy hotels and credit cards and cell phone, then you are in some serious trouble. Nevertheless, he did not seem to be the con artist. He was genuinely impressed.

What the fuck?, he said. *You have Indian visa?*
Yeah, they told us if we want to stay longer we should get a visa.
But it is for one year?
So?
Nobody can get a visa for longer than a month or two. We have to go there and extend it every so often. And they gave you a year, just like that?
I guess so, we were sincerely confused. Did not have a clue that our visa was such a big deal.

He was clearly an outlander with his share of tales. Had been in India for who knows how long, and the Himalayas and Nepal. We told him about our plan, to travel around India's coast, us loving the beach and all that stuff. We figured a month should be enough. We would go to Bombay, then along the coast, to Kerala, then to the tip of India and then turn north to Madras, and Calcutta and then back, full circle to Delhi.

Nah, don't do that. It is waste of time, he said.
What else?
You guys like the beach? Yes?

We nodded our heads.

Goa, he said.
Goa, what? we said.
Goa is nice place, you will love it. It was Portuguese colony till recently. They are all catholic there and it is a Hippy colony of sorts.
There are Hippies there?
Kind of. More like the children of the Hippies. Some of them are in their fifties, and their kids are Hippies. But, it is not just Hippies; there is a nice vibe over there. Beach communities.
Tourist?
Yes. But also some cool people too. They'll love it over there. Yes?

He turned toward the American guy who was with him. Or maybe he was Dutch too, we could not tell, but he spoke like an American. A stoned American.

It is all right over there. Fuck the chase. You have traveled a lot man. I say you stay in Goa. Savor the moment. Smell the roses, you know, that shit.

Yuri and I, we exchanged our glances. We do not change our plans easily, but those two, they made sense, and they projected some confidence. They seemed all right. They certainly knew India. And beach communities? They got us on beach communities.

So what else did you guys do here in Delhi?
We did some sightseeing.
You mean like museums and shit?
Kind of, we saw some fortress and parks, no museums.
Like a tourist, ha? He teased us. He winked at the other one. *Good boys, ha?*
No, nothing like tourists. It is… you know…. we like the old monuments and parks. I did my best to mend the situation. But my idiot friend had to interject:

And the zoo. We saw the zoo.

Fuck, I wanted to kill him. *Afghanistan, yes, Iran yes, talk about that you moron.* But the zoo? Who in his clear mind admits to an outlander that we like the zoos? Not surprisingly, they picked on that:

Zoo? Please do tell. He said sarcastically. *Was it a petting zoo?*

Yes, yes, very funny.

I decided to go for broke and tell the way it was:

What can I say, we like zoos. In New York, we went to the Bronx Zoo, in London and Singapore we visited zoos. Barcelona, that was a great zoo. You can learn a lot from a zoo.

Really? We got their attention. *So how was Delhi's zoo?*

We told them about the fine-looking park, a well-maintained garden with Indian finger food, how we strolled around, in that shady, pleasant and not very crowded place, among locals and without any tourists around. The animals were OK, the tigers in particular. We loved the big cats, and one of the keepers, in order to impress us I guess, he invited us inside behind the official cages. This was enclosed room with a number of smaller cages, where they kept the tigers. For, unlike the lions, tigers are solitary and they often kill each other if kept together for too long. So they rotated them around and that room was where they kept them when they were not on display. It was fascinating. The room was small and the cages tiny, so we were just a few feet away from the beasts. They growled, they snarled angrily showing their teeth. The whole scene was primordial, with the tigers' rumble echoing in that small room.

The keeper, in order to show off, he brought us to a corner cage where a young female resided. She was on the floor, squatted down, ready to charge, her eyes fixed on us, and her teeth showing out. Then she jumped. And we freaked out. The roar, it was unbelievable. And so sudden. She was squatted down, some ten feet away in one moment and a millisecond later, there she was, right next to us, smashing on the steel bars of the cage. But these bars, they were some ten inches apart, enough to stop the tiger, but not enough to stop her paw. She slammed into bars, and one of her paws went between the bars, way out of the cage, some three or four feet out of cage, her mighty paw was. She took a swipe at Yuri, and I could swear, her claws missed him by a few inches only. The Indian zoo keeper had a blast. *Tigress, ha! She new, she wild. Ha, ha.*

Zoos? Never thought of that, the Dutch said. *Maybe we should go visit, ha?*

He looked at the American, who returned his blank stare. He just gazed back at him, pulled one long smoke from his cigarette, and then looked around, pointing at that colossus breathing by my neck:

Why the fuck do I need go to zoo? I have Zoo right here.
Ha, ha, you got it, the Dutch said.

We got their attention and we felt more secure, now confident that we would not be ridiculed in this street. Encouraged like that we went further, and we offered yet another risky endeavor of ours:

We went to the Circus yesterday.
Fuck! No? Circus? Who are you guys?
No, no, you do not get it man. This is not your Amsterdam, flashy and perfect circus. This was an Indian circus. This was a circus, within a circus.

And indeed, it was something else, that circus was. It was local affair, of course, the two of us being the only westerners among that bunch, the middle class Indians, with their whole families, all excited and pumped for the spectacle, which by a western standard was nowhere near a professional show. A Las Vegas type display, this was not. It was much better than that. It was a real circus, the way God intended, the way it had been conducted for the last five thousand years. Yes, there was glitter and light, but on a human scale, and the locals, they truly enjoyed it. They boasted and cheered, they applauded happily when an act was performed well and they screamed and feared when the acrobats missed. And miss they did. A lot. The trapeze girl fell down, almost outside the net, almost killing herself, and the crowd was in shock, concerned and fearful. So when she tried the same act some minutes later, it was all so much better, so much more exciting and

127

personal. The fellow sitting next to us, he turned toward us, so proud, so sincerely happy for her: *ha, what a brave girl, did you see that?* The stunt she performed wouldn't have qualified for a warm up act in Vegas, but here, it was spectacular.

It went on like this for a more than hour, under the colossal tent, and tropical night with no air-conditioning or even fans, the way God intended. The fakir and his twisted, pretzelled body, the elephants performing and missing, and the jugglers attempting feats they were not prepared for, it was all so charming and touching. Not only because of the acts but because of the audience. The kids with their lollipops, clearly brought here at a great expense, they have enjoyed the spectacle, one they will remember for the rest of their lives, one bigger than all the Vegas shows combined. The parents sat nearby, swollen with pride to provide such a treat for their kids and for themselves as well, all happy, and proud how great their country was, for even these westerners, they were so impressed. Never mind that the acts, on their own, were mediocre at best. It was circus within a circus, a show, within a show. And then they were tigers.

Tigers. Again?
Yes, pay attention. Now comes the crazy part.

At the end of this circus, there was the big cats' act. Typically, in such cases, one sees a bunch of lions and a tiger here and there. But not in Delhi. Here, there was only one lion, a large male, and dozens of tigers. They paraded the lion first but when a colossal tiger entered the crowd erupted, as if saying, *see our tiger, it is bigger and stronger than that puny western lion.* And boy, this was a giant Bengal, a capital example. We had VIP seats, just a few feet from the circus ring, seats we could have never afforded in the west but in India we could. To see these majestic animals, and so up close, it was exhilarating. A cage was constructed, but this was not the usual sturdy cage, but a makeshift collection of aluminum interlocked fences, some ten feet high. So these tigers, these wild animals, were just few feet from our faces and a shaky, flimsy cage, between us and them. And, to make the things worse, there was nothing on top. The fence was ten feet high, but a tiger, if he really wanted to, he could have jumped over that fence. Our only hope was that he did not really want to.

So, like in any true adventure, where one is thrilled and scared at the same time, we enjoyed the show, all too wary of the tiger's sneer and growl, some few feet from our faces and beyond that flimsy cage. It was so eerie. We were scared to return the tiger's gaze. Between the acts, the closest tiger, now alone and restless, he would turn toward us and stare us down, his head just inches from ours. In a regular zoo, protected by the steel-framed cage we would have gladly returned the gaze, but not over here, not beyond that fragile, shaky fence. Here, we lowered our eyes, as true subordinates, careful not to offend the king. The trainers brought in some of the usual gizmos for a big-cats act, a makeshift ladder and boxes that tigers would climb and then jump from one to another or a through flaming ring. Except, once the tigers climbed on these boxes, which were some eight feet high, they were above the makeshift fences. Somewhere, half way through this act, one of the felines, way up above our heads, he leaned out, his head completely out of this cage. And he stared at us. We were sitting some ten feet down, completely unprotected, and a tiger could have easily chosen to jump down in our comfy, VIP seat. We just looked at each other, scared and confused: *Is this part of the act or something is going wrong here?* And then it got worse.

It got worse?
Shut, up, let the man talk. You dimwit.

The tigers, some dozen of them, in this flimsy cage were on display and the public went wild. The excitement was so high that they forgot about their assigned seats and they rushed down, toward the VIP seats to see better. But they did not stop there; they stepped over our seats and went to the fences. Dozens and later hundreds of Indian youth were on the fences, holding the bars with their bare hands and cheering and shouting at the tigers. Two of us, we could not believe it: *are they crazy?* The tigers, already outside their natural element, crammed into a small cage, were surrounded by hundreds of humans, shouting, yelling and shaking the fence. They growled and roared, and one could tell they were nervous. The trainers tried to control the beasts, their whiplashing all too frequent now, but the tigers disobeyed. I could clearly see, and I will never forget that moment, one of the tigers, sitting on the top of his box, his head above the rim of the makeshift fence, he disobeyed the trainer, did not want to come down, and he turned toward the audience, the frenzied, crazy audience. He extended his paw, slashing toward the Indians, his mighty claws on display. But he was not behind the cage. He was completely above the rim of the fence and could have jumped down at moment's notice.

One could have seen that this was all too serious since the announcer was yelling something over the speaker, not in English any more. But the sound system was nowhere near as powerful as the screams of hundreds of Indians, all too happy to see tigers up so close, completely unaware that it all could go terribly wrong in an instant. We were scared shitless, but mesmerized as well. Were we to witness a tiger charging humans, here in front of our eyes, us being two of those humans? We left our

130

seats, and moved ten-twenty feet away from the fence. We stayed like that for a good few minutes, and I could see Yuri's eyes, just like mine, watching the tigers as well as searching for nearest exit and planning an escape route if it were to come to that. It did not, but boy it came close. The crew managed to empty the cage and remove the tigers, who were all too happy to escape that hell, and the crowd, the crazy screaming crowd.

See, I told you. Circus. It is something to see.
???!!!!

They were mesmerized, could not say a word, but we could tell, by their faces, that they were utterly impressed. We clearly managed to save face and prove that we were not the sissy tourists. And then, there was one more thing we needed to ask. And for this one we could not beat around the bush. This we could not spin, for it was as touristy as it gets. I was hesitant to ask, but I had to, these two knew so much and could help a lot.

We plan to go to Taj Mahal. I know, I know it is touristy, but we want to see it.

I did my best to damp the inevitable scorning that was to follow. But apparently, it was unnecessary:

Taj? Taj Mahal? Ooooh. Yeah man, you must see that. You must see Taj before you die man.

Hilda the monster

Mike-the-bike, or Mikey, was his name. That was what
we called him. His real, Indian name was
Muhokloprotharaty....or something unpronounceable like
that. But he dealt with bikes. He would rent them and lend
them to us, so, Mike-the-bike, it stuck. He was part of our
crew. The only Indian among us. He came in, rushing. His
sandals splashing across the beach sand, he walked
briskly toward Ben's shack, toward us. We had already
finished our morning swim, Yuri and I, and had our tea
and morning snack. Cockney boy was sitting nearby,
quiet as usual. It was late morning, the sun already high
up, we sat in shade, under palm trees, with the Rolling
Stones playing in background, waves rolling on the beach
and an ocean breeze in our hair. Morning Nirvana in Goa.
Mikey, he broke in with his enthusiastic face, all red due
to his brisk walk, huffing and puffing:

*New shipment just came. Anjuna beach, you wanna
come?*
Shipment?
*New girls, I checked, two of them, perfect, Tuna fish and
King fish.*
?????
*Yes, yes, you know, one pretty and one ugly, they perfect,
they alone. We go? I take the ugly one, no problem.*
*I do not know Mikey. It is a long ride, back and forth. It
will take us half a day.*
You be sorry. They are alone, ready to take.
I'm lazy Mikey, there is plenty of action here, in Baga.
The pretty one, she like Monika, you like.

So we went there. Mike-the-bike, he was a good kid,
good-looking too, probably from a better off family, him
hanging around, on motorbikes, not working, and preying
on the tourists. They would come in batches, these

132

tourists, they followed the world cyclic ritual. Unlike us, the outlanders, who came and went at random times, these guys, they were predictable, and they followed the weekly cycles, to combine the weekends into their itinerary, to maximize the fun and excitement, to squeeze an extra day away from their offices. So, on Saturdays they would come and on the Sundays that followed, a fresh batch could be seen strolling around, all excited, and confused as well. Luckily, there were not too many of them. The majority of westerners, in these parts, they were old timers or drifters like us. Needless to say, we had no idea what day of the week it was, or even what month. Cockney Boy, he did not even know what the year it was, him being stoned for few decades now. Only thing we could tell was that the Monsoon was over, and that was about it.

We rode our bikes over there. Mikey, he secured an extra bike for me, free of charge. The ride was fine, as it always was here in Goa. We did not rush, just gently glided through the country roads, littered with palm trees and sandy beaches. Anjuna beach was not my favorite. It was a nice beach, smaller than Baga, the cliff coming close to the ocean and the sand strip much narrower, and the rocks protruding from the sandy shore. It was beautiful, but too desolate for my taste. Too far from the town and the mingling people and the market and the inns. But, some people like that stuff, desolate beach. We arrived after half an hour. It took us some time to disembark and push the bikes over the beach and toward that shack/restaurant/gazebo they had over there. As I said, it was a small beach, and they had only one place to chill. The place had two large elongated wooden tables for people to share, on each side a wooden bench, right there on the sand, and the ocean, just ten, twenty feet away. Too close for my taste.

It was a windy day, and as we pushed our bikes, my hair got out of my ponytail and into my eyes and mouth. We wrestled with the wheels stuck in the sand, slowly getting closer to the shack, not wanting to leave the bikes unattended on the road, and while laboring like that, with all that hair in my eyes, I saw the two of them. Tuna and king fish they were. They sat alone, in the corner of one of those large tables, shy, a bit confused. Mikey, he did his homework, the devil. He knew where they were gonna be and when. And he was right, the cutie, she was like Monika, a blonde Monika, slender, pale and delicate. In the corner of my eye, still wrestling with bikes, I could tell that they noticed us.

We go in, talk?
No Mikey, chill out.

Mike-the-bike, he grew up as an Indian boy, and in his culture, there was no dating. One does not approach a girl and ask her out, in India. And now he was thrown into this world and this new concept, with young and scantily dressed girls, seemingly just waiting to be picked, and to him this was all confusing. He did not know where to draw the line and he would approach a girl, and then, with no warning or any preparation, he would just bluntly say: *you want to go bike ride with me, yes?* This did not work that well, obviously. It might have, if it were not for the fact that Mikey was a skinny Indian kid. So he had me with him, except that now he thought that all I had to do is ask and it shall be given to me. I knew better, of course. So after we parked our bikes, we approached. Nonchalantly, we strolled slowly toward their seats. And the Tuna, well, she was something. A thick, strong, German girl, not fat, but stocky with all that white flesh, she was a specimen, a true Bavarian peasant girl she was. As we approached he saw me shaking my head, from left to right, and the smirk on my face, so he commented:

I like them like that. I like fat legs. White and fat. Crazy,
yes?

I wasn't complaining. We set nearby the girls, pretending
we did not see them or that we did not care. We ordered
some beer, chatted a bit, with that wind messing my hair
constantly. It was a bit annoying, but exciting as well. So
finally I asked:

You've been here long? How is this beach?
No, no, we just came.

The reply was enthusiastic, which was all I needed. After
that it was easy, a piece of cake. We talked about Baga
beach and how it was much better over there, how we had
parties and we had bunch of friends, how we hung out,
did some cookouts, and how Mikey was the main bike
guy in the town. He joined in, and he spoke eagerly and
passionately, like a true Indian would, which was not the
way one talks to the girls, at least not the first time you
approach them. But it worked. Hilda, as we learned her
name, she seemed very interested, and she knew a lot
about bikes and machines in general, for apparently she
was not a peasant girl. More of a factory worker she was.
One could see her big working hands, with calluses and
all. Mikey, he was in heaven. This was the furthest he has
ever gone talking to a western girl. It went on like this, for
quite a while, blonde Monika and I exchanging a few
looks and keeping it cool, while the two of them yakked
and yakked forever. He did not use his favorite line, afraid
that it would spoil everything, so I had to intervene:

Hilda, you can go with Mikey, on a bike, the ride, it is
something.

She looked at her companion, the blonde Monika, and then at Mikey, and then at me, and since nobody objected, out they went. So it was me and the cutie now. We talked and we flirted. I played it cool and slow, because I did not want to rush it, but also because I sensed that something was off. Something did not add up. She let Hilda go too easily, should have been more resistant, hesitant. In order to help Mikey, I played the well-known con, giving all the attention to the ugly girl, which was designed to put the girls off-balance. The ugly one, all too happy to be in a center of things for once in her life, she ecstatically joins the conversation, while the pretty one, confused and jealous, she tries desperately to regain the attention - she so obviously deserves- so she too, jumps in. But this time the cutie, she was genuinely happy for Hilda. Too happy. Something was off. I knew it. And then she told me. About her fiancé. Back in Germany.

Fuck, fuck, I knew it. I rolled my eyes, pissed off and angry. She saw this, and then I felt bad, which made the whole predicament much more complicated. I knew, exactly, what was to happen. I was about to get stuck into this nightmare, where I had to fake the conversation and find a way to get out. If this was Yuri and not Mikey, I would have stayed a few more minutes and then I would have disappeared. Somehow. Who the heck wants to talk to a girl in Goa about her fiancé? If this was Yuri, I would have left him fight his own battles. But this was Mikey, this was his only chance to score with a white girl. He had no prospects alone, against the two of them. So I had to stay. I tried to make the best of it, she was pretty after all. But Monika, she was not. A simple factory worker on a two-week vacation to Goa, she was. There was nothing for me to talk with her, and I tried, boy, I tried. Mikey, he took his time, the devil. I asked her if she wanted to go for a ride, and she refused, anticipated some sinister motives. I tried selling Baga beach, figuring out if I managed to get back to my crew, I could save the day, but she would not budge. It was hot and I wanted to go for a swim, which too was rejected. *Fuck, fuck, Mikey, you owe me one.*

Later, the two of them came back, and then Hilda offered to show him her room, which meant that I had to spend couple extra hours with this pretty simpleton. I felt sorry for her, but, as I said, Anjuna beach, it sucked, there was nothing there, just the beach, so when the sun went down, I could not leave this little girl alone, for she would have gone straight to her room, and kill Mikey's night, the best night of his life. And that I could not have on my soul. So I stayed. For hours. The music from jukebox in background, me sucking on my beer, her starting to feel guilty and confused, she would say things like: *I am sorry, we should go back, check on them,* which I wanted to do, but could not. Both Hilda and Mikey, they deserved that night, and she knew it. I abhorred small talk, never learned how to do it, so I just stared at horizon, first at the dying sun and then at empty darkness. It was painful.

Later, much later that night, two of us, Mikey and I, we rode home, him smiling all the way, glowing in the dark he was. The crew was there, waiting for me at Ned's cottage. Mikey went to his place. He seldom hunged out with us at night. They saw my face, solemn and dark, pissed off for wasting the whole day. I was frustrated and angry, and they were eager to hear what happened, but I was not in much of the mood, for storytelling. Eventually, I calmed down and I explained what took place. Yuri was quick to offer a console.

I told you, you dumb fuck. Always want something else, don't you?

But Monika, she was much more understanding:

137

You did the right thing, I am so happy for Mikey.

She sat on my lap, and she played with my hair, seductively. She pulled it out of my ponytail, and let it cover my face, the way she liked to do. And she kept saying, *he was a good boy, he helped a friend, didn't he?* She kept saying that and she kept teasing me, which by now was her routine. Ned, as usual, he did not care. She rolled a joint, which was the first one for me that day, since I never like riding while stoned. We smoked it together, she kept it in her hand giving me a smoke here and there, and sometimes she would blow a puff into my mouth, her lips just an inch away from mine: *he was a good boy,* she kept saying. It went on like that, for quite some time. After a while she curled into my lap, like a cat, her being so small and all. So, I guess, it was worth it.

Later, some weeks later, I saw Hilda again. She was in Baga. Apparently she moved in. The cutie was nowhere to be seen. I did not make much out of it, at first, but as time passed, I would see glimpses of her, here and there, and she clearly tried her best to avoid me. Mikey, he told me that she decided to stay. Her friend went back to Germany but Hilda, she stayed behind. For good apparently. She was cashing her unemployment checks, which, in India, was more than enough to keep her well-funded. He told me that he was not with her any more but that his friends would go to her, every now and then. And indeed, I would see her, in the corner of my eye, always with a different Indian boy. As time passed, our paths would cross, occasionally, and she always felt a bit embarrassed, for by now we all knew her reputation. But she stuck to it. Good for her. Hilda the monster, devouring Indian boys, them all too eager to oblige. She stayed in Baga, even when we left, some months later. I bet she is still there.

Clank, clank, clank

The clerk was right. We were skeptical, of course, since the locals, they exaggerated a lot. But he was right, this was a comfortable ride. Our first train-ride in Asia. The memento from a long dead empire and its grip on this world, clearly visible through these rail-tracks and the cars, still running. Not as smooth as they used to be, but they did the job, clanking, *clank, clank, clank*, through the endless subcontinent. Our seats were assigned and there were only a handful of passengers in the cabin, the two of us and a few-well dressed Pakistanis. The window offered an endless procession of mountains and deserts and towns and rivers and meadows. It went on like that forever, and it was comfortable and clean, infinitely more so than our bus rides through the Turkish steps and Afghan deserts. Especially the Afghan deserts. The cabin had leather seats, firm but nice. The leather was worn-out, smoothed by the years of usage, but intact, with no holes. There were six seats, three on each side, passengers facing each other, and a large window on the side, our side, since we made sure to have the window seats. There were small fans attached on each side of the cabin, high up, where the luggage was kept. Most of the time they stayed shut, for we would lower the window, just an inch, and the breeze from the moving train was enough to cool us down.

But, as we learned quickly, the trains, here and in the rest of the world, do not move much. Particularly here. They would stop ever so often and then they would stay motionless, for who knows how long, minutes, hours, who could tell. And these intermissions - the two of us waiting, not sure for what and why, hoping that the train would finally move, which it eventually always did - these endless delays, they do a number on you. Our co-passengers, the well-dressed and polite upper class Pakistanis, they were oblivious to this, and they managed just fine. They were all right, these passengers, not intrusive and easy to ignore. They let us be, which we appreciated. Well-mannered they were, but boring as hell. The whole ride was boring as hell. Comfortable and cozy, perhaps, but dull and monotonous for sure. Nobody was pulling my ponytail or pointing at us. There were no turbans or scarred faces. Nothing was happening inside, and the only interesting stuff was outside, through the windows, where the subcontinent presented itself. The scenery, viewed through this large window and under this smooth ride, was much more entertaining than the crew inside. So we worked the windows, we stared at the countryside. For hours. The train clanking, *clank, clank, clank.*

When we boarded, many an hour before, in Quetta, we were thrilled. The train station itself, it looked nothing like the bus station, which, over there, was just an empty field where buses would disembark. No, the train station of Quetta looked like the real deal. There was a building and kiosks. There was even a waiting room. And although the whole city, as well as its surroundings, looked like Afghanistan, that train station had all the trademarks of British India. It looked like Europe, a shabby and poor part of Europe, but Europe nevertheless. We were happy to trade a bus ride for a train, any time. Boarding a train in Turkey, Iran or Afghanistan would have been either impossible or impractical. The buses were a lifeline over there. Here, it was the other way around. The trains ruled this world, the subcontinent. At the beginning, the train was half empty, not many Pakistanis traveled to Quetta apparently, but later, it filled up. We were ecstatic, eager to embark, to finally have a decent trip, where the seats are comfortable and where one could stretch legs, go for a walk now and then, and even read a book.

The very fact that we were in a train and not in a bus that the ride was smooth and seats comfortable was a telltale sign that we had entered a different kind of Asia. But it was more than that. Everything smelled different. The train, it had a decent restaurant car where one could get some finger food and some snacks. Even some cooked meals. It was a very different food from the meals we have seen so far. Quetta and Teheran and Istanbul, they all had their own cuisine, but the flavors, the spices and the overall theme was always the same: roasted vegetables, rice pilafs naan bread and lamb. But not here, not in this train. Here, one could tell that we entered the whole new world. For here was the realm of Curry, strong, ever-present and unavoidable Curry. One could feel it, embedded in every fabric of the train, in the hallways and the cabins and the seats. The food in that restaurant looked as if from a different world. Which, of course, it was. Tempting it was too, but we did not eat local food while on the move. We had learned our lesson, a long ago, after that incident in Morocco. So we stayed put, and the savoring, it had to wait for some other time.

We tried to kill the time. We read our books, for an hour or so, glancing through the windows every so often. We sat there, most of the time silently, us not needing to talk much. At times, one of us would go out of the cabin, to the aisle, for a short walk. To stretch our legs and go for a stroll along the train, exploring, trying to find something interesting, except that was nothing there, just endless procession of identical cabins, with six leather seats - smooth, shiny, brown leather seats - some with passengers and some empty. Restless we were, going in and out, visiting the restaurant and ordering bottled sodas or chocolate, making sure that the food we ate was western, factory-made, always wary of diarrhea we were. Since the toilets in that train, they had to be avoided. We had checked on that. And then back to our seats, the book, the

141

window and the silent, polite passengers. And the train clanking, *clank, clank, clank*. Boy I missed those crazy Turks and scoundrels of Afghanistan.

The passengers and the conductors and the service in the restaurant, they were all pleasant. We did not have any objections, but we missed the endless processions of different ethnic groups, coming and going, the way they did in Turkey and Iran. The bizarre ride in Afghani bus was infinitely less comfortable than this journey, but it was not boring. It kept us on our toes, hour after hour something was always happening. But not here, nothing happened here. And the train stops, they were the worst. They were designed for trains and not for people. Elsewhere, at the bus stops, we would all get out to eat and to rest. We would all mingle, interact, the passengers and the driver, during the warm desert nights, with roasted pistachios, hot tea and friendly locals and drivers as well. But here, the stops only meant intensified boredom, stale air and the heat. Hellish heat.

After a while and a dozen or so of these long breaks we ventured outside the train. This was tempting but risky, very risky. We had no idea how long was train to be stationed, a few minutes or half an hour, for it all seemed random to us. There were no friendly locals and passengers, like during the bus stops, to call on us. There was no driver to walk around and make sure all his passengers were in. Nope, the train worked differently. It stoped at random, stayed as long as it wanted and then suddenly, it moved. All one could count on was a long whistle blow, or two, some yelling from conductors and there it went. And if you were not on board, well, good luck to you, left alone, with no phones or internet or any idea how to get your luggage. Which is why we never went out together. One always stayed in to guard our stuff. We aimed for bigger stations, indicating a large town or a city, with dozens of kiosks and eateries and boys carrying snacks and food for sale. We figured out that these were major stops and the train would likely be in for quite some time. It was on one of these stops that I was left behind.

I went out, curious to see the merchants, to have a peek at one of the many cities that we had passed by, and just to stretch my legs. Typically I stayed just ten-twenty feet from the train, walking along it, checking the local shops and merchants who were scouting the train, walking along the cars and selling their goods to the passengers at the windows of their cabins. I made sure the train was in the corner of my eye, and as soon as the whistle would blow, I would run back in. Yuri did not like these excursions: *Stay put* he said, *what the fuck are you risking it for*, he said. But I could not resist. At that time, the city looked promising, looked like a big place and the train station was obviously a major one. I was confident that the train would stay still for quite some time. By now I had perfected my method and pushed my trips even further, into the buildings and waiting rooms, keeping a close watch on that whistle and making sure that I could run to the train in time. Except this time it left without the whistle.

Instead, the half of the train, our half, detached from the main part, and then it just left, without the whistle. I ran like crazy, Yuri was yelling from the window but to no avail, I could not catch the train. I ran like that a good quarter of a mile, the locals yelled something to me, but the train, it was just too fast and it disappeared ahead of me. I walked back, angry as hell. I had money and my passport on me, I always did, but I had lost all the contacts with my companion and my luggage. I had no idea what to do. Catching the next train for Lahore, was the obvious solution, but how often did they go? How

143

many train stations were there in Lahore? How would I reestablish contact with Yuri, with no cellophane or internet? I was freaking out like that, cursing and walking around, pissed off at everything, this stupid country, stupid train and stupid people, who, incidentally, came to comfort me. They did not speak much English but they all kept saying that it is good, do not worry, it is OK, and they smiled back at me. It went on like that for a good ten minutes, myself angry and pissed off beyond description. Then one of the fellow Pakistanis, pointed toward me, and toward a distant rail track:

Look, your train.

He was pointing toward a different train, on a different rail tracks, some few hundred feet ahead of me, pulling in. I looked at him, puzzled, *Is he crazy? This is not my train.* My train left ten minutes ago. But then I saw Yuri's face, waving from the window, laughing his eyes out.

Ha ha ha, you stupid moron, I told you not to go out.

Apparently, the train spilt in two at this major station, and our portion was reattached to a different train, on different tracks, and that is why there was no whistle, since the train was not really departing. After this incident, we added another protocol to our travels: always establish a prominent landmark in a city of our destination and meet there a day or two later, if we ever got separated again. We never got separated again.

Later, in the cabin, during this endless boring ride, we spotted this lady and her companion. They were a bit older, probably in their fifties, well-dressed, she in more traditional sari-type clothes and he, in a western, three-peace-suit. They sat across me, next to Yuri. Quietly, deep in their thoughts, just like us. He would take a

144

newspaper and read, occasionally leaning toward her, pointing something in the paper, and commenting, her nodding her head. They spoke the local dialect, not English, although the papers were definitely in English. They embarked, some halfway through our journey and the two of us, by that time, got oblivious to the train and the long stops and the endless *clank, clank, clank* in-between. They did not bother us, they kept their distance, but not like the Indians, who were to come later. No, these two, they kept the distance as if they were superior to us. This was rather strange, for we had gotten accustomed to people finding us unusual and peculiar in these parts, and they would either stare at us or tried to avoid looking at us, but this was the first time that they looked down at us.

The two of us, we were used to this kind of treatment in Europe, where on every country border, they would examine our passports and compare the clean-cut photos in there with our appearances. And they would ask endless questions, about the purpose of our trip and where we were staying and for how long. Hard questions to answer, two of us just drifting from place to place with no idea where to stay and for how long. Like criminals they treated us. Not so much in the Latin parts - Spaniards, Italians and Greeks - they were O.K. but the northerners, they were annoying. The people, they would stare inquisitively, as we were investigated by the border police. Although, once inland, the Germans and the Dutch, they were fine, the common folk, they were OK. Except for the Brits. The Brits, they would put you down. When you ask for directions or a hotel or a train schedule, they would give you this look. You know the look. Fucking, stuck-up Brits. But that is a different story.

Both of us noticed this putdown. We did not say anything, did not need to. We were both surprised, for here, in Asia, as well as Africa, people did not do this to us. If anything,

145

it was the two of us that would look down on people. Now, to be honest, we did look strange, after a week or so in the desert, with those scumbags. Our clothes dirty and dusty and stained, unshaved, my hair a mess, all in ropes. We probably smelled funny too, not having bathed since Teheran or was it Istanbul -some ten days ago. The lady, she even made a gesture to this account. Was it directed to our strange look or odor, I could not tell. But still, we were in Asia, and we were not used to this treatment. After all, there were so many people smelling funny and looking dirty, in these parts. Puzzling, this all was, until he asked us to close the window, apparently the wind was blowing too hard at his face. He spoke rather harshly and in a condescending tone. Which was expected. But he also spoke perfect English, a Cambridge accent, the whole nine yards. Which explained everything.

Then they got hungry. He stood up, like a true gentleman, and unwrapped something from the luggage stored above our heads. There were two dishes, nicely wrapped, in aluminum plates. She nicely arranged the meals, two plates, one with some yellow aromatic rice and pieces of meat and vegetables, a Biryani for him, while she had a plate of plain rice and some curry sauce on a side, and some vegetables as well. There were also pieces of naan-bread, and pickled mango chutney, all nicely arranged and it all smelled fantastic. I could not help but stare at them, two of us hungry for a proper meal. They noticed this, obviously, which only added to their arrogance, and smirks.

Then they started eating. They did not have any utensils. Instead, they used their hands. Bare hands! Unwashed hands, in this dirty Pakistani train? Yuri did not care much, he managed to detach himself from these things, but I could not believe it. She would pick a lamp of rice, with her fingertips, and then she would dip this, the rice

146

as well as her fingers, into the curry sauce, and then stuck the whole thing, the rice, the curry and her sticky fingers into her mouth, and all this with unwashed hands, in this filthy train. And she was looking down on me? It was bizarre. We had seen some strange things in our travels and we had learned to have an open mind and not condemn the people. But not these two. Nope, these two, stuck-up phonies, they deserved it. So I stared them down, with a discussed grimace on my face, as if saying: *what a filthy animals you are, and you are looking down on me.* Yuri did not care much, he read his book, but she saw my face, and she twitched a bit, for she realized that to a westerner, their behavior was disgusting. Confused, she hesitated, murmured something to her husband, who replied something to her in a local dialect. The two of them continued to eat the way they did. They had to for there were no utensils, but they kept their faces down, staring at their plates, embarrassed to look up. And I kept staring at them, with that grimace on my face. They really pissed me off.

Boy, I miss those crazy Afghans.
Shut up and read your book, he said.

So I did that, and the train, it kept clanking, *clank, clank, clank*, for the next thirty hours or so.

147

Taftan

The gate finally opened. There were a dozen or so of us. We gathered there and in an orderly fashion, we proceeded. The border crossing consisted of a small metal door with a wire fence stretching for miles and miles, in both directions, cutting this desolated desert in two, one side Iranian and the other one,.....,who the heck knows. Was it Afghanistan or Pakistan, on the other side, there was no way to tell, for on the other side, there were no officials, just Mujahedeen. The two Iranian policemen came by in their Jeep, they assembled a small makeshift table and two chairs, placed them on the dirt, in front of that metal door, and they processed us quickly. We were the only westerners and they were bit puzzled, but that was all they were, just puzzled. It was obvious that they could not care less. It was a hot afternoon in Iranian desert, them eager to finish their shift, lock the border gate, close up this fence and go back to Zahedan. And if these two westerners were crazy enough to leave Iran and enter this God-forsaken shithole, what did they care?

Once we were on the other side we instinctively sensed the danger. This was a whole new world, and hazardous one at that. In twos and threes, they circled us, they came and went, never talking to us or addressing us directly, but with their harsh faces and stern looks, they just measured us. We did our best to look rough and tough and being a foot taller than the rest of them helped. But our faces, although dirty and unshaved, they were no match for this crowd. They had those ominous-looking faces, skinny with their cheekbones prominent, their eyes a bit slanted, almost Chinese, big crooked noses, and the turbans, and the scars. Most of them were shaved, but some had beards, thick black beards. They would come close, some foot or two away from us, but not like the usual inquisitive locals that would just come and stare at you as

148

a novelty, and then leave. No, these guys, they would not stare, they would pass by, and in the corner of their eyes, they would measure you up. None of them came close alone, always in the company of another man or two. We felt like two grey wolves sniffed by a pride of jackals.

There were no cars or telephone posts or electrical wires anywhere. No traces of anything belonging to 20th century or for that matter 19th or 18th one. The scene was medieval, as if we were transported thousand years back in time, somewhere in the middle of The Silk Road, among the caravans and the Bedouins. At our right, some few hundred feet back, was a settlement of tightly packed shacks and barracks made out of tin, plywood and cardboards. Some few hundred of them, but there were no streets or anything like that, just a cluster of dwellings. Taftan, it was called. The town, it was most likely just a temporary hub for these nomads, and many of them were outside, wandering. The whole place looked unreal. The endless stone desert. Not completely flat for there were some, barely noticeable, rolling hills. They were flattened, these hills, and not visible until one looks at the horizon. The soil was bizarre as well. The flat, hard surface, almost like a cement floor, with a thin layer of dust on it. And the rocks. Millions and millions of fist sized, sharp-aged, grey rocks. As if someone painstakingly placed a rock, and then a few inches besides it another one and then another one and like that forever, in all directions, as far as eye could see. And here in this desert, now that wind had died out and with no pollution or any traces of civilization, here the eye could see forever.

The jackals were getting on our nerves. Their inquiry did not lessen. Not at all. Dressed in those baggy, striped gray pants, with long sleeved shirts that covered their whole upper body, all the way to their knees, they kept walking around us, and they kept sizing us up. Others, presumably a different ethnic group, had those long Arab-type tunics, covering the whole body. But these were no Arabs, these men, they wore those large black beards and they looked much more sinister. Everybody had some simple sandals and there were no shoes of any type, and no visible weapons either. Which was a good sign. We all knew that knives must have been common among this bunch, but mere fact that they did not flash them out, and that nobody carried AK47 visibly displayed, clearly indicated that some level of law and order was present. Someone, somehow, did impose a certain rule of conduct, a civizaition of sorts. Probably a warlord, hidden in the Kasbah of Taftan. Surprisingly, we were not scared. The adrenaline rushed through our veins, we were alert, edgy and angry, but not scared. The fear, it creeped in later that night. However, the nerves were getting the better of us. One of the buggers, he came too close to me, and this was probably the third time he did that, passing nearby, sizing me up, in the corner of his eye, figuring me to be the weaker of the two, he just walked by, almost touching me with his shoulder he did.

I gonna smack the fucker to the pulp if he comes again, I said through my clenched teeth.

I said this in our language, my fists closed tight, eager to cut the chase and show these five-foot-four skinny midgets that they cannot fuck with us. These two buggers, the ones that just passed by, their combined weight was less then Yuri's alone. *How dare they*? A simple provocation from our side, followed up by a quick beating, would have sent a message. And it was a viable option. In fact, by the looks of things and the jackals' daring sniffs, it seemed like the only real option. We had to do something.

Steady, steady. He replied, quietly, still in our language.

150

I could not hold it any longer. The two of us, we had been standing like that for quite some time. Had it been an hour?, I could not recall. We could have sat down, we had those army-type, rough duffle bags, which we could have used as seats to avoid the sharp rocks, but we had to stand tall, and together. We were a much more formidable obstacle that way. And these animals, they respond to shit like that. We knew they would, we learned our lesson, growing up in that street of ours. Our neighborhood, The Godforsaken District as it was called, and we, the inhabitants, we were known as *the Forsaken*. It carried a lot of creed, downtown and in the clubs, to be one of *the Forsaken*. Tough place it was. I remember, very well, when my cousin got beaten so badly, him screaming in pain, on his knees. We all watched and I, scared shitless, I didn't do squat. We were both only ten. And later, our buddy, Danny, he had beaten two bullies, all by himself, which was a hell of feat, but why did he have to massacre them, smashing their heads on the concrete floor, blood, teeth and pieces of face splattered all around? No police ever came, to our neighbored. Knife fights and bloody noses were common in our school backyard and Danny, he got expelled for beating up the superintendant. And this was middle school, not the high school, where we all went together. So, we saw our share of a rough crowd, and we knew how to stand our ground, but this bunch looked much more sinister than anything we had ever seen before. Or after.

And that fence, the endless fence with the gate now closed, it kept us in here, like in a cage. Iran, on the other side, it looked so splendid at that moment, and if it were not for the razor sharp wire on the top, we would have probably jumped the fence. And spend the night in Iran. And night, it was approaching. Slowly, the shadows were getting longer and the prospect of spending the night, here, among these thugs, it made us shiver. And the fear, it was sneaking up on us. I had had enough, so I walked away from Yuri, went out to stretch my legs, which disturb the jackals a bit. Some of them stopped cold, and the few that were just about to approach, they quickly changed direction and walked away.

I walked toward the sunset, for it was hypnotic. Here, near the equator, there are no long, lingering sunsets. The sun does not hug the horizon like it does up north where we lived. Here, it drops straight down, but it does so in spectacular ways. The visibility was infinite, you could see forever, and the sun, the huge, dark-orange, perfect circle in the distant sky, it slowly went down. The air was dry but the dust particles, over the stretch of hundred miles of flat landscape transformed the otherwise too-bright star into a gentle red giant. It was a sunset from a different planet, as if we were in the Star Wars universe looking at some other sun. Hypnotic, was the only word to describe it, for one could actually stare, directly at the sun, its warm, soft, red glow shining back at you. There were few of the Mujahedeen praying toward this sun, which on its own was beautiful. To see these battle scarred warriors, with their small Persian rugs prostrated on the floor, facing this beautiful sunset, kneeling down, humbled, against Allah, it was something, I had to say. I walked toward them and the sunset. Yuri, he ran after me, grabbed my shoulder and pulled me over.

What are you doing you idiot?

I looked at him, puzzled. I did not say anything, for it was obvious, I wanted to stretch my legs and walk a bit toward the horizon and to see these praying warriors, up close. He saw my face and he understood what my intentions were so he added:

You cannot walk in on them, not like that; he nodded toward the few bearded devils praying on their rugs.

You cannot walk between them and the sun. You are going to get us killed you moron.

He pulled me back, strongly and harshly. He was resolute and I was confused. And conflicted. Angry for his abrupt intrusion, for nobody yanks me like that, but, at the same time, I was pleased that he saved me from a costly blunder. For he knew more about Muslims that I did, him having spent some time in Iraq.

Hallo, hello, and welcome to Taftan.

The voice came from behind. We turned quickly and we looked at the stranger. He approached us and by the look of him we were certain that he had just appeared to this scene. He did not look like the rest of this bunch, not by any means. He did not have the tunic. He wore pants and a long-sleeved shirt, but his pants were not baggy, his attire was white and perfectly clean with no stains, which in this place was nothing short of miraculous. He had small spectacles, like John Lennon did and he carried a small book on him, the Koran presumably.

You are Muslim? He nodded toward Yuri.

I had long blond hair, tied clumsily in a pony tail, unshaved, with dirty jeans and t-shirt, I certainly did not look like a Muslim, more like an angry hippy or a biker I was. But Yuri, well, he was something. Bald, with a mean, thin black mustache, his complexion, dark for European standards, but just right for these parts. Him standing well north of six-feet and two hundred pounds, he looked like a Sultan's bodyguard, a Janissary of sorts, and to be honest, some of his ancestors might have been Janissaries, the Ottoman's elite infantry.

No, I am not, but I have many Muslim friends.

That was true. And that was very well-received.

Very well, very well. Welcome. Where are you going?
To Pakistan.
So, to Quetta you want to go?
Quetta?
Yes, that is a splendid town, over in Pakistan, and you are in luck, there is a bus, leaving soon.
Bus? Now? Thank god.
Yes, yes, praise Allah.

We were relieved. Ecstatic. We did not need to spend the night in that horrendous place where a knife in-between your ribs was well within the realm of possibilities. We spoke happily, elevated that finally some trace of civilization has shown itself. And Al Mashir, which was his name, he spoke eloquently and he was pleasant. But it was more than that. Much more. For the jackals, they disappeared. All of a sudden, as if someone had slammed a fist on a kitchen table and all the cockroaches just ran away, so did they. We were in the middle of this field, having a friendly, quite intellectual discussion with Al Mashir, and nobody bothered us and nobody dared to come close. Except his student, a bearded fellow, shorter and less prominent than his teacher, but still dressed in white and with a book. We spoke of religion, and we learned that Al Mashir, apparently a Muslim scholar, had a great admiration for the Christians, them being of the same book as he called it. Jesus, or Isa, as he was known in Koran, was considered a great prophet, an equal to Abraham and Mohamed, the latter being the top honcho of course. He abhorred the Hindus and the Buddhists, which were the scum of the Earth, apparently.

It went on like this for good ten or twenty minutes and then the bus appeared. It was a funny-looking vehicle, that bus. Half the size of a regular bus, with its hood protruding, not unlike buses from the 1950's or American school buses of today. But that was nothing compared to the paint job. The bus was decorated with thousands of silly colorful images and glitter. The base color was red, faded red, with a ridiculous amount of blue and yellow imagery and decorations. The flags and ribbons were everywhere and broken pieces of mirrors, glued to its exterior, they shimmered, reflecting the red glow from the warm giant at the distant horizon. As it approached us, the Afghans running alongside, the bus stopped, right in front of us, as if four of us marked the exact spot for the bus stop. The doors opened, and two of us, we were hesitant at first, but after Al Mashir's, *Go on, go on, buy the tickets*, we ventured inside and purchased two tickets. Except, there were no actual tickets, the driver took the money and he nodded his head, as if saying, *I know you, you can ride, but now get out and let the rest pay for the fair*. So we went out and more people came and did the same. There were some dozen or so passengers waiting outside. When this was over, the driver closed the door, and went for a drive. Him and his assistant, with the windows opened, they drove around in large circle and yelled something like: *Albajkur, albuhood, albara,*...apparently calling for more passengers. They made two circles like that, and then ventured out, presumably making a large, last drive-by around the whole of Taftan. That did not take too long, Taftan being rather small and compact. So after ten minutes they were back, completing the full circle. They parked, right in front of us again. They spoke something to the crowd and to Al Mashir and he relayed the message:

155

Sorry, it looks like bus will not go tonight.
Why?
There are not enough passengers.
But it is almost full?
No, no, we need more people. Will try tomorrow morning.
But, overnight, who will come? The border is closed and
there are no roads to Taftan.
They will come, they will.
He said so with a smirk on his face. We froze. This meant
we had to spend a night, here in this wretched place. This
meant we would not be able to sleep at all. We had to stay
alert the whole night, here at this very spot, since for sure
we were not going to enter the Kasbah, not now and
certainly not in the middle of the night.

We have no place to sleep. Can we just bunk in here? We
pointed to the floor.
Nonsense, we will find you a nice place. Don't you worry
about it.

So he did. And so we spent a night in Taftan.

Al Mashir took this picture.

The Oblivion

It was a sticky, warm and humid night. We did not mind. The scents and the soft chanting engulfed this place. We walked around, mingled with the crowd, which was not too large, at least not for Indian standards. There was some kind of temple there, nothing spectacular, in ruins and quite old. There were flower petals everywhere and the smoke from the incense sticks saturated the air. The place was quite well lit, with strings of faded yellow light-bulbs hanging on the wires above our heads, every yard or so, hundreds and hundreds of light-bulbs. Their yellow glow reflected from the walls of these ruins. The trees were magnificent as well. They stretched way up, well above the hanging light bulbs, so we could not see how far up they went, the night being moonless, or maybe just cloudy. But the limbs of these trees, the ones closer to the ground, they suggested magnificent creatures. Thick and strong these branches were, and very unlike the ones we had seen so far. The bark was smooth and polished. It was very light in color, almost white and it shone, reflecting the faded glow from the light bulbs above.

There were monkeys all around, on the top of the ruins and on the trees. Quite large monkeys, reddish in color, like miniature baboons. They were not aggressive, and for the most time they stayed up there, hanging by the branches or in-between the ruins on top of the temple. Occasionally, one would come down and snatch something from the ground, a piece of fruit or a candy, dropped by the tourists. We had been there for some half an hour now, ever since the bus stopped. All the passengers disembarked. They mingled around, aimlessly, the two of us included. We boarded this bus, some ten, maybe fifteen hours ago, and we had spent the whole day with this bunch, the upper-middle-class Indians. Rather nice people, friendly and polite, and after a while, one

157

couldn't help but befriend some of them. Most of these passengers, if not all, were couples, alone or with kids and sometimes with grandparents. They booked this trip, the one day sightseeing family trip, but after a long day, most of them were fed up with these extended, unscheduled stops and inevitable delays. They were ready to go home. Two of us, on the other hand, we did not mind this digression. It was all right with us.

This is all scam, he said, the well-dressed Indian fellow.

He was the one that helped us with a menu that morning, when this bus had pulled over for a lunch break. Two of us, we were afraid to order any food, always wary of eating on the road. But he insisted that we should try something, claiming that the place was clean and the dishes would not be spicy. He handpicked a few things for us. And indeed they were fantastic, fragrant rice pilafs. They were very light, almost too light for there were only few skinny pieces of chicken in there, and I do not believe I have ever seen skinnier chicken leg, just a bone and a minuscule amount of meat. And there were not much vegetables either. Nevertheless, it tasted incredible, the aromas and the smells from the spices fooled our senses, you would think you are eating a rich, meat and vegetable dish, while in fact, it was just well spiced fragrant plain rice. It did the job, it filled us up.

This is just a tourist trap. This is no Buddha's grave, I tell you.

He was throwing a tantrum. Mainly because he was right, this was indeed a tourist trap, but also, because he was embarrassed in front of us. He felt that he had to defend his country and his culture and to show these two westerners that he too, was angry and frustrated, with this obvious con. Except the two of us. We were not angry.

158

We knew that this could not have been the actual Buddha's resting place, as the bus driver announced, for if it were a genuinely accepted resting place of Gautama, boy there would have been thousands of annoying Western followers and the whole circus that comes with them, Hare Krishna idiots and all that crap. But no, this was a much more secluded, intimate place of worship. We were the only westerners and there were some pilgrims there, a few dozen or so, and there were some chanting monks, and the incense and flower petals, the whole nine yards. But also, some tourist kiosks selling Buddha's memorabilia, and our fellow Indian companion, fuming:

Look at that, they just want money and we are already late. It will be midnight before we are back in Delhi.

We couldn't care less. Somehow, all this was just a trifle. We could see that the driver had no right to stop here unannounced, just to collect a fee from the local merchants as a reward for bringing in tourists. And we knew that these stops would result with us being dead tired once we reached our hotel. We knew all that, but we were not upset. Which was rather strange, the two of us not known for our tolerance. But, with that Buddha smile plastered on our faces, we mingled around, oblivious to any tourist traps, bus delays or similar little pitfalls. We were never big on that eastern spiritual crap, nirvanas, inner energy and alike. That was for the fake hippies and annoying westerners, not for us. But, something had happened earlier that day. It was hard to describe it, but we both knew it, we both sensed it.

We booked this trip, a one day sightseeing trip to the Taj Mahal, in a way a true tourist would have done. An Indian tourist, of course. There were some fancy, air-conditioned buses leaving daily from Hiltons and Sheratons of Delhi, but that was out of the question. Of course. We avoided

159

that crowd at any cost, us preferring the locals. For a moment we considered going on our own, by train and then by local bus, but, the buddies at our street informed us that it was not worth it, those train-to-bus transitions never work in India. *Just take the bus, it is easier*, they said. So we did. This was our first bus trip in India, and we were unprepared. The railway, it had been built by the Brits, while the roads were built by the Indians and one could tell. It was not Afghanistan, but it came close. There were no highways to speak of, instead, one-lane, half dirt half asphalt roads were the norm, even between the major cities. The bus would stop and go. It navigated potholes and shanty towns, while the children and the livestock shared the road with the traffic, which was very sparse. Here and there, the road would straighten, and would look like a two-lane highway, only this time the traffic would pick up. But this was Indian traffic. There was a camel pulling a cart with a gigantic haystack, bigger than our whole bus, and the tiny Indian fellow on the top of this hay, he took it easy. The camel, she moved slowly, one leg at a time, our bus followed, at this easy strolling pace, for more than half an hour. But we did not mind, and our co-passengers did not either. We were all excited, for the trip, for the Taj.

And the Taj, it did not disappoint. There are many places on this planet, that look magnificent on a post card or on TV commercials, but the Taj, it looked better than any post card, better than any poster. There were thousands people over here, but the place was not crowded, it easily accommodated these guests, as it was designed to. The garden that lead to the Taj, was some quarter mile long, with a perfectly symmetric, shallow pool, that reflected the Taj itself, in wonderful proportions, all harmonized with decorations, plants, flowers as well as people. Versailles paled in comparison. The gate that led us to this garden and the pool was perfectly carved, so much so that one could step back, some forty-fifty feet, and align the exact contours of the distant Taj with this stone carved gate entrance. Tourists swarmed the place, but thank God, the vast majority of them were Indians. We savored the moment, we did not rush toward Taj, but instead, we explored the park that led to it. We would sit on a bench or on the grass nearby the pool, and reminisce and we would soak in the moment, slowly advancing toward that marvelous oracle that awaited us at the far end of this park. We progressed slowly, as if afraid that once there, the magic would evaporate.

But it did not. For once we reached there, and once we stood next to the monument itself, we realized that we were in the presence of something different. Something dignified, something magnificent, and we felt as if we had entered the world of Arabian Nights and Prince Ali, which in a sense, we did. Taj was big, bigger than one would have imagined and it was all marble. But not just any marble. This stone, it was soft and warm and the texture was hard to describe with words only, for one has to feel it. We were asked to go barefoot, this being a Muslim place, and we were able to feel the texture, the warm marble, smooth and polished, yet not too smooth, for it was not slippery but rather easy to walk on. It was a marble floor and yet one felt as if it were a soft carpet. The inviting, almost pliable texture, it radiated the balmy, pleasant heat, since it had been baked on sun for better part of a day.

This lavish marble, it was not just reserved for the main steps or the shrine itself. No, it was everywhere, every single piece, every single nook and cranny, all the surrounding structures and the steps for the adjacent, hidden entrances, the roof, every single detail was carved in this praised marble. And this marble was heavily decorated, in particular within the tomb itself. Thousands, probably tens of thousands of flowers with petals of different shape and colors were plastered on every single piece of stone. But they were not painted. No, every single flower, and every single petal, and every single leaf, was an actual, hand-carved semi-precious stone, in the shape of a petal or a leaf, and these semi-precious stones were chosen in the appropriate color, and they were embedded, by hand, into the marble. And there were thousands of flowers and tens of thousands of petals.

We would go in and out of the main structure, which was rather crowded. We walked around the majestic terrace, for behind the Taj, there was a river, and the Taj itself was on a hill at the bank of this river. On top of this hill was the whole structure, the extended elevated terrace, with four smaller towers on each corner and with the shrine in the middle. The whole structure, every single piece of stone, was done in that magnificent marble. We walked behind the main monument, the shrine itself, and on that large terrace. There were not many people there, just an empty patio, with the view of the river below and the valley that stretched forever. We stood there, for quite some time, enjoying the view, and only once in a while, one of us would leave to mingle around, and explore the place. After a while, we left, and we walked toward a distant hill, some half a mile away, with a different fortress, made out of red brick and not nearly as pretty or well preserved as Taj. But it served as a view point. We climbed there, alone, for there were no tourists.

And then we saw it. Two of us, we have witnessed some magnificent things while on the road. We have stood by giant, three-hundred-foot sequoias, we saw Niagara falls, and Mont Ararat, we witnessed the Sahara's sunsets and sunrises as well, but that sight, that was something different. That was something out of this world. The river was orange, almost golden in color, and in a distance a lone fishing canoe and a thin silhouette of a fisherman standing tall, throwing his net, with the Taj in the background. The river, it curved gently, passing close to the Taj, and then it disappeared into the distance, its color getting more golden and shiny, as it approached the sun, which gently hugged the distant horizon. The Taj itself, it was engulfed in a reddish haze, standing proud, on the banks of this river.

With that in front of us, our mood, it suddenly changed. Everything changed. It all felt eerie, and quiet. There were no sounds to be heard. For this was a peaceful, powerful feeling. At that moment, both of us, we knew it. We sensed it. Something profound had happened. This trip, and this whole journey and our friendship, it all made sense. We did not talk about it. Not then, not ever. We did not need to. Our demeanor had changed, our lives had changed. We stood there, mesmerized. And only occasionally, one of us would stand up, stretch the legs and walked around that fortress, looking in some other direction. And wherever we looked, we encountered the same incredible calling. On the opposite side, toward the east, the sky was already dark, and one could see India standing there, as it has done for thousands of years, the villagers in a distance, tending their buffalos as they did since the dawn of time. There were no flashy hotels and fancy parties, just the cradle of humanity, in front of our eyes, and two of us, soaking it all in.

Dead Souls of Tabriz

The ride was long but not unpleasant. It was cheap too. We did not have any local currency, but the taxi driver took dollars, just a handful was enough, us making sure to have plenty of one-dollar bills for occasions like these. It was August, in the middle of Iranian desert, but this early in the morning, it was cool. The sun, still very low on horizon, its rays protruding behind the distant mountain peaks, was shining at our faces and we were blinded, us travelling east, toward this sun. The shadows, they were long, and the sun, it painted a nice picture on this strange landscape. It was yellowish and sometimes reddish in color. And the valleys, they quickly turned into ragged, rocky hills and then gradually, these yellow hills and their huge boulders, they grew larger and larger. Before long, we were traversing through sandstone canyons, cut deep into the mountains. And the sun, it disappeared, and one could only see it shining at the top half of the mountain peaks, all bright yellow, way up, high above our heads, for we were in deep shade, down at the bottom of this gorge. But we were too tired to appreciate any of this. We just wanted to get to the town, Macu it was called, or at least that was what they told us at the border. We just wanted to sleep. The taxi driver got us a hotel; we paid extra, for him and the hotel owner, and quickly went upstairs. We crashed, fully clothed, on a bed, the first one in three days. And what a three days.

We woke up much later, around noon, but surprisingly, the desert heat did not materialize. We expected a hot, scorching day, but apparently this high in the mountains, it did not get very hot. Or was it because of the canyon and its shade? It was hard to tell. Our room, it had a small balcony, and two of us, now rested, we surveyed the town from our position, high above the street. And Macu was a strange place. Cut deep into a narrow mountain gorge, many of its buildings were carved into the rock, straight out of the mountain faces. All buildings were stone built, but this stone, it was not white or granite grayish, but yellowish and soft and porous. So not only that the whole town had this yellowish glow, but everything looked rugged and unpolished, because the faces of all the buildings had this rough, coarse surface common for the limestone. And the dust was everywhere. The day was not windy, so the air was crisp, clean and fresh, but a thin layer of dust covered the streets and every surface one touched.

We stood like that, observing the town, quietly, with the smirks on our faces. We felt proud and accomplished. We could not help it. Just a few days ago, we were in Greece, on a beach, swimming and sunbathing, contemplating: *Is it possible to travel through Turkey and Iran and toward India?* Iran, in particular, was on our minds, for that was an obvious obstacle. And here we were. In this strange town, already well within Iran, and nothing seemed to be out of whack. Everything seemed OK, and ordinary. Except the scenery, which was indeed bizarre. But that was fine. By then we had realized that Asia, it is different. Here, the landscape changes so frequently and so dramatically. Just yesterday, we were on the other side of Mount Ararat, where the endless steppes and green pastures dominated the scene, and now, just an hour drive east, we were in a place that resembled Arizona and in a town not unlike a dusty dwelling from an old Western movie.

We strolled down that street, next to our hotel. There was a small eatery nearby, so common in these parts, selling some tea and some sweets, for there was no coffee in Asia. We were not hungry. We seldom eat breakfast, but we ordered one baklava, just to munch on something, while we sipped the strong black tea. The tea was served in small, glass cups, not much bigger than an espresso cups one finds in Italy and Greece. We were content and proud at the same time. Self-congratulatory as well. And for a good reason. We just crossed the fucking Iranian border. On foot. We were thrilled that all seemed to be working well. And all this happened so fast. We were alive and ready to embark. Ready to move forward.

Boy, that was crazy.
Yeah, it was.
I mean, we walked into Iran man. We slept on the floor of the border post, in our sleeping bags.
Yeah, I know. I was there.
C'mon, admit it. This is nuts. We are in Iran man. We are going to India. Nothing can stop us now.
Shut up, you dimwit. This is just the beginning. There is a long way ahead.

Stupid buzz-kill, he was. Of course I knew that things might get rough, and that the road was a long one, ahead of us. I knew all that. But so what? Can one get happy and thrilled, now and then? And what a better time than this one, for how often can one say: *Yesterday we crossed the Iranian border, in the middle of the night, on foot.* But no, not my friend, he had to play Cool Hand Luke all his life.

Fuck you, I said, *I'll enjoy the moment and you can play your games.*
I sipped on my tea, leaned back on the chair and took a long drag from my Camel.
You stay here, I'll look for the bus, he replied.

All buses, they went to Teheran, so the bus, it was easy to find, and even my friend with his broken English managed to get us one. Once aboard, we realized that something was odd. The bus was nice and clean, too clean for this dusty town in the middle of nowhere. We did not say anything, but our faces said a lot. We looked at each other, gesticulating and smiling, as if saying: *boy this ain't that bad at all*. The interior was dark red, and the seats were covered in soft, rich fabric. The whole bus was carpeted and there were no visible stains or pieces of garbage on the floor, and it did not smell funny. All the things one would expect to see in a bus, in this part of the world, they were not there. We did not complain. We got into our seats, a bit too small for our frame, but comfortable nevertheless. The rest of the crowd did the same. Strangely, although all seats were taken, there were no standing passengers. Everybody had an assigned seat. At first, we did not make much of it, assuming that there were not too many people willing to travel in and out of Macu. And then, there was the driver. He was unusually polite and courteous. He greeted each person and he made sure that every passenger was seated comfortably. This was a bit strange and unexpected, but this too we dismissed: *we just got lucky with a polite driver*, was what we thought.

As we embarked, we cleared the canyon very quickly and the scenery changed dramatically, as it often did in Asia. Before long we were out in an open, endless highland, and the sun, now high above our heads, it burned bright. And one could feel the desert heat. The small windows, on the roof of the bus, they were opened and the hot dry air, it blew hard, and it helped a lot. The bus ran smoothly over the highway, which was wide and straight. This unusually well kept, four-lane road cut through the semi-desert, up and down the rolling hills. The bus went fast, and non-stop. Which was another oddity. The buses, in these parts, they stop in every village and town, in order to pick up the locals and to stuff the driver's pocket. This was expected and common in much of the world, back home included. But not here, here, the buses run as they did in Germany and Switzerland. Our bus marched like that, hard and fast. And then it stopped. First, it slowed to crawl and then it completely stopped, right there on the highway, far from any exit or building or bus stops.

What a fuck? Did it break?
No, this is military checkpoint.
Checkpoint? We crossed the border a long time ago.
The country is at war. Remember? With Iraq. They will check our papers.
But you have been to Iraq, just a few months ago, they can see that in your passport!
I got a new passport you dimwit. Do you pay any attention? I've told you about it.

Three soldiers entered. Two of them with their machine guns ready, they stayed up front, while the third one, presumably an officer, he moved slowly, down the aisle, checking the papers. We could see, through the bus window, the military barricade stretching across the whole width of the highway, with sandbags and machine gun nests, and a whole bunch of soldiers behind it. The whole scene and the atmosphere in the bus, it was terrifying. This was our first encounter with a real war. Later, we would both had our share of war stories, from the Balkan war that was to follow, his tales being better than mine, of course. Like the time he was chased by Serbian mortar fire. Him, and his fellow scout, they were detected and they run back, and the mortars were closing on them, exploding some hundred yards behind them and then eighty and the just fifty yards behind. They ran like crazy, over an open field, but the mortars were getting closer, so they made a split-second decision, to lie down instead to run further. They were hoping that the Serb did not actually see them and that he was just guessing their trajectory and that once they stopped, the mortars would continue falling ahead of them. One had to be crazy as hell to lay down flat in the open field, with mortars aimed at you exploding all around. It was a fifty-fifty, life and death decision, and Yuri, he guessed it right. Who the fuck can compete with a story like that?

But that was a few years in the future, and at that moment, in that Iranian bus, we were green and did not know how to deal with these types of encounters. Did not know how to control our emotions. Those soldiers, they sent chills through our spine. The officer, the one that was inspecting the papers, he had a green uniform, with a black beret, a mustache and cool-looking, western-type, sunglasses. He looked more like an American soldier from the Vietnam War movies then a blood-thirsty Iranian extremist. As he moved closer, we got nervous. We had no idea what to expect. We did not have any official papers and we did not know if our passports were of any use. The Iranian Embassy told us that we do not require any visas, but at that moment we wished we did. Having some kind of paperwork, anything with the Iranian official stamp, would have made a huge difference. But no, all we had were our blank passports.

He moved, ever so closer, and the whole bus, it was eerily silent. The people would just hand the paperwork and he would look at them. Barely a word was spoken. The folk, it was obedient, but did not seem scared. This was not a picture of an oppressive regime mistreating their citizens, but rather an ugly face of war, where both, the soldiers as well as civilians, they played their parts. They had to, if they were to survive an onslaught from a well-equipped and well-motivated aggressor. The officer, he would shift his gaze, from the paperwork that he was inspecting toward the passengers, which too, he scrutinized, him searching for traitors and spies alike. His head, it moved slowly, from left to right, gazing at passengers with his eyes hidden behind the shades. And then suddenly, ever so slightly, his gaze jolted. Just for a fraction of a second, his head movement, from left to right, it stopped. We could tell, for it jolted in our direction.

And there we were, in a war-torn country, one at odds with the whole western world, us with no official documents. In the middle of nowhere. About to be interrogated by this menacing looking officer. *Is this how people disappear in Iran? What if he declares that two of us are western spies that sneaked through the porous Turkish border? What if he escorts us out?* We reasoned like that, scared shitless. Everything looked so much easier just minutes ago. *How would we explain that, yes, we are westerners, but no, we do not need Iranian visa, the Embassy said so. The fuck he cares about any Embassy.* We panicked like that, helpless and petrified. There was nowhere to run. All we could do was to keep our cool. And with poker faces we waited. And hoped for the best. It was finally our turn. We gave him the passports, not saying a word. We reasoned that the English was probably not the language he wanted to hear. He took them, flipped through the pages, stared at me and then at Yuri and then returned them back to us. Not saying a word. We played it cool. We nodded our heads, as if nothing happened, knowing all too well that it ain't over until it is over. But, it was over. He left, and the bus hit the road.

There were few more of these road blocks along the way. Every hour or so, and every time it happened, every time we had to play it cool and hand out our blank passports to a menacing-looking officer, that spine-chilling fear would come back, to hunt us. As time passed, we got a bit more comfortable, with the whole procedure, but facing such terrifying odds, it never got old, it never become routine. All that was needed was one, only one, pissed-off officer that had a bad day or that held a special grudge against the west, who could have just decided to take us out and do some interrogating. And why not? We were westerners, with no official documents or official business, traveling through this war-torn region. This was exactly what good spies would have done. But, this never happened. None of these officers ever questioned us, our passports, they opened all the doors. Magically.

The bus, it ran like that, fast and furious, eating miles and stopping only at these road blocks, as if trying to distance itself from the front line and the war, to cut deep into the mainland, as far as it could. Through the whole day, we stopped only twice, at one bigger city and at one short rest stop on the highway. The first real decent break, it happened fairly late at night, almost midnight. It was warm and we were pleased to get out. We did so, since at this stop, unlike on the earlier ones, all of the passengers took off, them needed to stretch their legs too. It was there when we first detected the echo of a forgotten civilization. The passengers, they were Asian, and thousands miles away from Europe's shores, but they did not seem Asian, or even Middle Eastern. The whole vibe was unquestionably European. The locals, they were friendly and courteous, but not intrusive like the Arabs or Indians. They kept distance, but not in a cold and suspicious ways the Afghans or Turks would do. No, they behaved in the exact way a French or German crowd would have behaved. They would offer a help if you expressed a need for it, and they would leave you alone if you wanted to. And you did not need to tell them so; they would just know what to do.

As we went out, leaving the bus, the passengers disembarked, one at the time, and the driver, still on his seat, he turned around and greeted every passenger with *Salam*, and every passenger greeted him back with *Salam*. One is accustomed to see this type of greetings coming from a crew of a passenger airplane, but not on a bus in

171

the middle of Asian desert. Later, we mingled around that shop, near the gas station off this highway. We needed some help exchanging our dollars and figuring out the prices of the local soda drinks, Persians not using the standard Arab numerals. We took these sodas, the Coca Cola knock offs, since the Iranians boycotted western products, and we munched on honey roasted pistachios, something that was recommended by one of those friendly locals.

Jesus, how many sodas did you drink?
I do not know, they are just 5 cents each.
But how many? Jesus, you gobbled ten of them man.
No, it is more than ten. Let me count.

We were sitting outside this little shop, with two plastic chairs and a metal table, and boatload of empty soda bottles on it. I counted some twenty or more of them. He finished about ten and I did the rest.

What the fuck. Why are we so thirsty? Was this pistachio so salty?
No, it is not the pistachio.
When did we drink the last time? Macu?
No, that was just a sip of black tea. The border?
No, we did not drink anything on the border.
Fuck. When did we drink? In that Turkish town before the border?
Yes, that must be it; that is when we finished our flasks.
Fuck, that is crazy!

And it was crazy. The midnight crossing from Turkey to Iran, sleeping on Iranian border post, the predicaments with the ride and lodging, all that commotion and adrenaline, and we forgot to drink. It was common for two of us to skip a few meals and go without food for a day or so, but forgetting to drink, for more than thirty

172

hours, that was something new. That was bizarre. And the craziest thing was, we did not even realize it. We were much more worried about the Iranian revolutionary guard inspecting our passports. We were not even thirsty, at least not until we finished our first Cola bottle that night. And boy did we devour those sodas. And the locals, ever so polite, they noticed this, and how could they not, with the pile of empty soda bottles on our table, but they offered only polite smiles and nods, not wanting to embarrass us. Later, we all went back to the bus and the driver, he waited for us, and he greeted every passenger with his *Salam*, and each of us nodded back and said *Salam*. Afterwards, all of us seated and content, he offered a prayer to Allah. They all repeated it, softly, and the bus, it marched on, over the highway, into the warm soft darkness.

We slept for the rest of the night, for there were no more road blocks and the ride, it was smooth and soothing. We woke up in suburbs of a big city, much bigger than anything we had seen in days. Probably as big as Ankara, which was a thousand miles ago. The bus navigated city blocks, intersections and parks. Stuck in traffic, it would slow down and it was there when we first really noticed the pictures. We had seen these photographs of dark, young men, plastered on the walls of Macu, and we knew what they were, but did not pay much attention. Did not want to. They resembled the photocopied announcements one often sees in western cities, "Missing cat" or "Garage sale", except that these were the pictures of the dead. The Iranians, they did not have much of the army, after their revolution, and these men, they fought almost bare-handedly against the well-equipped and well-funded aggressor. And they died. In millions. And this was how their fellow citizens honored them. We knew about this but did not want to think about it. We brushed it off, and it worked. Until we entered Tabriz, as this city was called.

These pictures of young men, thousands and thousands of faces, they stared at you. From the walls of buildings, and city squares, these faces, their eyes fixed on yours, they followed you. Like ghosts, coming from within these walls, they would haunt you. The bus would stop, waiting for a traffic light and inevitably, there would be a wall of a building or a gate of a park and on it, hundreds and hundreds of these pictures. The bus would slowly move along the long wall of a city block, and there too, thousands and thousands of faces. From a distance, they all looked alike, as if someone photocopied one picture and then plastered it all around city. But, as soon as bus would move closer, we could see that each of these photos was unique. Each one was a lost soul. There would be a skinny teenager, or a resolute fellow with thick eyebrows or frightened youth trying to look tough, each one different and each one someone's son. And each one dead. As we traversed this city, and it took a good hour or so, these pictures, they never stopped. Countless dead souls, trapped within those walls. I can still picture them in my head, after all these years.

The supper

With our feet buried in the soft, warm sand, and the Indian Ocean gently rolling just few yards behind us, we sat there on that long wooden table, the one that so prominently stood outside our restaurant. As an establishment, this place was not much, just a bamboo shack, covered with palm leafs, and a makeshift kitchen in the corner, the cook working hard, sweating back there, and Remi, as we called him, he served the dishes and made sure that all-was-well, as he put it. We came to his place quite often; the food was good, cheap and relatively clean. And the view was to die for, in the shade, behind that big beach house, under two huge coconut trees, just a few yards from the ocean. Often, we would just sit there and watch the sunset. But now, the sun was long gone, behind the horizon, resting deep below the ocean's edge and the moonless night was dark and warm, with a gentle breeze, reminders of a long gone monsoon, messing our hair. The feeble yellow glow from a dozen naked light bulbs, strung above our heads, helped a bit, but the light was dim, and it was hard to see what we were eating. The wind, it swayed the light bulbs as well as palm trees, so the light, it flickered and the whole ambiance looked as if we were under candle lights. Hundreds of candle lights.

There were quite a few of us, at this supper, with food, beer and dope a plenty, since Ned was paying. He had gotten some good news, apparently one of his Hashish shipments had arrived safely back home. The rest of them did not know about this, but he would tell things like that, to Yuri and me. I had no idea why. The whole crew was there: Toni the German, the Cockney Boy, Monica, Ned, Yuri and I. And the two girls we picked up that afternoon. Actually, it was all my doing, for my friend, he was an idiot, when it came to girls. Two of them were London chicks, on a two-week vacation, and with those cute

175

accents. Mine was quite the looker, an English-Indian. I figured, when in Rome,... Yuri ended up with the average-looking, a bit chubby, freckled English girl. And even with her, he could not score. He could tackle the Afghan Mujahedeen and Iranian Revolutionary guard, but with girls, he just could not do. He was shy, which could have worked, since girls, they sometimes dig huge, menacing-looking shy guys. But then he would say or do something dumb and awkward, and just bury himself. Often, with just one stupid remark, he would manage to kill my game as well. I missed our third amigo very much. He would have known what to do. The two of us, we had this third buddy, one that grew up with us, and the three of us had this bond, always together we were, except this time, the third musketeer, he could not make it, could not get his passport.

Remi, he brought more dishes, the usual stuff we had seen before, Biryanies, Naans, and Curry, but Ned, he wanted to celebrate, so he ordered a few special things, things we have never seen: Maili Kofta, Chana Masala, and Tandoori chicken. We drank the large-bottled, Indian Taj beer, smoked Hashish and there were a few lines of heroin, here and there, just to keep the things interesting. Cockney Boy, he was a man of few words and many joints, but that night, he was especially gullible. Our catch of the day, the two Londoners, fascinated him very much. The two of them, they knew his part of London, and it was funny to hear them converse, the seventy-something cockney guy with these two little chicks. He hasn't been back home since World War II, and he had some catching up to do. The girls, they gradually switched their accents, now much closer to Boy's, and it was amusing to watch. And watch was all we could do, for after while, that cockney slang, we could not understand.

Ned was unusually talkative as well. He pushed us to try more dishes and eat more, to drink more and to smoke more. *Try this, you have never had it this good,* he would say. And his dope was splendid. The two of us, we knew how to hold our liquor and our dope, and we would smoke a joint and then another one, and we knew how to tell when it got too close to the line, for if you cross the line, and get too high on hashish, it ain't pleasant. So we knew how to calibrate it and detect that boundary, where the high turns into paranoia. Except this time, for whatever reasons, was it the quality of dope, or the other stuff we took, the critical line, it never came. We would take a drag on a joint, get higher, and try a few more and more, expecting, that sooner or later, we would get dangerously close to the point of no return, where the high ends and the paranoia commences. This paranoia was not too dangerous, nothing like LSD, and all one had to do is to wait it out, for some 20-30 minutes. But Ned's dope was good that night and that line, it never materialized, and we just got higher and higher with no end in sight.

It worked for the two of us but not for a poor German guy. He took one joint too many, and he lost it. He spaced out. He had this guitar, and he played it well. That night he did Sultans of Swings, which ain't easy to pull off. But he did, until he got to the line: *Check out guitar George, he knows-all the chords,* and then he got stuck. He would repeat the same line and the same chord: *Check out guitar George, he knows-all the chords, Check out guitar George, he knows-all the chords,....,* and he would do it again and again. After the tenth time Yuri had enough:

What the fuck man! Get out with it.
I can't, I am stuck, I can't leave this line.

And then he would go back to *Check out guitar George, he knows-all the chords.* For half an hour he kept on it. It was annoying to no end.

Chicken-shit, cannot hold his dope, was what Cockney Boy said.

Later, I saw my idiot friend, trying his moves on that freckled English girl. He flashed his shiny Bowie knife: *who the fuck shows a knife to a girl?* But I did not care. The Indian girl was all over me, and I let him drown. My cutie, she was quite shy through the day. We met them at the beach, as expected, for it was there were we lived, spending most of our time in and around the water. The two of them were sunbathing, sitting on the sandy shore, a bit scared of the ocean, which was reasonable, the ocean being pretty choppy with monsoon still lingering in a distance. It was a fairly straight-forward pick, them glancing at us, our teasing: *You wanna go in?,* them answering laughingly: *No way, the waves are too big!,* us sitting next to them, a few niceties and that was it. We agreed for a date at Ben's hut for a coffee or tea, and they came. Of course they did. The English girl was rather reserved, but I could not figure out was it because she was shy or because of my friend's moves. The Indian girl, she was much more approachable but made sure to keep a strict distance. She stayed two feet away from me. At all times, no matter the occasion.

Later, we went to a shop, since they wanted to buy some good quality silk, and the two of us, we knew were to get it. By that time, we had befriended a few shop-owners. That was the way to make a living in Goa, to serve as a pusher and a glue between the westerners and the local shop-owners, them ever so eager to sell and make a profit, and yet not in tune with the westerners' customs and their uneasiness towards pushy and noisy merchants. Ned showed us the ropes. Typically, the tourists, they got screwed, except this time, for obvious reasons, we genuinely wanted to help the girls and made sure they did not get cheated too badly, with the price and the quality. And even there, she had to be jumpy. I would gently put my hand on her shoulder, just to point her in a direction of silk shawls, the very ones she looked for, and instead of responding with an agreeable smile of appreciation, she jolted, as if touched by electricity. And then a look would follow, the one that said: *how dare you touch me.*

So, it did not look good at all. A bored, chubby English girl and talkative, but obviously not ready for action, Indian cutie. I abhorred these weird situations when you were stuck with someone, did not know what to do or what to say, and yet, you couldn't just leave, because custom does not allow for you to say: *you know what, this is so boring for me, I'll just leave.* So we strolled around, for an hour or so, talking about stupid things, me basically shutting down and letting Yuri taking the lead, which was painful to watch. The cutie, she sensed my detachment, it was hard not to, and she tried to start up a conversation. This would work for a while, and then it would quickly die down as soon as I came within a two feet distance. I endured this for as long as I could, and finally, I had had enough, with the girls and with the stupid custom so I said: *You know what guys, I am bit tired from that swim, I'll go home to take a nap.* My idiot friend, not having a clue that his freckled girl was not interested, showed me his surprised face, as if saying: *Are you crazy? We are doing great.* Poor fool.

Yuri and his reaction, it did not surprise me, but the Indian cutie, she did. She said: *Ooh, our hotel, it is not that great, can we see your room?* This caught me off guard, and I hesitated for a second. Ordinarily, a request from a pretty girl, to see your room at a beach resort, under such a silly excuse, it is easy to answer. But in this case, I was worried that she might really be interested in a room comparison, and that once in there, this date would turn into a nightmare, with four of us sitting, bored and confused, in my room, and me, with nowhere to go. I did not have much time to think, and hedging my bets, figuring out that the nightmare scenario was more likely, I said, rather harshly: *O.K. but I am really tired.* I had to leave that option on a table, and had an excuse to chase them out of my room if necessary. But it was not necessary. They checked our place very quickly, just a peek inside and a declaration that it was much worse than theirs, but they had to admit that our room had a great ocean view while theirs was some quarter mile in the jungle. That was latter, but before that, while we were climbing upstairs, toward our room, while we were alone, the cutie and I, she grabbed my hand, leaned on me and whispered into my ear: *I am sorry, outside, with all these Indians watching I have to keep the appearance. Let us meet tonight; it will be easier to hide.* And the day, all of sudden, got much better.

Toni, the German Guy, he came out of his endless loop, and he managed to finish his *Sultans*, and he kept on with Dire Straits; the *Brothers in Arms* were next. The Indian girl, with her hands all over me, she kissed me and hugged me, and it was quite annoying. I pretty much ignored her, for it was obvious that I would score that night or the other. She did not seem to mind, for she too, was happy to get herself a white boy and was not looking for much more than that. Which was fine with me. So I kept talking to Ned and the rest of the crowd. I kept glancing at Monica, to see her reaction. If this was any other night, she would have been on my lap, flirting and teasing me, but now, obviously, with this little Indian slut all over me, she did not do that. I tried to see if there was any trace of jealousy in her, but I got nothing. She was attentive to Ned, but no more than usual. Deep down, I was hoping to detect a reaction, maybe anger or resentment, anything that would indicate that she was not happy, seeing me with that cutie. But no, I couldn't sense anything, not even a trace of discomfort. Not only that, but she seemed genuinely happy for me, she talked to the girls, Indian doll in particular, she asked the right questions and gave her the right amount of attention, not too little, not too much, as if nothing had happened. It drew me crazy.

We teased the German guy: *One more joint? No? C'mon, you are big boy you can take it.* He only smiled back, shaking his head from left to right, embarrassed a bit. *Beer, I'll take, but no joints, not tonight,* was what he said. So Ned got another round of Taj, and the joint, it skipped the German. Later, Ned ordered some sweets: fried bananas. It was out of this world. Just bananas, fried on some pancake dough, covered with caramelized brown sugar. Simple but delicious. We ordered and reordered, I guess the hash, it did its toll and the sweets, they tasted fantastic. Toni was done with his list and he asked for a song.

Play Dylan's Sara, I said, but Ned jumped at me,
No, no Sara, that chokes me up man.
I did not get it: *What do you mean?*
It does not matter, bad memories, he said.
OK, OK, play some other Dylan than, I said to the
German guy. So he did.

Later, we walked back home. Them, the Londoners as well as the rest of the crowd, they were ahead, in the dark, along the beach and next to the ocean. The ocean was at our left. We were going north, back to Ben's hut and our inns. Remi's restaurant, it was almost two miles down the beach, so it took some time. I liked to string behind, preferring the solitude, now and then. The night was balmy warm, and while the beach and the ocean was pitch black, to our right, some quarter- mile in a distance, the light bulbs from the occasional house sparkled. I walked like that, for a good ten minutes, alone, lost in my thoughts, reminiscing, the way I always liked to do. And then she came behind me. She slipped her hand into mine, and she squeezed it hard, much too hard to be unintentional. Monica, she just walked like that holding my hand. She squeezed it even tighter, and her small, tiny frame pressed on my side. She cuddled like that, leaning her head on my shoulder, except she was much too short to reach my shoulder, so she just rested her head on my chest, and we walked like that. Quietly.

Then she told me that one day we would meet up again
And things would be different, the next time we wed
If I only could hang on and just be her friend
I still can't remember all the best things she said

Or was that Dylan? It is hard to remember, with all that hash.

Sunset in Goa, Vagga Beach

182

If only

*There must be some kind of way outta here, said the joker
to the thief.*

He had to play Dylan, and of all the songs, he had to
choose that one. The two of us, we sat on our beds, well-
fed, clean and rested. We read our books, in this not-so-
shabby hotel, and we listened to music. We had arrived
early that morning, after a long, seemingly endless train
ride from Quetta. And Lahore, it greeted us splendidly. It
was obvious, from the moment we disembarked, at that
train station, that we had finally arrived. The grandeur of
Indian subcontinent presented itself marvelously. The
regal, colonial train station, with intricate iron-work
decorations, marble floors, high pillars, and dark, oak
benches in waiting rooms and those kiosks with
mahogany wood and the clerks behind them selling the
tickets. It all looked the way Kipling described it. The
people, the endless procession of different people, dozens
of ethnicities and shops and businesses, and rickshaws
and smells and noises, it was all there. And there were no
Mujahedeen, no scumbags of Afghanistan.

The city was safe and easy to understand. We got a taxi
and hotel very quickly. And the room was quite nice. It
had the bathroom and it was clean. Nothing splendid of
course, but compared to Quetta and Taftan, this was the
Plaza hotel. We showered, for the first time since who
knows when, we rested and we ventured outside. And this
was no Teheran either. There were no mullahs and
Ayatollah's pictures on the walls, and being a westerner
did not mean squat here, so we were free to mingle and to
roam. English was spoken everywhere, the rickshaws and
taxis were cheap, the restaurants and hotels affordable.
We ate well, we tried different restaurants, some rather
expensive looking ones, and our money went a long way.

We strolled around and enjoyed the scenery. We would randomly pick a motorized rickshaw-taxi and would let the driver bring us anywhere he thought was worth going. And they did very well, these drivers. We saw some splendid buildings and parks and fountains. And we rejoiced, eager and happy to explore the city. We rushed out to pluck the majestic flower, the Indian subcontinent.

Which was a mistake. And we should have known better. We should have learned from our earlier blunders, for two of us, we were no spring chickens when it came to travel. We had been on the road before, and we knew, we knew all too well, that this predicament, this slip, always comes back to haunt you. For sooner or later, you let your guard down, you let your emotion run ahead of your senses and then you crash. You burn out. For you see, once on the road, when you reach the goal, you realize that day has twenty-four hours. And without your boss or your school or your spouse to bug you, without a schedule to keep, and without any urgency to move forward and travel further, you quickly realize that twenty-four hours is a long period of time. One can rush to see the monuments and eat in good restaurants, but sooner or later you are stuffed and tired of endless buildings and castles so you go back to your room and then you realize that the day is still young and that there is nothing else to do. And you are bored. But that does not sit well with your emotions, for they tell you that something must be wrong, you must have fun, they tell you. You have reached your goal, you should be jubilant, happy, ecstatic. Except that you are not. You cannot be. The day is too long, and one cannot be overjoyed for twenty-four hours straight. And then you sit in your room, and the moron next to you is playing, *"There must be some kind of way outta here,....,*which only bums you even more.

Indeed, we should have known better. We should have been prepared, and learned how to deal with this predicament, for we faced it many a time before. On our very first escapade, when we were just kids, barely eighteen, backpacking through Europe. We saved some money, working odd summer jobs, some legal and some not as much. The two of us, we came from a poor country so the trip was rough and on a budget. I remember, very well, Mc Donald's was too expensive for us. We had to be careful what to eat and where to sleep, which was often in parks and train stations. We ate cheap, surviving on bologna, salami, and bread from grocery stores. But, that was not a problem, we barely even noticed it. We pushed through, we saw Venice and Florence where we picked those two Dutch girls, we slept in parks, in a shadow of the Coliseum in Rome, and we swam and horsed around on the beaches of Monte Carlo. The furthest point of our trip was Madrid and it was there where it happened, where we crashed, for the first time.

Not because we faced an obstacle or a problem, not because it was hard, but because it was easy. It was too easy. We rented a room, which in Madrid at that time was cheap and easy to do. We ventured out, checked Picasso's museum, we saw Guernica and the Prada museum as well. We saw a bullfight, and then we went to a park or two, and we strolled around and we ate in decent restaurants. Spain was much poorer at those times, an equivalent to our country, so the money we had, it was enough, and for the first time during that trip, we could actually afford a nice meal. Everything was lined up perfectly and we rushed out to see more, to do more, to have fun to be jubilant and happy. And then we crashed. We felt empty. We had planned to stay a few days in Madrid, since Hemingway liked it so much, but there was nothing to do. Another museum? Fuck no. Hungry? Nope. To see another bullfight? What for? We slept, and then walked the streets, hopelessly lost and depressed. *This is it? This is the grand finale of our trip? This is what we planned for months and months?* It was so boring and although we did not want to voice it out, both of us envied our friends that stayed home. We were young and we reasoned that it was the money. It had to be the money. If only we had enough of it, to stay in luxurious hotels and drive in fancy cars and eat at those glamorous restaurants, for sure, it would not have been this boring. *Look at those punks, at Hilton hotel, they know how to live. Not us.* We reasoned that way.

Since we could not have afforded such a luxury, we figured out, the next time, we would take more exotic, more daring trip, and then for sure, this predicament could not happened again. We should not crash. But, of course we did, again. We chose Africa, for our trip. We went to Morocco and then pushed further south to Mauritania, Mali, as far as we could go. And although we got robbed in Lisbon and although we had a terrible experience with scumbags of Tangier, we did not crash there. For you see, you do not crash at tough times, you crash at easy ones. It happened in Casablanca, of all places. It was suppose to be the grand finale, this is where Bogart said *"Of all Gin joints in world,...."* . This was Casablanca for god's sake, how could one be bored there? True, there were camels and the architecture was beautiful, the bazaars were busy and mesmerizing, the waterfront promenade was exquisite as well. But it was hot, the food sucked and the natives, they were annoying as hell. So, for most of the time we stayed in hotel room, resting, bored to death. And although this time, we were older, and we had more money and Morocco was very affordable, we still managed to convince ourselves that *"if only"* was the main culprit. "If only" we had more money and "if only" we were in those splendid-looking hotels, then for sure, *the rainbows and the unicorns,* they would have presented themselves. We reasoned that way.

In both cases, we snapped out of it, for we pushed forward, continued on the road, and the road, it does not care for your little depressions and hiccups, it moves ahead with all the pitfalls and the problems, the very ones you so desperately try to avoid, and yet the very ones that make the voyage interesting and worthwhile. For without them, without these obstacles, the journey becomes smooth and predictable and quickly turns into a drag. Comfortable, perhaps, but boring for sure. We knew all that. We were much older and more experienced this time and we knew that we had to keep it cool, keep going forward, and not rush it. Not to dash into euphoria and expect the bonanza of happiness, that was the creed. And yet, we failed, we succumbed to the expectations of ecstasy. It lurked within us, this expectation, as soon as we disembarked at that train station, for it felt as if we just entered a Kipling's novel.

We let our guard down. We rushed it. And then, inevitably, we crashed. Only this time it was not nearly as bad as before. The two of us, we learned how to cope with these things. And the road helped, it threw a curved ball at us, and a tricky one at that. There were no busses or trains for India and for sure we were not going back to Taftan. So we felt trapped and the sense of urgency, almost fear, followed, which was not pleasant but it was much better then boredom. Eventually, we figured it out, we boarded a plane. That forty-five minutes flight to Delhi burned the hole in our budget, but it was worth it. So, we pushed forward, we had to, and as one does so, one learns that fancy hotels and flashy parties, they are not the answer, they belong to the world of Coca Cola commercials, not the real life. For this journey, it is not about the rainbows

187

and the unicorns, it is about the memories you keep and friends you make, along the way.

------------◇-----------

Years later, many years later, one late morning in August, on the Mediterranean coast of Monte Negro, I was sipping my coffee, the strong Turkish coffee they serve over there. I was sitting in a cafe, right next to beach, and the sun was just coming out, behind the mountains. The water was crystal clear with no waves, glassy and smooth. The tourists, they came down already, kids splashing in the shallows and girls walking by in their bikinis. I had my book, coffee, my legs rested on the chair across the table. Leaned backward, I read. The owner of this establishment, my childhood buddy, as well as my second cousin, he waved at me and he smiled: *You know how to live man.* I nodded, smiling back at him. Content. The pine trees casted their shadows and the August sun was not too strong, at least not yet, and the view at the beach and this magnificent bay of Kotor in front of me with coffee and a book, it was heaven on earth.

Next to me was a table with some tourists, college kids, two girls and a guy. They yakked something, but I did not pay attention. This was just a noise in a background, mixed with the chatter coming from the beach. Then suddenly, their yakking got louder and more coherent: *Whoa! Look at that. That is life, these guys, they have it all.* I had to look up, and indeed, across the bay, some quarter mile ahead, behind the dock, there was a yacht. And it was an impressive one, some sixty feet long, white, with beautiful streamline design, it slowly emerged behind the dock. It shimmered in morning Mediterranean sun. But I did not care, I went back to my book. The college kids, on the other hand, they could not stop yakking: *O boy, what I would give to be over there, look*

at them, they know how to live. Not like us, sitting here,
sipping cheap coffee, bored to death.

So, I looked again. I lifted my head, away from my book
and my coffee, for I had to see this. And they were right,
these college kids. This was not one of those boring
yachts that silently sail by, without a single soul on the
deck. No, this was something different. There were
people on board, some dozen or so people, running,
jumping, horsing around, clearly enjoying themselves.
Kids, as well as the grownups, some happy family, this
was. Privileged and happy. So I looked closer, and then I
saw something strange. That kid, over there on the left. I
recognized that kid. That was my daughter, and that lady
next to her, that was my wife. And then it dawned on me.
This was my uncle's yacht. My rich uncle would rent a
yacht and the whole extended family would go for a ride,
every morning. And it was fun indeed, the first time and
the second. But after a while, it became a drag, and I felt
bad, to break my uncles heart and to tell him that I do not
want to go, so I snuck out, to this café at the beach. Since
here, with a good book and coffee, here it was heaven on
earth. For I knew, all too well, that not all that glitters is
gold and you cannot buy the stairway to heaven. But these
college kids, they did not know that. How could they?
They were just kids.

The magic bus

The air was crisp and surprisingly chilly. This early in the morning, the desert, it looked very different. The plateau, its flat hard surface with millions of small, fists size rocks scattered all around, was still there, as far as the eye could see, but the colors, they were different. Everything was clean and fresh and bluish in color. And the sun, shining from a distant horizon, its rays pocking our eyes, it was getting stronger by a minute. We knew that this freshness was about to disappear, and we were hoping to get out of this place as soon as we could. The bus, the same crazy bus that should have departed yesterday afternoon, it was there and the passengers were embarking. The Afghans did not bother us anymore. They did not approach us with their inquisitive, harsh stares. Instead, a more reserved, respectful demeanor was on display, and some of them even offered a friendly nod. Was it Al-Mashir's intervention or was it our survival of the night that impressed them, it was hard to tell, but they kept their distance, and that was all we wanted.

Al-Mashir, he was nowhere in sight, and frankly, after that last night, we did not care, just wanted to get the fuck out of here, that was all we wanted. The bus was tiny, not unlike an American school bus. It was small and cozy, so much so that we could not stand straight, since the ceiling was just five foot high. And the seats, they were petite and uncomfortable, very much like school bus seats, designed for a short ride and not for overnight trips. The two of us, we sat together, which was a challenge. We were too big for these seats, but then again, tucked in like that, we felt secure. Our frames, much larger than the Afghans' were on display, for all of them to see. And saw they did. We could tell by their looks, they would turn around, poking each other, as if saying: *Look at those two giant foreign devils, crammed like that.* And yes, we were crammed, but we did not mind. Confident and thrilled we were. Our disproportional size, so clearly visible in this tiny bus was sure to keep the scoundrels in check. Plus, it was only a matter of time before we were to depart. We had to leave Taftan, this shithole town, in this godforsaken corner of Earth. The sooner the better.

The bus was not in hurry. The driver, he yelled and called and gesticulated, for apparently he wanted to sell more tickets, although clearly the bus was full, and all seats taken. But, he managed to incite a few extra passengers, who climbed on the top of the bus and sat there. Apparently, this bus was a two-decker. The upper deck consisted of people sitting on the roof. Strangely enough, this upper deck, it looked much more comfortable that the bus interior. Our entire luggage as well as some huge bulky cargo, most likely clothing items wrapped in large bags, was all up on the roof. On this roof, the Afghans had a large tent-like cloth, which was then wrapped tightly around all that cargo. They wrapped it into a bulb, like a giant burrito, stuck on top of the bus. It covered the whole length of the bus, as well as the width, and it was some five feet tall. It would have been impossible to climb and stay up there if it were not for the many ropes, tightly secured, crisscrossing this burrito. The Afghans, they would pull themselves up, using these ropes and then they would sit comfortably, as in a sofa couch up there. They tucked their legs and arms around the ropes, so they would not slide off the bus, and they sat there contentedly, leaning on their sides, as if on a sandy beach. The two us packed like the sardines, we envied them.

The bus finally departed, but not before it took a few more drive-bys around that clearing, and then, one more, last circle, around the whole of Taftan, the driver desperately trying to sell an extra ticket. But there was nobody left, no new passengers embarked, and the bus, driving slowly like that, along the brinks of this godforsaken town, it gave us a chance to see Taftan up close, one last time.

Fuck, I can't believe we slept in there.
I do not want to think about it. OK? Zip it! Is what Yuri said.

The Afghans sitting next to us, some younger, some older seemed friendly, curious. Excited, as much as we were, they wiggled in their seats, talked enthusiastically among themselves. They would throw glances at us, but rather friendly, curious glances. After a while they started unwrapping their turbans. The first guy we saw do that was the fellow across the aisle. The tough looking son-of-a-gun, with his crooked nose, scorched skin and those tiny, mean looking eyes, he slowly raised his hands, and started unwrapping his turban. These Afghan turbans were like caps, made of tightly wrapped cloth, bluish in color, like Bedouins. His hands worked diligently, but not frantically. It was like a ritual for him. He untucked the loose end of this cloth, and then unwrapped two or three feet of this turban fabric, with most of the turban standing up, on top of his head. Then he wrapped this loose textile, like a shawl, around his face, making a face mask. He went twice around his head making sure that his face was covered and only a small slit for the eyes was left open. He looked like a bank robber in old western movies, or a ninja warrior.

We looked intently, for we have never seen or heard of such a ritual. It was fascinating, because by now, essentially everybody in the bus was engulfed with this procedure. As if we were witnessing some ancient ceremony, where everybody followed the same ritual: Slowly, in measured ways, they unwrapped a few feet of the turban cloth and, in a dignified, almost ritualistic manners, they wrapped it back around their faces, leaving just a small opening for their eyes. They were so preoccupied with this procedure they did not even notice our stares. For here, in Afghanistan, we could not take a careful look at the people. Any inquisitive stare from our side was reciprocated by menacing stare back, the way a stray dog with a bone would do. So, for the most part, we had no chance to examine their faces. This time, they let us do it, for they all seemed to have forgotten about us and now they were concentrated on this ceremony of theirs. Once they were finished, and by this time the bus was done with the last circle around Taftan, they looked back. But not angrily. Rather surprised they were, as if saying: *You are not going to do this?* Some, more sinister of them, they threw a sarcastic smile back at us.

Soon after, we found out why. The bus, all its windows down, to bring in some fresh air, or more likely because there were no glass windows to begin with, it charged the desert. Literally, it went out towards the desert, for there were no roads, just an endless flat stone plateau. There were no traces of any civilizations, like a town or a building in a distance. Nothing. There were no tire marks either, so the bus driver, he had to navigate this desert the way a Bedouin would, by relying on his memory and the position of distant mountains. He seemed confident and he gunned the engine down. The bus jerked and rushed forward, through this hell. And in an instant we learned the reason behind the Afghan's ritual. It was the dust. A huge cloud of dust, it engulfed the whole bus and everything inside. In matter of seconds we were covered with a thin layer of very fine, powder-like sand. Not like the usual beach sand, but more like baking flour. The Afghans, anticipating this, had made the face masks and they all bent their heads down, so not to look forward, for the sand, it was so fine that even with your eyes closed, it would sneak in. The two of us, we could not believe it:

Fuck, fuck, it is in my eyes, in my mouth in my ears.
Ha ha, ha, this is crazy,

We laughed like that, to brush off the shock, wandering: *Is this a temporary thing, until we hit the road? Or, maybe the whole ride is like this?* Caught by surprise, unprepared as we were, we just laughed it off, and franticly tried to find some piece of cloth to cover our faces. In the corner of my eye I saw that mean son-of-a-gun, sitting across the aisle, his head bent down, leaning on the seat ahead of him, him laughing, enjoying our predicament. Our luggage was up, on the roof of this bus, and since it was hot we did not have any extra shirts on us. We did the only thing we could, we leaned forward, our foreheads resting on our elbows anchored on the seat ahead, we covered our mouths by pulling our shirts up, over our noses. We had to keep our eyes shut, and in this bizarre position, both of us leaning forward, our heads bent almost at our knees, not seeing each other, we exchanged a few words:

Shit, I hope this does not last.
Don't bet on it.
This is inhumane. Nobody can endure this for too long.
There must some kind of road coming soon.
Don't bet on it.

My partner, the somber, precautious fellow, why did he have to be correct all the time? This ordeal, it did not end soon. Far from it. And the dust, although annoying, it was not the main torment. After a while, one adapts, one keeps the head down, eyes shut and breaths through the shirt. Irritating, but manageable. The bumps and the constant shaking, that was the real torture. The bus, it went full

194

steam ahead. It clocked some fifty-sixty miles per hour, an impressive speed for such a piece of shit machine. The desert was flat, but far from a paved, highway-flat, and every small bump would amplify itself into a big bounce. We, as well as the rest of the Afghans, were sent flying off our seats, some foot-two high in the air. And as this ferocious little bus ate the desert, it encountered millions of those fist sized stones that littered the floor, the true source of our agony. We could have managed the dust and we could have adjusted to a large bounce, every now and then, but this constant rattling: *Rat-rat-rat*, the bus shaking as if we were sitting on a washing machine during the rinse cycle, that was excruciating. Imagine if someone strong, much stronger then yourself, takes you by your shoulders and starts shaking you violently. Now imagine if this shaking does not stop after a few second. Imagine if someone is shaking you violently like that for hours. And that's how it was.

And then the music started. It came from small speakers, mounted over our heads. We did not notice them at first, but once the screeching started we noticed them all right. It was very high-pitched, screaming music. Indian singers, very much like Bollywood-movie music, with singing distorted by these cheap speakers and the volume cranked unbelievably loud. It was painful. The roar of the bus, the stones hitting its floor, the tires rumbling and engine as well, it was noisy as hell, but this squeaky music, it was played so loud that it dwarfed everything. We were angry with the driver and we lifted our heads trying to sneak a peek around the bus, risking the sand in our eyes. We expected the same angry reaction from our Afghan co-passengers, and they did look back at us, but they smiled approvingly, some even moved in the rhythm of this music, obviously enjoying the show. We retreated back to our fetal positions, our heads bent down, our eyes closed, sitting crammed like that next to each other, shaking relentlessly. We suffered in silence, the machine slowly grinding us to a pulp, *Rat-rat-rat.* It went on like this for a good hour, until the tire blew off. But we did not know that, all we knew was that the bus had stopped and that we could walk out of this horror.

At first we did not mind the heat, happy to stretch our legs and to be on firm ground was all we cared. The Afghans, on the other hand, they knew better. They did not mingle around, instead they promptly squatted near bus, on its shady side, claiming their spot. The wind, it was howling and for a while we did not feel the heat, although the sun, it was way up above our heads, baking the landscape. Gradually, we managed to assess the situation. There was the bus, its front left tire flat, the two drivers working hard to replace it, a bunch of Afghans squatted on the shady side of this bus, clustered together, like the penguins during a winter storm, and the two of us, dazed and confused, standing out, unprotected, under this unforgiving sun, with no shade in sight. And the sight, it was terrifying. Observing this landscape, devoid of any trace of civilization, with empty wilderness as far as eye can see, we started to worry. *What if they cannot fix the tire? What if this new tire blows off as well?* Clearly, nobody was coming to help us, this being the only bus in a hundred miles radius. To walk back was an option, but frankly, we could not even tell in what direction was "back". The wind erased the tire marks and the plateau was empty, with no landmarks, save for those, still distant, mountains ahead. With the sun, so high up, it was hard to tell the east from the west.

We could not detect any discomfort among the Afghans, which was reassuring. We knew that in a case of real danger, they would have reacted. Like jackals, they would have growled and they would have barked. Instead, they just hung about there, quietly, weathering the heat, which by now was becoming unbearable. We came closer to the bus, hoping to find a foot of shade for us to squeeze in, but that was reciprocated by scores of angry faces and fuming snarls. So we backed off. The drivers, apparently used to this type of predicament, they were prepared and they were efficient. There was a stash of spare tires on this bus, and they managed to put us back on track rather quickly. With mixed feelings, happy that we were not left to die in this desert and yet not looking forward the hellish ride which was to commence, we opted for the upper deck. We grabbed the ropes and we climbed up. The handful of Afghans already situated up there, they did not seem to mind. They were friendly and they showed us how to secure our position. The thick ropes, which were securing the bulky roof cargo, crisscrossed the roof very tightly, but as soon as we sat on it, the cargo would sink in, like a sofa chair, and it was easy to pull the rope over our legs, closer to our waist, and then with our arms free we grabbed another rope and held it tight. The Afghans, they laughed approvingly and they seemed genuinely excited. And this enthusiasm, it rubbed on us, as we sat there, comfortable, way up, far from the dust, with a wind in our faces, happily waiting for the ride to begin.

And the ride, it did not disappoint. This high up, we were spared from most of the dust and although we were exposed to the scorching desert sun, the speeding bus generated a hard wind which kept us cool. The screeching music, so prominent down in the cabin was absent here on the roof. And even the horrendous grinding, *Rat-rat-rat,* it was muffled by a five-foot thick soft cargo below our butts. That was all perfect, the way we hoped it would be. And the view, it was magnificent. We smiled at each other. The Afghan youth sitting next to us smiled back, heartily. The landscape, this high up, it was even more menacing, for the horizon, viewed from this height, stretched even further and the world around us, it was even emptier than we imagined. As far as eye can see, and we could see forever, there was nothing. Just the yellowish flat plateau, everywhere one looked, and those mountains ahead of us, ever so distant, no matter how hard this little bus tried to reach them, as if they were pulling away from us the faster we tried to catch up with them.

There was a jolt, every now and then. We felt it but we dismissed it. At least at the beginning. Everything else was perfect, so a big swing in a random direction, as if a boat had encountered a rough wave, we absorbed. Our body would tighten, we would hold on the ropes, as tight as we could, and then we would swing back. The same way we did while sailing the rough seas back home. Except, these random swings, back and forth, left and right, they kept coming and coming, way much more frequently than on a sailboat. Moreover, while sailing one can see the wave coming and one can get ready for it, but here on the top of this roof, these rolls, they kept coming with no warning at all. The swing, it would toss us violently, in a random direction and all we could do was to contra-react. We would fall on a side, hitting the soft cargo we were sitting on, then we would clinch on the ropes, with all our strength we would pull ourselves up, in a sitting position, and as soon as we would recover, another jolt would come, and then another and another. The hell on earth this was, and we learned, all too well, why nobody with the seats down bellow ever came up. One had to be a stupid foreigner to do such a dumb thing.

It was just basic physics, and I should have known better. Those bumps we felt in the cabin, the times when we flew off our seats, a foot or two in the air, here, on the roof, those bumps would amplify exponentially. A little jolt in the cabin meant a violent swing on the roof. It was too late to do anything. We could not scream or ask for help.

Nobody could hear us and even if they could, they wouldn't have cared. The only thing we could do was tough it out. Our faces pale, we kept our eyes fixed on horizon, trying to keep our heads still. But this was a losing battle. The bus would toss us viciously, way off balance and we would lose the horizon and our heads would shake like in a bubblehead toy. This induced an immediate headache followed by nausea. We would have vomited, but luckily our stomachs were empty. We did not eat anything that day, nor the day before. We could not talk to each other and we could not adjust our positions. All we could do was to keep on keeping on, to hold on for our dear lives, tightly squeezing those ropes and counter-reacting the brutal jolts that nearly tossed us off that bus. It went on like this for more than an hour. The worst hour of our lives. By far.

This ferocious tempo, it was tough on us, and it was tough on the machine. So it broke down. Again. This time it was not the tire, the two drivers were working on something under the hood. The question: *What if they cannot fix it?*, It was not on our mind, not this time. All we wanted was to get the hell out of the roof, and reclaim our seats. We had to reclaim them since here, in the Orient, once you vacate your seat, you lose it. Most of the passengers stayed inside the bus, since this was not a tire issue, and, as expected, there was an Afghan, sitting there, comfortably stretched over both of our seats. As soon as we entered the cabin, he turned his face away, playing his ignorance, as if saying: *Your seats? What seats? These are mine seats.* And I was ready for the confrontation and the yelling, us pointing to the seats him pretending not to understand and his co-passengers yelling back at us, supporting their kind. This was how these things were usually settled. But this was Afghanistan, not Turkey, and these buggers, they were all armed, and knives they were a plenty. So I flinched. As tired and frustrated as I was,

199

and as much as I needed that seat, I knew I had to be careful with this gang.

But my worries, as how to proceed, they were unwarranted. The bugger, he did not look at us, he just looked through the window, as if minding his own business, pretending he did not see Yuri coming toward him. And my friend, god bless him, he did not even bother explaining nor asking for the seats. He did not care for the Afghans and their knifes. He just grabbed him by the collar, and, like one would pick a little child, he lifted him up and tossed him in the aisle, right in front of my feet. He did this brutally, one hand on the collar and the other clenching the Afghan's throat, so the poor fellow could not scream. His signature move. Then he dropped him on the floor and even stepped on him, as he moved to our seats. I followed, stepping over the frightened Afghan. I put on my tough face, as tough as I could muster, as if nothing had happened and as if this was how we always did our business. But I was frightened. Shocked actually. We just humiliated one of their own, and these tough son-of-guns, they were angry. There was no way this would end without a fight. There were too many of them but in these closed quarters, inside the cabin, our size was much more advantageous and I knew we could hold our own.

It was the knives that worried me. I did not want to come to that. No knives, that was all I was praying for. And, as I sat there, my right hand on the handle of my bayonet, hidden under the shirt, for we were not stupid to keep the knives up with the luggage, with a corner of my eye checking the crowd, I prayed: *God, I can fight, I will fight, but no knives, God please no knives.* Finally, I mustered enough courage to look around and examine their faces and determine which one will attack first. I expected the angry stares and disapproving snarls, but none of them looked back. The poor bugger, the one that was ruffled, he disappeared somewhere, and the rest, they were all preoccupied with their own business, looking straight ahead, avoiding my eye-contact. Even the tough-looking fellow across the aisle, he quickly turned his head away from my stare, his head bent down, in a submissive position. It took me a few seconds before I realized that there was not going to be any fight. Yuri, the grey wolf, he just taught them a lesson, destroyed one of their own and the rest of the jackals, they just licked their wounds. My face, it changed, from a stern, tough-looking one, into a more cynical one. I enjoyed staring them down, their heads, quickly bowing, as soon as I would look in their direction. And Yuri, he did not even care. He just leaned toward the window, ignoring the crowd, looking at something outside, for he knew, instinctively he knew, that this bunch would bow down, as soon as they encountered a true show of force. It was good having him on my side.

So the bus, it continued its ferocious ride and so we endured, in that fetal position, our heads on our knees, with the dust, and the screeching music, and the relentless shaking, *Rat-rat-rat,* for hours and hours to come. Not until much later, in the wee hour of the next day, in that gorge in the mountains, did we have a chance to rest for good. In the mean time, the torment continued, except that after a while, our senses, they were numbed, and all the anguish, somehow, it faded away. The body felt it, but somehow it learned not to register. We were quiet, did not talk at all, we stared at the floor, through our squinted eyes. We could not even look at our surroundings, for any peek through the widow, it was reciprocated by the wretched dust in our eyes. And there was nothing to talk about. Just to endure it, the way we use to do back home, during open water swim marathons. You hunker down, you plow through the best you can. Except this time,

201

giving up, it was not an option. The bus would stop at somewhat regular intervals, roughly every hour or so. Apparently the engine had to cool down. It took us several hours before we reached the foothold of those distant mountains, and it was there, where we had encountered the first outpost. The first trace of civilization.

It was not much, this outpost, just a shack, made of plywood and tin, but it meant the world to us. Flimsy and shabby as it was, it represented some hope, some humanity. We spent a good portion of that day rushing through this endless desert, covering hundreds of miles in the process and encountering absolutely no trace of the human race, not a road, not a sign. It made us feel so small, so helpless. We had no idea how much of an impact this isolation would have had on us. For one does not appreciate this intrinsic need, a desire, to see something, anything, made by humans. It is only after one traversed hundreds of miles of an absolute, endless emptiness, that one fully appreciates this desire. It lay heavy on us, much heavier that one would have imagined. We did not even realize this until we saw that shack. And it was not only us. The Afghans too, they seemed so jubilant and cheerful to see a human dwelling. Even the drivers were happy to have made it this far, within the reach of a civilization, albeit scrubby one at best.

Inside the shack, there was a small bakery, a large clay pot, heated by wood and used to make naan bread. The patron would make a dough, flatten it in his hands, like a pancake, and then he plastered it on the side of this large, hot clay pot, where it would bake, for a minute or so. With his dirty hands he would peel the finished product and sell it to eager Afghans. We passed on the food, since hunger, we could endure. It was the thirst that was becoming an issue. We were hesitant to even look for water, for god only knew how contaminated it would have been, in this dump, hundreds of miles from any proper plumbing. But, incredibly, there were ice cold Coca Colas available. This was nothing short of miracle. In the middle of a desert, in this god forsaken corner of earth, there was a shack and a generator, which in turn was used to cool the soda. There was a large styrofoam box, some four-five feet long, not unlike the one used to store fish on commercial vessels, filled up with water and chunks of ice floating on the top, and Coca Colas at the bottom. The best Coca Cola commercial, if there ever was one.

These chunks of ice, they were almost gone, so the water was cold but not exactly ice cold. Obviously, this did not mater, here in the middle of desert, at high noon. All the Afghans, as well as two of us, we stormed the box, trying to grab a bottle or two. Normally, we would have to wait for our turn, but due to the earlier incident, the Afghans, they made some room for us. We gobbled the sodas, like camels we drank, some dozen bottles we devoured, for these were small 200ml bottles. While doing so, we stood by, observing the crowd. We watched the rascals, their ritual of buying naan, eating it plain, them coalescing in groups of two or three, keeping their eyes down, passing by us, in submissive manners. Then we saw him. A tall, bold, Asiatic-looking Afghan, he picked a bottle, and held it in his hand, measuring. And then he returned it back. He picked another one, which too he held, for a while, only to discard it as well. Then he left. Without drinking. Apparently the sodas were not cold enough. We saw what he did, and we nodded, and he offered a thin, veiled smile and nodded back, appreciating our admiration.

The Holy Man

Years back, when I was up north, I met this guru, Cockney Boy was telling the story, one of his many. *He was old and skinny. And dirty, he was the real deal, not like that phony over there.* He pointed to a holy man, sitting some twenty-thirty yards away. We looked at Ned, to see if he agreed, for we all thought that this nearby guru, that he was the real thing. Ned, he nodded his head, and made that facial grimace, as if saying, *Cockney Boy, what does he know?* We were all sitting on the floor, next to the campfire, at this hippie festival, of sorts. These were not the new-wave, fake hippies. These guys were for real. Most of them in their fifties, many with kids, they settled here, some twenty or so years ago, in the nineteen sixties and seventies, and now they lived, peacefully, in these communes, and they met regularly, every Wednesday at Calangute beach. Here they sold their produce, the things they farmed and the things they consumed, and some drugs as well. One could munch on Hashish-brownies and Space-cakes, the latter, having LSD mixed into the icing. But, these guys, they knew how to handle their drugs. After all, they were still alive, after all these years. And I had to say, they looked pretty healthy. But, oblivious to this, to the surrounding and the music, and some distance chanting, the Cockney Boy, the old bard, he was telling his tale:

And this guy, this skinny fakir, he was something. The villagers, they told me to see him, that he is the wise-man and holy man, no less. This was a long time ago, the nineteen sixties or maybe even fifties, I do not remember. I do remember that I was young and that there were no cars or motorbikes anywhere. One could go for weeks, roaming the countryside, without seeing a vehicle, only the ox-carts and the pedestrians. I do not remember even

204

seeing a bicycle. And if you think, being white in India is a big deal now, boy you should have seen it years ago....

He went on like this, as he often did, on a tangent, reminiscing about the good-old-times, and the times before that. I zoned out. The chanting and the music and the brownies, they did their toll. The ground, it was spinning, but not too much, more like gentle waving, back and forth, as if I were on a sail boat. As I was listening to the old man's tale, I focused my attention on that guru, across the meadow, for we were on the top of the hill, overlooking the ocean, and the grassy meadows, they were all around us, as well as the palm trees, hundreds of tall palm trees, with their coconuts, hanging up there, way above our heads. This guru seemed so distinguished, and as I stared at him, for who knows how long, I realized that he barely ever moved. He just sat there, peacefully. And his facial expression was a mystery. Not angry or proud, not condescending or happy, a mask it was. I could not read it. The mosquitoes would bite you, or a flare from these many campfires around would land on your face, and you would twitch or jolt, but not him. His face was perfectly still, not a single muscle moved. At least I could not detect any. The grass and the sand were soft, but after a while, sitting in the same position, your butt and your legs would get sore, and you would move and readjust, shift the body weight from one side to the other. You would do that, but not this guru. He just sat there, content and almost immobile. And when he did move, he did it so slowly, in continuous, measured ways, as if he lived in a slow motion universe.

I was young man than, and crazy, so I roamed like that, seeking something, I guess. I could hear Cockney Boy's slang. Hard to understand he was, but we got used to his accent, or maybe he mellowed it down, for these types of occasion? Either way, we managed to follow these long tales of his.

They told me that the holy man, he barely talked to anybody, hadn't spoken in years, but if he sees a white man, maybe he will say something. And the villagers, they wanted him to say something, for apparently, any word out of his mouth, it was God sent. As I said, I was younger than and I believed in that crap....

There were many children around, which was unusual, for these were white kids, not the brown, Indian kids that were so commonly seen. These little hippies, the sons and the daughters of hippies, they ran around cheerfully. The younger ones played, while the teens manned the kiosks. They sold tomatoes and zucchinis and other vegetables, or cheese, home-made cakes and other western dishes. There were only a few garments for sale, for unlike back home, in the west, where a hippie flea market would have been all about the accessories, the silk shawls, earnings and hats, here it was mainly about food. These people, they were able to get cheap clothing and frills from the Indians, but western type food and vegetables, that was much harder to find. So, this weekly flea market, it served as a community supermarket, to stock on the items they did not manufacture. The whole place had an obvious, easy going, let-me-be vibe. It was not pretentious or judgmental. And it was festive, with many flags, hung on the strings, between the palm trees, among the inevitable naked light bulbs, and the campfires and the music. But not from the speakers, this music, it came from the groups that gathered around their own campfires and a guitar or two they brought in. Our gang, it had its own camp fire, and the musician, the German guy. Except he was not playing his guitar. We were listening to the Cockney Boy's monologue.

The locals, they told me that the fakir and his house were not there, but some few miles outside the village. So I asked: He has a house? Which kind of fakir has a house? They do not have anything, let alone a house. And they answered, yes, yes, he has a house, but he does not live inside. It is an empty house and he sits, in front of his doorsteps, for many, many years. More than thirty years, they said. That is all he does. He never enters the house. Well, that I had to see.....

I zoomed back to our guru, sitting nearby. A group of fake hippies approached him, them singing and chanting. You could tell they were fake by the way they dressed, all in colorful attire, silk shawls, acid washed jeans and alike, which was the right dress code, except these bozos, they were too clean and tidy, and they smelled good. They resembled the pictures from fashion magazines more than the old-timers nearby. Plus, only idiots would try to engage a genuine guru with this hare-rama bullshit. Fortunately, one of the actual hippies, an old-timer with some authority, he intervened. With some urgency, but without yelling, he chased them out. He approached quickly, his face stern, and his hand motion gesticulating the well know, *off, off you go,* notion. They scattered promptly, and he sat, nearby the guru, not too close, more of a guardian then a companion he was. The holy man, he slowly turned his head toward him, and with ever so small facial expression, he acknowledged him and then went back to his world. At that moment, I realized that this guru, he was apparently their guest. They fed him and let him stay here, at this turf of theirs. For apparently, right there, where he sat, it was his home as well.

So, I went to see him, said Cockney Boy, *at his place. And, just as villagers said, there he was, sitting at the doorstep of his home. This was not much of a house, just a flimsy broken shack, but still, rain or shine, this fakir, he*

207

would not go inside. The villagers, they would bring him some food but not much, for he was as skinny as hell. And dirty. So I asked him, why don't you enter the house?

I wait, he said.
Wait for what? I asked.
Wait for lady luck.

I did not get it, how could I. I looked at him puzzled, so he told me his story:

Many years ago, I lived in this house, the very one behind me. I had wife and kids, did my chores, tended my field and my animals. I did not have much, but I worked hard and I managed. One day, the lady luck, she knocked at my door, but I was too busy. I had many things to do, so I did not recognize her. I let her slip away. Well, only later did I realize who she was, but it was to no avail. The famine came, the kids died and my wife left. So, here I sit now, and wait, for if she ever comes back, the lady luck, I will recognize her and I will greet her with my arms open.

He finished his story, took a long drag from his joint, stretched his legs and leaned on the palm tree trunk behind him. He sat like that, on the floor, comfortable and content. He did not even look at us, his mind drifting, his gaze, fixed to the distant horizon, he was in his world. And for the rest of the night, he just sat there, quietly, with that tiny little smirk on his face. Cockney Boy, the living legend he was.

India, her Majesty

Up, up you lazy bums, let Baba teach you something today.
???
Hey, what did I say? Up we go! Ha, ha, ha.
What the fuck? Ned? You all right?

We looked at him, wondering, did he go mad? Ned, he was never like that, cheerful and springy. And what on earth was all that: *teach you something today?* We had just finished our morning swim and we were exhausted, resting at Ben's hut, drinking Indian tea and munching on a small chocolate bar, and bananas, the way we did every morning. He knew he would find us here, since the two of us, we were more disciplined than the rest of these beach bums. Except the German guy, who was with us, already done with his morning gig. Toni organized these morning fishing trips for Australian tourists. The local fishermen would take a few tourists, one per each of their long slim fishing canoe. Early in the morning, at sun-break, they would sail out, with the ocean smooth and glassy. It was pretty cool. These tourists, they would fish with the locals, by hand, throwing the small nets, the way it has been done for centuries. It was a great fun for them, and it was profitable as well. Toni charged a few hundred rupees per head; him keeping the lion share, but the fishermen, they got their cut, as well as free helping hands.

So, there we were, all three of us, tired and happy, enjoying the morning in this tropical paradise, and this huge bozo, all jumpy and frantic, he was killing our vibe. We laughed at him, and pretty much ignored him, the two of us not in a mood to vacate the cozy bamboo chairs, our feet, buried deep into the warm sand.

Take it easy man. It is too early, what's the rush?
No, no, off we go, I'll explain later.

He switched to our language, so the German Guy would not understand, which added to the urgency. Reluctantly, we followed. We did not have much choice, for who would want to offend the seven-foot-giant. We walked up hill, him marching ahead of us, his head bent down a bit, with his huge steps, he charged that hill, two of us barely able to keep up the pace, his one step as big as our two. We cleared the beach and the town square and moved up the street, among the shops. The day was sunny, but not hot yet, and the streets were near empty and clean, and air was crisp, with never-ending morning ocean breeze doing its thing. The neatly spaced, one-story white buildings, selling the tourist stuff, they just opened, with only a merchant or two in there, and no tourists in sight, this early in the morning.

What do you see?

He was holding a silver ring. We were in one of the shops, and the owner, he stood nearby, quietly and respectfully. He did not hassle us or offer the usual Indian: *Come to my shop sir, very good price sir.* No, this guy, he just nodded his head, and let Ned in. Then he moved aside, and Ned took over, freely moving around the shop, as if it was his.

I do not know Ned. I see a ring, a silver ring. Cheap silver ring.
Do you see the stone?
Yes, yes I do, a white stone, somewhat translucent white stone.

I answered, a bit annoyed, glancing at Yuri, who too was confused.

See, when I move the ring, gently, from left to right, see the stone now?
Yeeah, cool, there is this white line across and it moves inside the stone. Nice.

I faked the enthusiasm, still not having a clue what was going on and still wary not to offend our good jolly giant.

It is not cool you moron, it is very profitable.

Then he switched to our language, so the merchant wouldn't get the details. And the merchant, he just nodded his head, understanding the necessity of such a procedure.

You know how much is the ring?
I do not know Ned, I said lazily, being confused and bit irritated by this interrogation, *some 30 rupees or so.*
Yes, he sells it for 30-40 but the wholesale, he will go down to 20-25.
OK?
You know how much we sell this ring, back home, on the islands, to German and Italian tourists?
You sell these back home?
Pay attention, you dimwit. Of course we do, everybody does. Didn't you see those kiosks with rings and silver jewelry, and silk shawls, back home? Concentrate!

He was getting a bit irritated with me.

They sell for 10-15 dollars back home.
Fuck! That is thousand percent markup.
No, try more like two thousand percent, if you negotiate well.
Whoa! We can make a fortune. I can buy hundred rings and make thousand bucks.

Yes, and the best thing is, they'll all fit in your pocket. Light and small they are.

Whoa! This is fantastic, I looked at Yuri, him smiling enthusiastically as well. Not much of a businessman, my friend, but he trusted me, and he could add two-and-two.

I told you Baba will teach you something today. Ned said cheerfully.

And then he added:

But, you must learn a few things. The stones, they are not all the same. This white one, with the line inside, that is a Moon Stone, this one here that is Tiger Eye and this, the black shiny one that is Opal. And that is it. You stick with these three. The rest, one can by in Turkey and it is easy to get to Turkey. But, these three, they only come from India, and there are not many of us that travel back and forth. These you can sell back home easily.

Thank you, thank you Ned, we really appreciate this.

That was Yuri. He was not much of a businessman, could not talk to a girl, but my friend, he knew how to deal with these situations, this mano-a-mano stuff; that he knew. I was too excited with the news, and my mind was racing with the numbers, how much cash we had left, how many rings we could buy, and thing like that. So, I completely forgot courtesy. And Ned, he appreciated Yuri's call. He nodded his head, and his huge hand shook mine and Yuri's.

And it is easy to smuggle them in, he continued, *the customs at the borders, they never find them, they do not care for rings, it is drugs they look for.*

212

Next, we went to another shop, across the street, where a similar protocol followed: the owner stepped aside and Ned, he took over and showed us the ropes. This was a silk shop.

OK, let me test you. Look around, which is the best shawl, which is the best item?

This time, I was not bored or irritated. Far from it. My eyes focused, I examined the shop, the fabric, the texture and the colors. The most visible items were those simple, common, silk shawls, ones that every hippie has. Cheap, purple colored, and with very few silk threads in them. But, after a few glances around, one could see Ali-Baba's treasure hidden behind. Some of the fabric I picked, it was out of this world. Rich and vibrant, this texture, it was hard to describe. Under your fingertips, it was heavy and smooth, and slippery; it felt as if one was touching a living thing. They were beautiful. Then I found it, the silk rug. I never knew that they made rugs out of silk, but this thing, it was straight out of Arabian nights. A small, three-by-six foot rug, some quarter inch thick, exceptionally well decorated and the silk, the rich and thick silk, it was alive. One would hold the rug, and then it would slip, it would wiggle through your fingers, as if you were holding a cat or a snake. I held it like that, mesmerized, and the merchant, he said:

The kid, he has the eye. That is the treasure my friend, the best I have.

Ned agreed. He shook his head, smiling. Approvingly. And I stood there, all proud and happy.

Yes, that is the best piece he has, and the most valuable. But that stuff, we do not sell. That stuff is too expensive for these schmucks. There is no profit there.

And one could see that the merchant agreed, him nodding his head.

Now, this crap, he took the cheep hippy shawls, *this stuff sells. It is super cheap here and we sell it for thousand percent markup back home. And, these too, you can fold so tight that hundred of these would fit in your pocket.*

So which one do we buy? The rings or the shawls?

You buy both, if they get you for the rings, then you still have the shawls. They sell a bit harder, but they are much easier to smuggle. Just shove them along your other cloths. The rings, if the customs picks on you, they are harder to explain.

After that, it was easy. Ned, he opened the doors and two of us, we just followed. The treasure hunt commenced, in Goa, and elsewhere in India. We found the goods, almost everywhere we looked, for this was where the Silk Road began, some three thousand years ago. The treasure was all around us, not exactly in plain sight, for one needed to look closely, but it was there all right. Yet, the trade in India, it was conducted differently, and the whole experience was a bizarre one. To cheat and to trick the opponent was not just common or expected, no, it was much stranger than that: it was almost impolite not to cheat. Bargaining, cheating and lying, it was so deeply rooted into the fabric of the trade, that they would actually get annoyed with you if you were honest. Like that fellow in Delhi, who was irritated when we accepted his first offer. It was a good offer and the two us, we took it. One should have seen his face, visibly upset, with himself, of course, since he knew that he should have started higher, but he was annoyed with us as well, for what kind of schmucks were these to just accept the first offer? We should have had some decency and pretended that we wanted a lower price. If for no other reasons, than to show some respect.

They would swear on their children or dead parents, they would cry and laugh, whatever was needed, and yet, there was no chance, no remote chance, that they would be honest. They would lie, deceive and cheat. With the price, which was obvious, but also with delivery, with the promised packaging and the timeline. Anything that could go wrong would go wrong. Never, in million years should one pay anything in advance. They would even laugh at you as if saying: *You actually expected him to deliver? But you already paid him, why would he deliver the goods now? He has the money*. That was the attitude. We got burned on perfumes. Which was my idea, but like many others, it originated with Ned. He told us how he smuggled bricks of hashish, by wrapping them in some Indian perfumes, to mask the scent, in a case the border police used dogs, which they seldom did. We did not want anything to do with hashish, not after that Morocco hassle, but the perfumes, they made sense. Pure sandal-wood oil as well as patchouli, they sell with thousand percent markup, and unlike the shawls and the rings, which if discovered are hard to explain, *Why do you carry a hundred shawls?*, having a small, four-ounce bottle of some aromatic oils, that was easy to justify. The border bozos, they had no idea that these oils were worth their weight in gold. The problem was, we could not actually test if the oil we bought was hundred percent pure. We had to trust the merchant, who was a honest-looking fellow, and who swore, on his mother's grave, that he had hundred percent pure sandalwood oil. And it smelled fantastic, but when we tested it in a lab, back home, we learned that it was diluted to less than ten percent purity.

215

But, the two of us, we have been around the block, so we had some tricks of our own. We knew their Achilles heel, which too, we learned from Ned. It was the girls. These devils, they were suckers for slender, white girls. Which is why Monica accompanied Ned on most of his trades. We did the same, except, I did not want to use Monica, not like that. And it was easy to find a substitute. Like that little Swiss junky. Blond, pale, smooth-skinned, she did not mind showing her legs and whatever necessary, to score some dope, so she followed us like a puppy, us always having a good stuff, courtesy of Ned. So, I brought her with me, in a back room, where deals were made. She set on the floor, her legs crisscrossed, her skirt high, way up to her thighs, and her loose shirt, barely covering her arms and shoulders, she giggled and flirted, mainly with me, and mainly for dope, but to those merchants, this was pure magic. To see a white girl, half-dressed, sitting on the floor of the back room, this was better than a Las Vegas show. And boy did they pay the price. Their guard down, they forgot to bargain and cheat and deceive, they would accept my offers, and they would bring more goods, for a great price, just to keep her in there a bit longer. And if I did not like the price, I would pretend to leave, and they would quickly agree, desperate to score a glance or two of her white legs.

Typically, these back room deals, they were one-to-one affairs. You and the owner, and the endless bargaining. But, my little blond, she was a sensation, so the room was crowded. We had a few distinguished visitors, all too happy to participate. One of them was a gemstone dealer, and he pulled a crazy stunt. In his feverish enthusiasm, he produced a small box, which he kept in his pocket, and inside was a white silk tissue, which he unwrapped, and showed us a magnificent ruby. His hands trembling with excitement, he gave this ruby to her to examine. And the stone, it was huge. I had seen rubies, a quarter size of that one, selling for thousands of dollars. To hand such a treasure, to a stranger, just to hold it like that, it was bizarre. But, then again, one has to understand how magical this was for him. As an Indian, this poor fellow, he had very little interactions with women, any women, and now, he had a chance, to sit across this blond fairy, and stare at her thighs and her slender white legs. She held the stone in her palm, close to her lap. Trembling with anticipation, he moved closer, to show her the intricate details of the stone, but mainly to feel her scent, and to be in proximity of this divine creature.

And the stone, it was perfection. In India, they cut rubies differently, they polish them in an oval shape, and the stone, cut like that, once exposed to light, it produces three bright lines, deep within the stone and these lines they intercept in a single point, forming the ruby star. And as one gently moves this stone from left to right, this star, it moves along. The sharper these lines, the better the stone, and this was a superb stone. As big as her fingertip. But he did not stop there, the merchant. No, he produced another little box, which contained a bunch of sapphires. One large piece and couple of smaller ones. These stones were way above my price range, but he was not showing them to sell, he was showing them to score a few more minutes with Aphrodite. And then it happened. His hands shaking, he dropped the smaller sapphires right into her lap. The stones, they rolled down, between her thighs, on the straw mat we were all sitting on. She pulled up her skirt, and moved her butt, a foot away, so merchant could pick up the stones. But her move created a shock, her skirt was way up and she was practically naked, only her tiny white underwear covering her. And nobody was looking at the stones.

Except our poor gemstone dealer, who instantly forgot about the half-naked girl and started yelling, for us to step back so he could find the stones, for even the smallest one was worth a few hundred dollars, which in India was an annual salary. He found five but was not sure how many he had. Was it one large and five smaller ones, making the six, or was it a large one and six smaller one? He was not sure, but I was, for I saw the sixth stone. She was sitting on it, her thigh leaning over it. I was not sure did she do it on purpose or not, but I leaned over, and with my hand firmly on her thigh, I lifted her butt off the mat, and then scoped the sixth sapphire of her inner thigh. To see a girl caressed like that and to see me handing the sapphire back to him, it was transfixing to them. She gave me this surprise look, but I was not sure if she was surprised that sapphire was there, under her butt, or if she was surprised that I did not let her steal it. I knew I could have done that, and two of us could have split the score, but I felt sorry for the merchant, and he was eternally grateful. And the whole gesture, of me returning the sapphire was greeted with a genuine admiration. The whole bunch, they approvingly nodded their heads. After that stunt, among these Goa merchants, I walked on water. The little junky, on the other hand, she never spoke to me again.

As we opened these doors of Ali-Baba's treasures, we uncovered, yet again, that India, her majesty, can be beautiful and can be cruel, but it was never dull. On our daily jamborees with our crew, besides the usual chat about daily stuff and our traveling adventures, now included the tales about the treasure hunts and crazy things we encountered. We all talked about it, except the German. He stuck to his fishing trip business and few other legitimate trades. It was easy for him. His unemployment checks, they came regularly.

We visited that fur guy. You know the one next to the market?

218

Ooh, I know him, the weird looking one. And?
Boy, it was crazy. I bought a fur coat, some kind of wild cat, beautiful thing. But then he brought us in his back room. Actually, we were already in the back room, but this was a small partition within this back room.
Ha! He must have had some crazy shit in there.
Yes he did, and it sent the chills through my spine.
Really? Chills? What did he show you?
You will not believe this, he unrolled a Tiger Hide. Right there on the floor in front of us. Can you believe it? He had a Tiger Hide.
No way! That is impossible. What did you do? Did you buy it?
Fuck no! It was cheap actually, a few hundred bucks. But I could not look at it, I almost punched the guy. Fuck, I am still shaking, just thinking about it. You know how much we love Tigers.

The rest of the crew went silent. For this was some shocking stuff, and it took some time to process it. To know, that among these houses and a friendly-looking crowd, among the innocent silk shawls, sandals and earrings, there were dead tigers and leopards. Killed by poachers. If these people can tolerate such crazy stunts, who the hell knows what else was in there. It took some toll on us. Then Cockney Boy spoke:

Tiger Hide? That's nothing. Once I bought a little girl.
Fuck, what are you saying? You hired help?
No, no, I bought her, from her parents. She belonged to me.
How old was she?
I do not know, some nine, maybe ten years old.
Fuck, you pervert.
No, no, it was not like that. She just cleaned the house and took care of me.
So, she was just the help, that you hired?

We tried to reassure ourselves that Cockney Boy, he did not actually purchased a person but rather, just hired house help, like live-in maid. Albeit, a rather young one. We tried to play it down, but he was resolute. No, he paid some eighty pounds for her, which was a lot of money back then, he said. And her parents, they were just passing by, selling the surplus children. Or, more likely, these were not her parents, but middle men, who bought her from the villages nearby. Either way, as he explained, he owned her, fair and square, the same way one owned a cat or a dog. She was of use to him and he treated her well, she had plenty of food and nice shelter. She was better off than dying of hunger in disease ridden shanty towns.

Fuck it! Fuck it! So, what did you do with her afterwards?
Well, let me see. This was many years ago, while I was in Kashmir, ... ,I 'm not exactly sure.
Ooh, yes, I remember now, I sold her back to that Indian merchant, right before I left for Delhi. I did not want to drag her around, with me.

India, her majesty, sometimes cruel, sometimes beautiful, but never dull.

Hesitant, at the edge of the continent

I could hear him clanking those rocks, and that *clack-clack* sound coming underwater, even though he was more than a hundred yards away, far down the beach, underwater, banging the two rocks together. I was submerged, my head underwater as well, and I could clearly hear the rocks, and the clanking sound they made.

Do you still hear it? I could see him yelling, from the far.
Yes, I can still hear it, I shouted back.
Fuck, this is unbelievable. How far am I? Some hundred yards at least? What is the science here, you nerd?

But I had no idea. The two of us, we lived on the beach, our whole lives, but this phenomenon we have never encountered. I guess this beach, with its rocky pebble floor and oval shape, somehow amplified the sound, and with no people or boats around, this sound traveled far and clear. After this, it was my turn to clank the rocks and I could see him, all excited, jumping out of water, on the other side of the bay, yelling:

Yes, yes, I can hear the rocks! Fuck this is unbelievable.

Like a kid he was sometimes. We had come to this beach, some few hours earlier and managed to kill half a day, just horsing around. We did not want to leave, since the beach, it was far from the town center, and it took us a while to get here. So, naturally we tried to make best of it, and hung around as long as we could. We did not get these Greeks. Who the fuck builds a city on the shore of Mediterranean sea, and then decides to move the center some five miles inland, away from the beach? Why bother? Our place, the city we grew up in, it was ancient as well, two thousand years old, but it was located smack on the beach. Even the town hall, it is on the beach, some twenty feet away from the ocean. *That is how you build a Mediterranean city you schmucks.* But we loved the Greeks, funny and friendly they were, them thinking we were Serbs, which was not far off. And the girls, little hairy devils, it was hard to find a pretty one but we suspected that these fellows here, they were like the Turks and the Arabs, hiding the best of their assets, away from the foreign devils.

Nevertheless, there were plenty of tourists to compensate. We stayed in a hostel, and here in Athens, like in Barcelona, the hostels were unisex, boys and girls sharing the rooms. Even the showers down the hall, they were communal, naked boys and girls bathing together. The two of us, we did not complain. We shared a four-bed hostel room with two New Zeeland girls. We did not ask for it, we just paid for two beds and the receptionist assigned us the bunk bed, one of the two, in that large room. Yuri made sure to be on the top bed, the kid he was. The two girls occupied the other bunk bed. They were outlanders like us, beautiful, green-eyed freckled girls, bit stocky and their faces sunburned, as if they were farm hands. But funny and easy to talk to they were and they made quite an impression on us. The two of them, some twenty years old, on the road for more than six months, drifting from place to place, had been to India and Turkey and half of Europe. They would work part time in more affluent countries, Holland and Denmark in particular, and then spend their money at cheaper places, Greece, Turkey and alike.

Later, after that clanking rock experiment, the two of us, we moved to a local eatery, a cheap place overlooking the beach. This was not a fancy, touristy resort beach, but a simple bay for locals to gather. And the eatery, it had a few plastic tables, placed out on the road, us facing this road and the beach behind it. We munched on Gyro, had some soda and later we had Turkish coffee, except here, as we had learned already, one must call it Greek coffee. A bit tired, washed out after spending a few hours on the beach, we enjoyed the food and the view, the sun getting closer to the horizon and embarking on its long descent. We did not talk much, but we knew that we had to make a decision. To go or not to go was the question. Although we never put it that way, *of course we go*, we said to ourselves, but it has been three days already, here in Athens, and the two of us, still hesitant to proceed further. *Why hurry, we have the girls and the city to explore and life to live;* was what we told ourselves.

And the girls, they were eager, so even my idiot friend, he managed to score. And they were not clingy, they let us explore the city on our own and would hang out with us only if we felt like it, and increasingly, we felt like it. This arrangement, it was tempting, and as skeptical as I was to have a girl for more than a day or two, I had to say, those two, they were something to consider. They could not believe we were about to go to India, by bus.

But why not take a plane?
C' mon, it is not the same. You know it.
But how are you going to traverse Iran?
Not a clue.

Two of us, we did not plan this trip in much detail. The main source was a book, written in the seventies by a hippy back home, who traveled from Amsterdam to Delhi, by bus, for apparently at that time there was a bus route like that. That was all we had on us. That and a few conflicting details regarding Iran. On Afghanistan, we had nothing. We reckoned, once on the road, we will figure it out. Yuri, he even suggested to bring the girls with us.

223

No way, not a chance. What the fuck are we to do with them if we get stuck in Iran or Afghanistan? Just leave them there, on their own?

Yeah, look at them, they are tough they can take care of themselves.

You schmuck, there is no way you would dump a girl like that, give me a break!

And he knew I was right, for he would never do a thing like that, the sucker as he was. And he knew that I would, as I had done it before, when necessary, when they become too annoying and clingy, like that girl in Marseille. An experience I did not care repeating, so I was adamant, *If we go, we go alone.*

So we go tomorrow? For sure?
Yes we do.
We could hang a few more days with the girls you know.
You would like that would you?
Yes I would.
Fuck it man, we either go or we don't. OK? You wana take that train back home?

He did not care for that train ride, I knew that. From Belgrade to Athens, it was only five hundred miles, a distance that should have been covered in four hours if we were in France, but here, at the backdoor of the continent, where Europe blends into Asia, it took more than twenty four. And it was not only the time delays that startled us, it was the whole ride, the whole package. It was a prelude for times to come, except we did not know that. But we did sense it. We could tell that something was weird and unfamiliar. The very first few hours on that train exposed that bizarre ethnic interplay, the one we would encounter so many times later on.

The train, it was full, there were more tickets sold then seats, obviously, so the hallways were filled up with people. That was not too strange except that the cabins, they were half empty. This was an overnight train, with six-seat cabins and nice, cozy, cushioned seats, three on each side and a sliding door separating the cabins from the narrow hallway. And, while most of the passengers were crammed into this slim corridor, essentially all of the cabins were occupied by just two fellows, each one sleeping comfortably over those three seats on the side of the cabin. Two guys, laying over six seats and the crowd, dozens of us, like sardines standing in the hallways. Two of us, we did not get it.

What the fuck, why don't you get in? We asked a passenger.
Shipptars, he responded.

This was the name Serbs used for Albanians. And the Albanians, although puny and short, they had this fearsome reputation. They all stuck together and many carried knives, so these Serbs, they were scared to push them too hard. Occasionally, a fellow Serb, he would open the sliding door and ask for a seat. This was a logical thing to ask, since each of these two jerks were prostrated over three seats. The normal thing to do would have been to move and let the person sit, but these punks, they answered rudely in their broken Serbian: *My friend, he go restroom, he come back, I keep seat for him.* And then they would just slam the door. This was an obvious lie, for this answer was repeated several times for several cabins, and we all knew it was their way to take all the seats. We all knew that, but nobody did anything. Such was *Shipptars'* reputation. This was the time for me to shine. I knew how to deal with these punks. All I had to do is to pull a Monte Negro card.

225

I entered the cabin, just a few minutes after they chased the poor Serb, and as I opened the door they quickly resume to their mantra, *My friend is coming,...,*except this time they were angrier and more arrogant, surprised that anybody would dare disturb them so shortly after they just chased that guy out. But I did not care:

Yeah, yeah, fuck your friend, I'll sit here and when he comes I'll deal with him.

Then I grabbed the guy's legs, pushed him harshly and then positioned myself comfortably over the two seats, him being squeezed into a corner one. I even cursed at him, rather elaborately, in his native language. Yuri, he was surprised, for it was a custom for him to lead and for me to follow, but he quickly got with the program, and he tossed the other punk in the corner and grabbed the remaining two seats, all for himself. And the Albanians, they did not say squat. Not only because we were rude and harsh and much bigger than them but because I switched to a Monte Negro accent. We all spoke the same languages, the Serbs and the Croats, but the accents, they were very distinct. And the Albanians, they quickly recognized the slang and realized that we were not Serbs but probably Monte Negros, and they for sure were not to mess with Monte Negros. I knew that, because as a kid I spent a few years in Kosovo where I learned some of their language as well as some of the custom. Now, to be fair, I was Monte Negro on paper only, a far cry from a tough fighter I was, but I looked like one, I spoke like one and boy did I behave like one, and for these Albanian bums that was more than enough. And, my cursing, in near perfect Albanian, it was an icing on the cake. It scared the hell out of them.

Later, when we woke up, the Albanians as well as the Serbs, they were all gone and different ethnic groups, mainly Gypsies and Macedonians, populated the train. This was rather new and strange for us, this procession of ethnicities. We were puzzled and confused. One moment you would take a nap and the next moment the people around you, they were all different, somehow. We have never seen such a thing, but that was just a glimpse of things to come, the kaleidoscope of ethnicities, Hazars, Armenians, Kurds, Pashtuns, Azerbaijanis, Persians, … , and who the heck knows who else was about to be paraded in front of us. And the Asia, it showed yet another face, some few hours later, when we crossed into Greece. For the Greeks, god bless them, they run their country in some bizarre ways. The train, it barely moved. It would run for some ten, twenty minutes and then it would stop for half an hour, often at random places in the middle of fields, nowhere near a city or a post. And when it moved, it moved so slowly and at times, and this is god's truth, it moved backward, for miles and miles. It would go back to a town we have already visited. Excruciating this was and those last hundred miles in Greece took almost ten hours to cover. It was Zeno's paradox in practice, the closer we got to our goal the slower the train moved. So, there was no way we would have taken this trip back home, with the tail between our legs, and only two cute girls to show for.

So you are going tomorrow? For sure? Two of them asked.
Yes, we depart tomorrow.
So we celebrate? Tonight?

The girls they were troopers, I'll give them that. That night we celebrated with ouzo and coffee and baklavas. The strong coffee would jazz us up and ouzo, the sweet liquorish brandy, it would mellow us down and baklavas, well, they just tasted good. The girls were good companions, they knew what to say and when. Impressed with our decision, they did not try to persuade us, now that we have made up our minds. It all felt strange, them being extra agreeable, as if we were the bullfighters before the fight or gladiators before the games. Going on such a mission, hazardous and crazy, willing to risk your life, it had such a strange effect on the girls, like an aphrodisiac it was. Two of us, we were conflicted. We liked the attention but we were wary about the motivation. The night, it was long, and the hour late and at one point we had to go back to our room. And the girls, they decided to switch partners that night, each of us ending up with a different girl, a farewell present that was. And a very good one at that.

The warm asphalt, the deserted train station, the scruffy untended palm trees around us, a gust of wind swaying the palm branches and playing with the garbage on the floor, the plastic bags gently dancing on the pavement, carried by this late morning breeze. The Mediterranean sun, it was getting stronger, the two of us alone, at the far end of the train post, on the open field, waiting for the train, the ever-so-late Greek train, that was to carry us to Istanbul, far away from the beloved continent. The time passed slowly, two of us reminiscing, the station almost empty and only a handful of westerners, with their backpacks, stretched out over the quarter mile long tracks. We were restless, would sit down and wait and then walk around, up and down, and then occasionally one of us would walk up to the station to by a snack or a drink. The girls, they stayed at the hotel, two of us, we sneaked out earlier, quietly, without saying good bye, not wanting to spoil this adventure with unnecessary sentiments. Many things went through our minds, and it all felt like the time in Gibraltar when we were departing for Africa, except that time, we were naïve and ecstatic, not realizing the perils of such a trip. This time, we knew better, and the feeling, it was strange, like before a race, your mind is made up, you are about to start the long, open ocean swim, and you are calm and in a zone, and yet you worry. You try not to think too much about the predicament and yet, you cannot help it. Finally, in a distance we saw the train.

Fuck, I hope this will not be Africa all over again.

Well Yuri, there is only one way to find out.

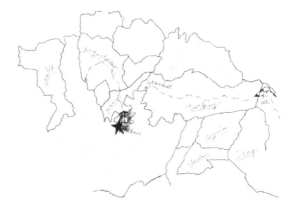

Many years later

We left India a few months later. We did not take the same route back, making sure to avoid that trip through Afghanistan. Instead, we took a plane back home, like true tourists would. Ned was puzzled: *I never figured you for sissies*; he said that, for apparently he and Monica, they always took the land route to Europe and back. But we had had enough, of deserts and Mujahedeens and besides, we had stuffed ourselves with Indian goodies, silver rings and semiprecious stones, silk shawls and exotic perfumes, and some other stuff, better not be specified in detail here. By doing so, we seriously depleted our cash reserves. This was the time before credit cards and ATM machines so getting the funds to pay for a plane ticket back to Europe was a challenge. Eventually we found the way, we always did. We hooked up with two sweet Polish girls, blond and tall, but plain looking. I never managed to figure those Poles, so many unattractive, dull looking blonds. But that is a different story. These Poles, they were tourists, and they were all around Delhi. Apparently there was a direct flight from Warsaw, which on its own does not seem unusual, until one realizes that all this was happening during the Cold War and the Iron Curtain. The Soviet masters restricted the poor Poles from traveling outside their domain, but apparently India was OK.

This was the winning ticket for us. Our passport allowed us to travel freely, through the western as well as the eastern world. Naturally, we booked the plane, but here too, we needed some trickery. The only way to pay for the fare was to use Polish currency, but nobody in Delhi could find Polish zlotys. It was possible to exchange dollars for zlotys at the counter of the Polish airliner, except they used a ridiculously high, government-controlled exchange rate. But, we had the two blonds with us, and they arranged everything, and we got us the zlotys. All said and done we bought ourselves a flight out of India for mere $20. A great deal if there ever was one. We had a layover in Tashkent, a God forsaken city in the heart of the Soviet Union. The airport was eerie, dark and cold, with no modern TV displays and with more uniform personnel than the passengers. After that we spent a few days in Poland, desperately trying to find a good looking blond, but with not much luck.

---------------◇-----------------

I stayed in touch with Toni, the German Guy, for surprisingly long. For almost ten years we would exchange a letter or a postcard, every once in a while. Eventually we lost touch, but, from what I gathered, he got married to a local Indian girl and has a family. His last letter came with a picture of him, in front of Ben's hut, with the palm trees in the background and two brown little rascals, playing in the sand. He had a huge joint in his hand and it looked as if he was about to pull a smoke out of it. Except, this joint, it was a prank. Almost a foot long, with a smoke coming from its burning tip, this was Toni, showing us, that he still remembered the good old days, and that crazy night when he was stoned dead, lost in the Sultans of Swings song.

Ned was arrested, and served several years in prison. And as luck would have it, he did his time in our hometown. But we never went to visit. Somehow it did not make sense to do so. A few years into his sentence the civil war broke out and Ned, being a Bosnian Serb, was released and deported to Bosnia. The government logic being: *Here are your drug dealers, deal with them, we don't care.* Later we heard that he enlisted and was fighting on Serbian side. That war, it was not my cup of tea, so I stayed neutral, but Yuri being Yuri, he volunteered to

231

fight on Croatian side. By what we gathered, our Ned did well. He become a well known figure, his nom-de-guerre was Captain Ned. To the Croats he was a war criminal but for the Serbs he was legendary warrior. Chances are that he and Yuri, they fought each other, neither of them realizing that the one was just behind the hill lobbing the mortars back at the other. The war is over now and his name disappeared from TV screens, but knowing Ned, I am sure he is alive and well. I choose to believe so.

I called to inquire about Monica, some years after Ned had left the picture. The phone number she left was not her own, but of her parents. It took some time before I managed to communicate to her father who I am and how I knew her. Eventually he warmed up, and his initial rudeness and hesitation disappeared. But this was a strange and awkward conversation. And very sad one. She was gone and they had no idea how she died and where. All they knew was that she passed away, alone, forgotten, in some dump, among the other junkies.

The Cockney Boy is long gone too, I am sure of that. It was a miracle that he lasted that long. His body might be dead but his sprit is not. It still roams the dirt roads of India, among the other ghosts and dead souls, stuck in there, among the hills and valleys of the majestic subcontinent.

As for Yuri? Well he is still around. I saw him the other day, he put on some weight but I swear he looks great. A few months after that trip he became a coach at our swim team and he did well. He climbed the ranks and rose to a high position, some kind of advisor to the national swim team, and he managed to attend Sydney Olympics. You can see him marching at the opening ceremony, among the athletes and the coaches. But still crazy, he is. Just a few months ago, on my regular visits home, he talked me into attending this regatta, a sailboat race. He always manages to talk me into doing something crazy. This race, it was supposed to be an enjoyable, a one day trip from our home town to a local island and back, twenty miles in total. A picnic really, except, this race, it goes on regardless of the weather, and the weather was horrible that day. A sunny, but chilly autumn day with a cold, gale strong, northern wind. It was howling steady at forty miles per hour with gusts exceeding fifty. It was like a blizzard. *Are you sure we can take on this wind?* I asked, but he assured me with*: Aah, nothing to worry about.* It is hard to say no to him, besides, he already secured two other crew members and I was not the one to chicken out. And these two, they did not seem that experienced, so I asked: *You don't have any safety vests for these two, do you?* And he gave me that look, an angry look, as if saying: *Are you fucking kidding me?* But he did not say that, instead he continued with the sail boat preparation and then he mumbled: *Aargh, those Americans, they made you soft.*

Well, long story short, it was arguably the worst six hours of my life. Right there with that Afghan bus ride, albeit the bus took much longer. There were almost two hundred boats at the start but most of them quit the race, turned on their engines and hid in the local coves and harbors. Several boats capsized and three had sunk. Only forty sailboats finished. Needless to say, we finished the race. Not only that but we won our category. And here comes the kicker, our category was: *the boats thirty years or older.* Naturally, no sane person would continue with such an old boat in that weather. Except us of course. For who other than my crazy friend would have kept going on, under hurricane type weather, in that forty year old, twenty-six foot long, piece of crap. For my friend, like a bulldog, once he starts something he finishes it. Regardless of the cost. By all accounts the boat shouldn't have survived. It was junk, with makeshift ropes, improvised equipment, some of which held together by a duck tape. And I am serious; he had duck-taped some parts of the mast. *Yuri, are you sure that duck tape will hold? Oooh, sure, don't worry about it.*

He sat on his command spot, with the tiller in his hand, controlling the rudder and issuing the orders. Within half an hour, the horrendous swell and gusts incapacitated the other two crew members, them pale and green-faced, they pretty much sat in the corner and vomited for the remaining five hours. I felt sorry for them, wondering if we should turn back, but Yuri just ignored them. This meant that I had to do all the work. Within an hour or so, it became clear that my friend raised too much sail. I told him: *No need to be a hero. This is a storm you moron. Do not raise the jib. Stick with the main sail,..., trimmed main sail.* But no, not my friend, he raised all the sails he had, and now we were under full gale, his rudder not responsive and us titled dangerously on the side, drifting aimlessly toward the nearby rocky shore. So, naturally he asked me to lover the jib. I knew that we were in trouble. Did not need him to tell me so, but he felt uneasy for asking me to do so. To lower the front sail, the jib, alone, by hand, in those conditions it was a tough job. He hesitated:

Wait until this gust is over then crawl over there.

Fuck, it Yuri. This is not a gust. It has been blowing like this for more than twenty minutes. I had to go now.

He just nodded his head, agreeing. And he gave me that look, as if saying:

Sorry buddy, you have to do it.

So, there I was, at the front of this twenty-six foot piece of crap, at the bow. I was lying down, on my right side, my leg and my right arm anchored between the rail, the boat near the tipping point, at ninety degrees, the bow, going in and out of water, caring myself with it. With my left hand, inch by inch I managed to pull down the sail. Every now and then, the whole bow would submerge below the waves and I had to hold on my breath, for I would go under the water as well. Once lowered, the few hundred square foot jib shook ferociously on that gale wind, and with the boat being basically on its side, it meant that most of the sail was in the water, so it took another agonizing ten minutes before I managed to pull it in, tie it down, somewhat, with his makeshift ropes, which came handy, I have to say. At that moment, I was not scared, just pissed at him. With jib down and trimmed main sail (my doing as well), he regained the control of the rudder and the rest was just the endurance. We were tossed and shaken, wet and cold, but out of real danger, as long as we held on tight.

Later, in a pub, with beer and pizza, we reminisced about the race. Some friends came and the rest of the crew was there, now rested and showered, they regained their color and were cheerful and happy to have survived, to tell this tale, for the rest of their lives. The TV was showing the footage from the race, "Mrduja 2017". One could see the carnage, the capsized sail boats, helicopters rescuing people, Coast Guard ships all around.

See! And you were complaining. Wanted to quit.

Yuri said that, pointing at TV and then at me. Mocking me. But then, once he was sure that the rest of the crowed could not hear us, he leaned forward and quietly he said:

235

You saved the boat, buddy.
I know, you schmuck.

We sat there, enjoying the beer and good food, learning more about the race, for at that time we had no clear picture on what really had happened. Had no clue on how many boats quit, sunk or were damaged, learning these facts from the TV. And as we did so, our deed, of finishing the race, it grew larger and larger. More people showed up, and the rest of the pub, when they learned that we were at that race, the very one shown on TV, they joined our table and the beer kept flowing and the legend only grew. And our crew, the incapacitated two, they were agile and eager, to share the stories and answer the questions. Around that time, I had a chance to tell Yuri about the book I wrote. *Yeah?* He said. *You did? Good.* Then he sat there quietly for some time, him as tall as ever, now heavier, nearly three hundred pound heavy, larger than life. My friend Yuri, he sat there and then looked at me and said:

Did you write about Taj? About that soft marble floor?
Yes Yuri, yes I did.